Masquerade in Blue

Masquerade in Blue

D. C. Brod

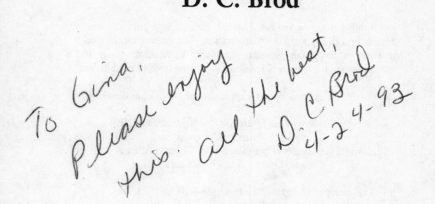

To Gina,
Please enjoy this. All the best,
D. C. Brod
4-24-93

Walker and Company
New York

First published in the United States of America in 1991
by Walker Publishing Company, Inc.
Published simultaneously in Canada by Thomas Allen & Son
Canada, Limited, Markham, Ontario

Library of Congress Cataloging-in-Publication Data
Brod, D. C.
Masquerade in blue / D. C. Brod
p.   cm.
ISBN 0-8027-5792-8
I. Title.
PS3552.R6148M38   1991
813'.54—dc20   91-10188
CIP

Printed in the United States of America
2 4 6 8 10 9 7 5 3 1

For Bruce Cobban

Sincere thanks to Rachael Tecza for her perception and support; and to Patrick Parks and the Elgin Community College Writers Center; the GFPs: John and Maria Alderson, Cecelia Downs and Thomas Keevers; and the Thursday night workshop regulars.

Chapter 1

THE RINGING BEGAN JUST as I pulled the door shut behind me, my key still in its lock. That's how close I was to a clean getaway. A stronger-willed person might have prevailed. But, to me, the call of the telephone is like a blank crossword puzzle or a Jack Nicholson movie — time expands to accommodate it. I let myself back into my office and grabbed the phone just as the answering machine was poised to take over.

"Quint. God, am I glad you're there." It was Jeff Barlowe, Foxport's answer to Woodward and Bernstein. "I need your help."

Bad timing. I made a noncommittal noise and glanced at my watch. Maybe this wasn't a lost cause yet. Airport traffic can be unpredictable, so I'd given myself plenty of time to get to O'Hare. But when Jeff said, "I'm in jail and you're my phone call," I had the feeling it wouldn't be enough.

"Jail? What'd you do?"

"Do? What did I do? Nothing. Not a damned thing. That's why I'm here. I didn't do a damned thing." There was a rise in Jeff's tone that sounded like the early stages of panic.

I was on the wrong side of the desk to use the chair, so I pushed a couple files out of the way and sat on its surface. "Okay, okay. Take it easy. Just tell me what happened."

"Nothing. That's it." He paused long enough to take a deep breath. "I got slapped with a contempt of court citation. That son of a bitch Kramer said I could sit here and rot until I tell him what he wants to hear."

"What's he want to hear?"

"I can't say right now."

"So, what do you want me to do?" I winced at the trace of impatience in my voice. There was one of those little cartoon characters on each of my shoulders. One had horns; the other wings. One chanted, "You should have let it ring." The other said, "Don't be a shit. The guy needs help." I picked up a glass paperweight and felt its heft and the smoothness of its contours. Inside was a tiny adobe house with windows rimmed in turquoise. "You want me to come down there?"

"No. I want you to send me a cake with a file in it. What the fuck do you think I want?" That settled it. Jeff only employed the heavy-duty four-letter words when desperation demanded it.

I returned the paperweight to its place on the desk and stood. "Okay, I'll be there. You need a lawyer or anything?"

I heard what sounded like a fist smashing into a wall. "I need a private detective, goddammit. If I'd needed a lawyer, I'd have called a lawyer. Okay?"

"I'll be there as soon as I can." Then, I added, "Just take it easy, okay? I'm on my way."

There was a long pause and an intake of breath. "Thanks."

Sighing, I replaced the phone in its cradle. This was a no-win situation. It was two o'clock. Elaine was probably above Missouri by now. Missouri or Illinois, it didn't matter; there was no way I could contact her. My choice came down to leaving Elaine stranded at the airport or Jeff stranded in jail and, ultimately, there was no choice. I could call O'Hare after Elaine's plane landed and hope that she would hear the page. Then I thought of the oblivious masses that streamed through those terminals. I'd probably have more success getting my message to her via carrier pigeon.

I looked at the phone. If I didn't show up, she'd call. I rerecorded my answer message, telling Elaine I was sorry, I could explain, and I'd reimburse her for a cab to the Jaded Fox, where I'd meet her.

Elaine was resourceful. She could handle a predicament. And when I explained what had kept me from the airport, once I understood myself, she'd understand. What was I worried about?

As I drove to Abel County Jail, I tried to concentrate on Jeff's situation, but my thoughts kept shifting to Elaine. It had been six months since she moved to Santa Fe to work for a friend who'd set up a small business out there. We'd kept in touch, and though she never said as much, I'd often wondered if there was someone taking up a lot of her free time. Why wouldn't there be? But maybe that was history now, because all of a sudden she was coming home. No explanation, just coming home for a while. That's what she said—"for a while." Whether that meant a week, a month, or until there was a crosstown World Series in Chicago, I didn't know. I wasn't sure how long I wanted it to be either. We'd had a few really good months together. Hardly enough to establish a habit, but enough to wish we'd had more time. Now it looked like I might get my wish, and the prospect was making me a little bit uneasy.

Maybe I was better off not thinking about Elaine. I switched on WGN and listened to the top half of the second in a Cubs/Mets game. Sutcliffe was pitching with one out, Johnson on first, and McReynolds at the plate. Now there was something to concentrate on — a double-play ball.

Abel County Jail is set back off Danziger Parkway an eighth of a mile. From the road, looking down the long, slow curve of a drive, it didn't look anywhere near imposing. With its lush, trimmed grass and marginal landscaping attempts, it might have been any number of government institutions. But as I inserted my car between the white lines in the visitors' parking area, the signs were there — tall, chain link fences, barbed wire, and barred windows. This wasn't the place you'd go to get Fido's license renewed. Still, it was a far cry from Joliet State.

I waited for Jeff in a small room with a long, narrow table and three folding chairs. In the middle of the table was a chipped, brown plastic ashtray. That was it. As I waited, idly looking for concealed cameras, I wondered just what I could do to get Jeff out. Finding no camera and no insight as to my mission, my thoughts shifted gears to the plane that was carrying Elaine. It was surely in its descent over Chicago by now. I sighed and moved to one of the spindly chairs and waited some more. Almost twenty minutes later, a guard opened the door, stepped back and let Jeff into the room. As the guard closed the door behind him, Jeff flashed him a scowl. I noticed that being found in contempt hadn't deprived him of his civvies.

"You get to keep your shoe laces too?"

He eyed me through the thick lenses of his wire rims and, in a voice taut and unnaturally even, said, "Let me get one thing straight here. Nothing about this is funny. Nothing." I thought for a wild second he'd been drugged or something. Then he shook his head and brought himself back. "Shit. Listen to me. I drag you out here then start wailing on you."

I studied him, a skinny kid with curly hair in need of a trim, a comb, or both. There was something about the way he carried himself, on the verge of exploding from repressed energy, that took at least ten years off his age. He still got carded occasionally, even though he'd never see his twenties again. Although he managed to harness his cynicism and energy for his job, he didn't have much time for the pretensions and bureaucracy that went with it. Next to Jeff I felt older and more a part of the establishment than I cared to.

3

"That's okay," I said, and gestured toward a chair. "So, tell me, what's this all about?"

Sitting with Jeff through the late innings of a tight game is like watching a lizard trying to keep its feet from scorching on a rock. He just can't sit still. Now, he couldn't even sit. With his head bowed and hands shoved deep into his pockets, he paced the length of the table. I waited and tried not to think about the DC-10s circling Chicago. Finally I said, "Jeff, talk to me."

"It's about keeping my mouth shut. That's what it's about."

Then, as though he'd pondered that notion as long as possible, he jumped subjects. "You know, when I was a kid, the absolute worst punishment my parents could inflict on me wasn't a spanking. It wasn't pulling the plug on the TV. It was sending me to my room and forcing me to sit in there with the door shut." He kicked at the table's leg as he passed it. When he spoke there was that eerie, hypnotic quality to his tone again. "I can't stand being closed in anywhere. Small rooms remind me of coffins."

"We'll get you out of here." I leaned on the table and tried to make eye contact with him. "Just tell me what happened."

He looked at me and said, "That's one reason I became a reporter. You know, no cubicles, no office hours." He turned away. "Shit. So what do I get locked up for? For being a goddamned reporter. That's great. Just great. Fan-fucking-tastic."

I wanted to throttle the story out of him. Instead, I swallowed and said, "Okay. You're in here for contempt. Can they do that? Isn't there something called reporters' privilege?"

Abruptly he stopped and, hands gripping the table's edge as though he were about to overturn it, said, "Can they do that? I'm in here, aren't I? Reporters' privilege means shit in this fascist town."

I let Jeff figure out for himself that he was edging toward the line that separates a sympathetic pawn of an unjust system from an asshole.

After a minute, he smiled slightly, nodded, and finally sat in one of the chairs. But he kept his hands moving. "Okay, it works like this. If they can prove that they've exhausted all other sources, if they can prove that I'm the only one who can give them the answer, then, yeah, they can find me in contempt."

"What was it? A grand jury hearing?"

"Yeah."

"Well, isn't there some limit? I mean they can't keep you in here forever."

He looked at me, his eyes narrowed, and I knew that was the wrong thing to say. "I know of one poor son of a bitch they locked up for forty-five days for not revealing a source." He paused, shook his head, then added, "I'll be a fucking lunatic way before then. I won't make it."

I jumped in before he could elaborate. "So, talk to me. What do you know that no one else knows?"

He took a deep breath and I tried not to appear too hopeful. "You've got to promise me something before I start. You have to keep this person's identity to yourself. If you can't swear to that no matter what, you might as well leave now."

That was tempting. I pictured Elaine watching other passengers meeting family and friends as they disembarked. She was looking for me, stepping aside so others could connect with friends and relatives. But I said, "Okay. I'll keep my mouth shut."

Eyeing me as though he might see the truth of my words written somewhere on my face, he said, "I mean it. No matter what you learn, you can't reveal this person's identity to anyone."

It was my turn to scrutinize Jeff. "This guy eat babies for breakfast?"

"Dammit, Quint, don't do this. I need a straight answer."

"And I gave you one." I leaned toward him. "As a professional, I'll keep my mouth shut because it's part of my job." I slid back into my chair and added in a softer tone, "And as a friend, I'll do it because you asked me to."

Jeff relaxed slightly. "Okay. Thanks."

"Who are we talking about?" I asked.

"You hear about Leonard Novotny, that land developer who was murdered a week ago last Saturday?"

"You mean the one they found in his office under a bunch of dead ducks?"

"Dead, blue ducks," he corrected me.

"Ah, yes," I said, as it all clicked together for me. For the past six or eight months, Jeff had been covering the exploits of a character known only as the Blue Fox who had become something of a local hero for his style and target selections. He first surfaced in the seventies, when people began to realize that the tumorous, mottled fish swimming and floating in the Fox River weren't an aberration. Agencies started talking pollution control, and to speed things up, someone started pointing out the worst offenders by dumping dead fish or sewage on their steps or stopping up their drainage system—"monkeywrenching" was the term the reports used to define this method of protest. The guy spray-painted his insignia, a blue fox's head, at every scene — hence the Blue Fox.

He'd been out of the news for almost ten years, then one day about a year ago he'd walked into the executive office of a major oil company we had to thank for a big oil slick off the coast of Alaska and dumped a bucket of sludge on their white, deep pile carpeting. No one got much of a look at him. Witnesses claimed they saw a guy dressed in a trench coat and wearing a blue ski mask pulled down over his face. After that he paid not infrequent visits to polluters, mostly in the communities surrounding the Fox River, and had lately begun to target developers who were turning the prairies and wooded areas into shopping malls and single family homes.

The Blue Fox's identity was a closely guarded secret but, for the sake of press coverage, he'd recently made himself known to Jeff Barlowe. The liaison had garnered Jeff some harsh criticism along with some damned good stories. But nothing's free, and he was paying for it now.

"This is the guy you've been reporting on?"

"Exclusively."

"Okay, wait a minute. Novotny died — what, ten days ago — and they've already exhausted all other sources? They're sure you're the only person who can tell them what they want to hear?"

Jeff scowled. "They've been trying to get me to cough up the Fox's name since I started doing these articles. The police and the mayor's office are getting pressure from the industries the Fox is embarrassing. They jumped at the chance to wring it out of me."

"Okay. So I'm here because you're going to tell me who he is, so I can get him to turn himself in so you can get yourself out of here."

Jeff's momentum flagged. "Not exactly. You see, when I was ordered to appear before the grand jury, I knew what they wanted out of me. So I contacted the Fox." He hesitated.

I was starting to catch on. "And he decided he'd rather let you rot in jail than turn himself in for murder?"

Jeff seemed almost embarrassed. "Yeah, something like that." Then he waved his hand at me to keep me from starting in on anyone. "There's more to it. The Blue Fox symbolizes a very powerful movement in this area. And it's so obviously a frame that — "

"Hold it. I can't believe this is Jeff Barlowe, whose middle name is 'objective,' talking here."

"What do you mean?" He leaned across the table. "C'mon, Quint. This is such an obvious frame, they must've been embarrassed to subpoena me."

"You've been in this guy's confidence, what, six months?"

"More like seven."

"Did you ferret him out or did he contact you?"

He hesitated, then said, "The Fox contacted me."

"So, we're talking about a guy who has a pretty firm grasp of the basic principles of publicity."

"What's that supposed to mean?"

"I think we're talking a good-sized ego here."

He shrugged. "Maybe. So?"

"It ever occur to you that maybe it's just big enough so he might put a bullet into a man's chest, then sign his work?"

Jeff scowled. "Listen to you. All this guy cares about is saving the environment."

"Or maybe Novotny walked in on him while he was redecorating his office."

"No." He shook his head and turned away. "I don't think so."

"What's this character's connection to Novotny?"

"Novotny had filed for a permit to build a corporate park—read tax revenue—on seventy-five acres just north of town. Environmentalists are up in arms. A chunk of the area is wetland. They claim it needs to be protected."

"Save the swamp?"

"Something like that."

"Didn't I read that Novotny was about to go ahead? He must have gotten his permit."

"That's the thing. He didn't. Not yet. But he was going to start building on a part that wasn't connected to one of these wetlands."

"That's legal?"

"Yeah, it's legal. It's just not too ethical. Lots of folks wanted him to wait. One group was trying to convince the Forest Preservation Commission to buy the land. But now," he gave a halfhearted shrug, "they're going to have to do some fancy persuading."

"Why would he want to build if he wasn't sure he could finish?"

"He figured he'd win and even if he didn't he'd just have a smaller industrial park. Either way the land was worth more to him than if he left it undeveloped."

I nodded, and then for my own clarification added, "So these

7

wetlands are spread out through the seventy-five acres. You're not talking about one big swamp."

"That's right. Anyway, Novotny was poised to send in his troops and start trashing nature."

"Then someone trashed him."

"That's one way of putting it."

"And I suppose this Blue Fox guy was leading the protest pack."

"You got it."

"What had he done? Before he supposedly killed the guy?"

"Well," Jeff smiled, "Novotny had this brand-new high-priced touring car. He goes out to his garage one morning and finds it filled with water."

"Blue water?"

"Yeah, but it was hard to tell because the windows were smoked."

"What'd Novotny do?"

"He called the Fox a terrorist. Among other things."

"Imagine that."

"Yeah, and he said he wasn't going to put the deranged judgment of a few fanatics before the good of a community. That plus he threatened to nail the Fox's tail to the wall, so to speak." He paused, then added, "He also said he was putting out a hefty bounty, betting that at least one of the Fox's confidants has a price."

"Interesting. And now the Fox won't turn himself in, and you're not going to cough up his name. So where do I fit into the 'free Jeff Barlowe' scenario."

"When I talked to him, he said he wouldn't come forward, but he did have some information that might help find the person who really did kill Novotny. I told him about you and he agreed to meet you and give you this information. On his terms."

"Where? When?"

"In the bar at The Den. Four o'clock."

"Today?"

He nodded.

Thumb and forefinger against the bridge of my nose, I silently calculated how long it would take Elaine to write me off. And at the same time I prayed for another chance.

Resigned, I took a deep breath and said, "What can you tell me about this guy? How will I know him? Will he be wearing a blue cape and Spandex pants?"

Jeff chose to ignore that. "Just show up. The Fox will do the rest.

He knows who you are." Then he cleared his throat and pulled himself up closer to the table. "If the Fox thinks you're being followed . . . if he thinks anything isn't on the up and up, you know . . . well, he won't show."

My jaw tightened and I studied Jeff for several long seconds. "How long am I supposed to sit there and wait to pass muster?"

Jeff finally looked at me and, with a small shrug, said, "Five, maybe. No later." I didn't respond and he quickly added, "I don't think that's going to be a problem though. Really, he'll talk to you."

What the hell, apparently I'd enlisted for the duration. "You've been digging around on this story since it happened. Any chance you're in here not so much because you can ID this guy but because you were on to something?"

Jeff frowned. "I wasn't. Not that I could tell anyway. You can take a look at my notes if you want. I'll get word to Tim. He'll let you have them."

I didn't need the little voice in the back of head to tell me I was investing more than a few hours.

"Are you absolutely certain this character didn't kill Novotny?"

"Why do you think I'm sitting here?"

I gazed at the small window in the door, which was the only indication that there was a world outside this room. When I turned back to Jeff, I could tell from the look on his face that his own thoughts were similar. "If you're wrong," I said, "you better be ready to break that other reporter's record."

Jeff sighed and shook his head. "No shit."

As I watched him, his features taut and his eyes dull, it occurred to me that you could do a lot worse than being stranded at the airport. Now I just had to convince Elaine.

Chapter 2

IF ELAINE'S FLIGHT WAS on time, it would be on the ground by now. It probably wasn't late enough for her to tag me a no-show, but I called my answering machine from a pay phone at the jail just in case. I had a pretty good idea how she'd react to the message I'd left her, but hell, it was better than no explanation at all. There were no calls, so I set out for my rendezvous with the Fox.

I drove with the windows down. It had turned into the kind of early fall day I'd hoped would greet Elaine — warm but with traces of fall in the air and in the trees, which were just starting to change.

When I first moved to Foxport, I used to go to The Den on a pretty regular basis. Maybe as often as once or twice a week. But since I'd moved to the second-floor apartment of a house on the river, I'd found another place that was within walking distance. I hadn't been to The Den in a couple months.

I got there at about a quarter to four and stopped by the pay phone in the foyer. Figuring I still had some time and Elaine should have realized by now that something was wrong, I tried my answering machine again. A beep told me to hold on for a message. I held my breath.

"Yeah, uh, McCauley." It was a man's voice. I exhaled. "This is, ah, Dick Powers. You were, ah, doing a, you know, a job for me. Well, it's not a problem anymore, so forget it. I hope you didn't do any work on this. You know, I hate to shell out money just 'cause I was a little paranoid. Well, ah, let me know." Then, with an awkward laugh he added, "Hey, good luck with that woman you're standing up."

Someday when I had the money, I was going to swear off wandering spouse cases. Half the time they reconciled, which was swell for them, but I'd spent the better part of two days watching Powers's wife scour Foxport's shopping district from one end to the other. If she was trysting, she must have been using a dressing room.

There was another beep followed by a long pause, then, "I don't believe it," followed by a deep sigh and another pause. Then, the voice I liked to remember thick with sleep but making me laugh — Elaine woke up with her humor intact — said, "Quint, this is great. I have three dollars and fifty cents to my name. No, that's wrong. I have three dollars and twenty cents. I just used thirty so I can spill my guts to your answering machine. I love it. Damn." Another sigh, then, "I'm going to make a couple calls. I don't know where I'll end up. Maybe I'll call you later." And she hung up.

I called American Airlines and had them page Elaine Kluszewski. And I asked them to do it again when there was no response the first time. No good.

I was thinking that I'd just lost my last chance with Elaine when I walked into the bar, almost five minutes early. It was a fairly small room, which consisted of a long, dark wood bar lined with stools and two raised tables at each of the four windows. Except for the bartender, it was empty so I took a seat at the bar and ordered a club soda with lime. Elaine's dad lived in Chicago. Maybe she'd call him. But we'd never met and I couldn't imagine introducing myself to him as the guy who stranded his only daughter at O'Hare Airport. This was not going to be the reunion I'd hoped for. Even if I explained and even if she understood.

The bartender placed my drink in the center of a paper napkin. "Tab?" she asked. She was tall with shoulder-length black hair and wore a red shirt that probably could have stood to have one more button activated. Hoping to get this over as soon as possible, I shook my head and pulled a five out of my wallet. I patted my pocket for cigarettes then remembered I'd left them in the car.

A couple minutes after four, a man walked in. He looked like he had a few years on me — mid forties maybe — and he wore a pair of khaki pants and a knit shirt. He glanced at me and gave me a quick nod before sitting at the bar. There was one empty stool between us. Was this him? Not exactly what I'd expected, but then what was the Blue Fox supposed to look like? Shiny eyes? Wet pointed nose? The shirt color was right.

He cleared his throat and ordered one of the German beers on tap. The bartender, with her back to us, was aligning a row of bottles and gave no sign that she'd heard him. But after a few seconds she moved toward the tap and slowly drew the beer.

"Where's Rob?" he asked as she set the drink in front of him.

"Doesn't start until four during the week."

Both the man and I consulted our watches. "He's late," he said.

He's not the only one, I thought.

She lifted one corner of her mouth in what I guess you could call a smile, and shrugged. "He'll be here."

11

He gave her the once-over in a not too subtle way. "How long you been working here?"

"A few months," she said as she moved down the bar, wiping out ashtrays that already looked clean.

"You from around here?"

I took my drink and sought out one of the window tables. I wasn't in the mood to pick up any new lines, and if this guy was the Fox, I was prepared to eat my wedge of lime.

Ten minutes later another man came in. He wasn't tall but solid with broad shoulders and the sort of tan you really had to work at. His hair was sandy-colored and was just starting its retreat from his forehead. Maybe he did construction. Or environmental work. Buttoning the cuffs of his red shirt, he approached the bar and said, "Hey, Julia, I'm running late. Say you forgive me. How'd it go?"

The bartender didn't respond, just crossed her arms over her chest and tried to look grim-faced. But she could only hold the frown for a couple seconds.

"I know, I know. I just missed the rush, didn't I?"

Julia relented and, assuming a less defensive posture, said, "I've learned not to expect you until a quarter after the hour."

"Guilty as charged," he said without a trace of remorse. He patted the shoulder of the man at the bar as he passed him. "Bissell, haven't seen you in a while." Then he lifted the partition at the waitresses' station and stepped behind the bar. "How's it going?"

"I seem to be managing."

Maybe it was time to call this off and start looking for Elaine. Then I remembered I was supposed to give him until five. I looked out the window. I liked Foxport with its small town atmosphere, which its citizens were trying to maintain despite the steady influx of people who were moving there because of its small town atmosphere. And the Fox River was a part of all that — it was the main reason I'd invested in a small business here. I'd lived near the Pacific Ocean for about eighteen months and though there's nothing like it, there's still something to be said for a river. It's like the ocean's this outrageously beautiful and seductive woman who's so volatile and passionate that in a matter of seconds her disposition can swing from serene to explosive. But she's adored despite her outbursts because you put up with a lot to get a lot. The river, on the other hand, isn't quite so gorgeous, so she works hard at being steady and soothing. But she's got her limits and though her anger is slower to build, to see her in full fury is to understand mortality.

To me, there was something about all that that was both hypnotic and affirming. I might not always live near a river, but I would always want to.

"Quint McCauley?"

I turned and met the gaze of the dark-haired bartender.

After a few seconds, I nodded. She seemed to be waiting for something more than my word on it, so I pulled out my wallet and showed her an ID. She examined it, folded it back into my wallet, and set it on the table. Then she regarded me with clear, deep brown eyes and said, "My name's Julia Ellison. I understand we have a mutual acquaintance who couldn't be here himself."

I blinked and swallowed. Boy, did I feel stupid.

"Let's go for a walk." It was more an instruction than a suggestion. I pocketed my wallet and obeyed.

There's a bike path along the river that stretches across three towns and then some. We walked along it, toward one of the two traffic bridges in Foxport. I'd rolled up the sleeves of my shirt and the sun felt good on my arms. Julia was watching the river, hands in her hip pockets, and seemed content to be doing this until I called the meeting to order.

"You aren't what I expected."

After a few steps she said, "What did you expect?"

"I've never heard you referred to with a female pronoun. What was I supposed to think?"

Finally she smiled. "Isn't it amazing how people will believe everything that is fed to them in a newspaper?"

"Isn't it silly how we assume we aren't intentionally being lied to?"

She pulled a strand of hair away from her face and I noticed her hand was small and square, its veins pronounced. "It was a convenient lie. By the time Jeff found out I was a woman, he was already using male pronouns." She looked up at me. "It wasn't an intentional deception."

"Why would Jeff assume you were a man?" Before she could interject, I added, "He isn't like that, you know. He wouldn't assume."

Unconvinced, she shrugged it off. "You'd have to ask Jeff."

"Whatever," I said. "I guess I'm not here to make any judgments. I'm just trying to get a friend out of jail."

She nodded and I saw that when her hair caught the light it wasn't black—there were shades of brown and red in it. "I'm sorry that happened, but I can't help him. Not that way." Her eyes were large but narrow with heavy lids. The effect was both attractive and disconcerting. "What I do is important."

"And what Jeff does isn't?"

"Excuse me for being blunt, but there are lots of reporters."

"And only one Blue Fox?"

She stopped walking, and waited until I looked at her before continuing. "Let's face it. When it comes to the environment, if it's not cute and fuzzy, it's hard to get the public concerned. Most people out there don't know how desperate the situation is. The movement needs extremists to let them know. People do what they can, as long as they don't have to go out of their way. They ask for paper bags at the grocery and then fill them with plastic liter bottles of diet whatever. It's getting late; they don't realize how late. Sure, there's a big environmental movement on now, but how long is it going to last? How long before it's replaced with some other cause the politicians and media decide to shove down our throats? Now is not the time to get complacent. We've got to keep the environment at the forefront of today's and tomorrow's issues. The word is preservation, not conservation. Development and destruction of this land have got to stop. We don't have any more of a right to this planet than the forests they're cutting down or the marshes they're filling in. This is war. The situation is desperate and sometimes desperate measures are called for." Her face was flushed and I figured she did a pretty good job of firing up the troops. But what about the casualties?

"I suppose that includes letting Jeff Barlowe sit in jail. Even though he thinks the same way about being cooped up as some people do of heights."

She looked away briefly. "If I step forward, even if I'm acquitted, the momentum is lost. It's gone. The movement can't afford that. It needs me."

"So does Jeff."

Abruptly she turned and strode toward the river's bank. I followed. What else could I do? When she got there, she squatted, arms wrapped around her knees, and stared into the water. I looked too, but saw nothing. After almost a full minute, she whispered, "There" and pointed at something in the shallows. At first I thought it was a bird's shadow, but then I saw its long narrow form wagging its way along the bottom. "That's a yellow perch. Ten years ago there were just a handful of these left in the Fox. And they were so full of pollution you wouldn't dare eat one. Now the river's brimming with them and the sight of a fisherman standing in the current with hip boots is a common one." She stood slowly, dragging her gaze from the fish. "And if it weren't for the Blue Fox dumping dead fish on the steps of the chemical companies and in the offices of the packing plants along the river, we'd still be stepping over dead fish and ducks as we take our scenic strolls by the river."

Her jaw muscles hardened and she stepped right up to me. She had to look up to address me, but not much. "So, yes, I'm sorry about Jeff. It's too bad he's caught in the middle, but there's a war going on here and he's one of the expendable ones. I'm not." She started to turn away, but stopped and added, "If you're having trouble with this, maybe we'd better call it quits. Jeff understands. He said you would find out who did kill Novotny, not try to talk me into turning myself in."

Before I had a chance to respond, she was on her way back to the bike path. What was it about this woman that made me want to forget my promise to Jeff? "Did you kill Novotny?"

"No."

She kept walking and I jogged up behind her. "But you were there, weren't you? You were in Novotny's office the day he died."

"No, I wasn't."

"Then who was?" I was keeping pace with her.

Stopping, she grabbed my arm, bringing me to a halt. "Whoever killed him. That was part of the frame. How dense are you?"

"How dense do you think I am?" And before she could tell me, I continued, "You say you weren't there, you didn't kill him. I say that's good enough for me?"

She held my gaze for several seconds, then, releasing my arm, nodded, and started walking again. We reached a foot bridge and she turned east to cross the river. "So, you think maybe I killed him." She spoke as though she were trying the idea on for size and kind of liked the way it fit.

"I think I'd be either dumb or gullible to overlook you." I stopped on the bridge and looked down the river toward the south, hands sunk in my pockets. "I can see you busily making your statement in Leonard Novotny's office. You're feeling pretty good, thinking about what he's going to do when he sees it. It's fun to conjure up images of a red-faced man swearing vengeance on the Fox. All of a sudden, he walks in. He's not supposed to be there. It's Saturday, for God's sake. Novotny always golfs or something on Saturday. He says something like 'Aha, I've got you now!' and you panic. He comes after you. You go for your gun — maybe you carry one in case of traps. So you don't have to chew your leg off. Anyway, before you know it, Novotny's dead. It could've happened that way."

I turned and saw that she'd been watching me and found my scenario amusing. "There are lots of possibilities," she said. "That's only one of them. And it's wrong." With a slight shrug she added, "If I had killed him, wouldn't I have tried to clean up the evidence?"

I smiled. "What? You bring paint remover with you on these little raids, just in case you have a change of heart?"

"How can you prove I didn't do it if you don't trust me?"

"I don't have to prove that. I just have to try to find the truth." I was leaning against the bridge, my elbows on its railing. Julia did the same.

After a minute, she said, "I guess I can live with that."

Pointing downriver toward The Den, I said, "You bartend full-time?"

"No. Just summers and odd hours during the rest of the year. I teach sociology at Abel County College."

"How'd you become the Blue Fox?"

"That's a question you don't get to ask."

"I see. You only answer the questions you studied for. Okay, how about this one: What do you know about Novotny? Who would want him dead?"

"Well, he ran the company himself, but he was grooming one of his kids to take over. He was married to Amelia Forrester. She comes from an old family in the area. Seemed out of place with Novotny. He was rich, but wasn't born that way. Used to work construction. Never got out of the mind-set." She clicked off the facts of Novotny's life like they were items on a shopping list. Then she paused, and in a tone that bordered on thoughtful, added, "Amelia's parents believed that she married out of her class." She smiled as though the thought amused her. "Appalling that a woman of Amelia's breeding would wind up with a guy from Cicero."

"How'd it happen?"

"I think they met at college. Apparently Amelia was going through her rebellious stage. You know, wearing berets and going to coffee-houses. Leonard Novotny must have seemed wonderfully Bohemian to her. The perfect date to shock her parents with." She glanced at me before looking down the river again. "Trouble is, she went ahead and married him."

"Mistake?"

"Yeah, but it's hard to say who was sorrier."

I nodded. "What about the kids?"

"A son and a daughter. Martin and Rebecca."

"Which one is running the show now?"

"Rebecca."

I pressed for more. "Tell me about her."

"Mid-twenties, University of Chicago graduate, more than capable. She may do a better job of it than her dad did."

"Will she continue with the industrial park?"

"She's supposed to start construction any day now."

"Without a permit."

"That's right."

"Who do they have to convince they deserve one?"

"The Army Corps of Engineers. You see, what a company like Novotny and Associates does, or says they're going to do, is for every wetland they fill in, they'll create another that's as good or better."

"That seems reasonable."

"That's what I mean." I'd struck a hot button and I braced myself accordingly. "People hear that Novotny's going to give them a new wetland that's even better than the original and they think 'What are these environmentalists bitching about now?' The thing is, have you ever heard of man doing a better job at something than nature?" And, before I could come up with a couple examples, she continued, her voice rising. "Wetlands are incredibly complex, balanced systems. You've got to think you can play God if you believe you can duplicate it."

When she finished, the silence hung in the air between us for a minute. I decided a new subject was the best way to go. "What about Martin Novotny?"

"Don't know much about him." The indifferent tone was back. "He's been on the West Coast for years. Hardly ever comes home. I don't even know if he came back for his dad's funeral."

"Why not?"

"I've heard there was some friction there. They didn't get along. I don't know why."

"Jeff said you'd give me some leads. So far you've told me nothing I couldn't have learned myself."

"I've saved you some time."

"I need more than that." She was staring down the river and I'd have given a month's pay to know what was going on inside her head. "Does anyone else know the identity of the Blue Fox?"

After a moment's hesitation, she said, "A couple people do. You don't need to know who they are."

17

"Do you trust them?"

"With my life." She met my gaze. "In fact, on several occasions I have."

"Are there any organized groups, aside from the Blue Fox brigade, opposing Novotny's project?"

"Yes, there's a citizens' group called SOW, S-O-W."

I chewed on it for a minute. "Don't tell me," I said, "Save Our Wetlands." She didn't correct me so I continued. "They have any political backing?"

Turning back to the river, she said, "Yes. David Reaves."

Julia didn't have to fill me in on this one. Reaves was the state representative for the district.

"You know, if Jeff needs a lawyer, he should contact Cal Maitlin. He's done some things for SOW and other environmental groups. He's an advocate."

"That's nice. But Barlowe doesn't need a cheering section right now."

After a minute, Julia said, "Will this take much longer, Mr. Mc-Cauley?" She was consulting a black watch with a large face. "I've got an appointment I've got to keep."

Thousands of responses flooded my brain and it's a real credit to my upbringing that all I said was, "Don't we all, Ms. Ellison? Don't we all?"

As I drove the short distance to my office, I thought about Jeff spending his first night in jail and me without much to offer in the way of answers. So far, this Fox woman had given me a lot to think about but no answers, and damned few leads that hadn't already been investigated by the police. But when you've got nothing new to go with, you go with the old and hope somebody missed something.

I wondered about Julia's age. I'd first placed her in her mid to late twenties and unless she was remarkably well preserved, I was sticking with that estimate. So that meant she'd have been in junior high or high school when she started this Fox business. Pretty damned precocious. Pretty damned unlikely. Was she from Foxport? Was her family still here? Maybe this Fox thing was something that had been passed on from one generation to the next. Actually, it probably didn't matter when she became the Blue Fox, just as long as it was before Leonard Novotny died. But if she wasn't the original, I sure wanted to know who was.

My office is in the back of an import shop called The Jaded Fox, which I own with a woman named Louise Orwell, who also happens to be my landlady. The office has its own entrance, that clients use. But when the shop's open, I usually enter through that area. Louise doesn't need my help running the place, but I like to visit with her.

When I walked in, she was showing a customer a pair of jade earrings. Louise smiled and said, "Ah, Quint." She kept talking, but I lost the rest because it was then that the customer turned toward me and I saw that Elaine Kluszewski had come home.

Chapter 3

I WANTED TO THROW my arms around Elaine and hold her for a long time. At least until the shop closed. But there was something about her posture and expression that suggested this wasn't the moment.

She stood, one hand resting on the top of the glass case, the other in the pocket of a long, faded denim skirt. A white cotton shirt with pale red stripes was open at the neck, and I saw that she wore the gold chain with the jade pendant I'd sent her for her birthday. Her mouth was a thin line drawn across her face. It didn't curve up or down. It was just there. She was waiting.

I picked up on Louise's narrative. ". . . so I told Elaine you wouldn't leave her at the airport unless you had a very good reason. Isn't that right, Quint?"

Never taking my eyes off Elaine, I said, "Yeah, Louise. That's right."

"Yes, well," she hesitated. "I've got to call that Mr. Edwards back. Yes, I'll do that now. Watch the shop for a moment, will you? I'll just be in the back." Muttering something about a shipment of cloisonne jewelry, she moved from behind the counter.

I stepped up to Elaine and, wishing I'd rehearsed something, said, "I'm really sorry. A friend of mine is in jail. He's not handling it well. I had to talk to someone . . . you know, to see if I could help him."

Crossing her arms over her chest, she looked at me straight on and said, "The governor?"

"What?"

"You had to talk to the governor?"

"No." Where was she going with this? "Why would I have to talk to the governor?"

She turned her head slightly so she was looking past me. "I guess I just assumed it was something really critical he needed. Like a stay of execution."

"Ah, no." I conceded the point. "It's not quite that bad." I sunk my hands in my pockets and kept going. "Almost, but not quite. He's in jail on contempt charges. He's a reporter and he refused to name a source. Add all that to the fact that he's claustrophobic, and he's in pretty bad shape. It was a now or never kind of meeting. I had to help him." I was getting no response from her, but I kept going. "Elaine, I'm sorry. If there was any way I could have done both things, I would have. But there wasn't and I had to choose. So, go ahead and give me some shit. I deserve it. But when you're done you've got to forgive me."

"Why?"

"Because if you don't, we can't go forward from this point. I'll never know why you came back and maybe you'll never know why either."

She regarded me for a long moment, then looked away, her eyes blinking rapidly. "Yeah," she said, her voice unsteady, "I guess you're right."

I waited for her to continue. When she didn't, I said, "I'll make this up to you."

A smile came to her slowly and she swept me with her gaze. "How?"

I thought I saw the smile reflected in the dark colors of her eyes, but you can't be too sure about these things. I wet my lips. "Well, first a tour of Foxport. There's someone I want you to meet. Then dinner. A first-class dinner. You know, champagne, edible fungus, the works. And then," I paused for dramatic effect, "I taped *Death of a Salesman*." That's Elaine's favorite play, though I've never figured out why.

Her eyes widened, but her voice remained even. "Lee J. Cobb or Dustin Hoffman?"

Damn. She was a purist so she probably preferred the earlier version. But I had to go with what I had. I swallowed and said, "Dustin Hoffman," adding, "John Malkovich plays Biff."

Several seconds passed before she said, "That's the one I like."

There are two major north-south streets in Foxport, that flank the river. I live on the one on the east side – Route 35. Along most of the river, the flood plain is pretty wide, but there's one spot about a mile north of my place where the road snakes right down to the river. And though the river hasn't gotten that high in years, it can be treacherous when it's icy or wet.

We drove past a new subdivision filled with homes that probably reflected their owners' personalities on the inside, but from the outside looked like they were all owned by the same person. Elaine said, "I didn't realize this area had been built up so much."

"You city folk." I adopted a slight drawl. "You think we're out here forty miles west of civilization, tiptoeing around cow pies and amusing ourselves by trying to spit cherry pits across the river."

She laughed softly—a welcome sound—then said, "Well, this is the end of the line for the commuter train, isn't it?"

"That's true." After a minute I added, "There's not an expressway or tollway entrance that's convenient to town." Chicago's expressways had been laid out back when Foxport was a far western speck on the map. A nice place to vacation, but too remote to be taken seriously. You'd have needed a lot of foresight to predict what it had become. Foresight or luck.

After a while, my commentary on Foxport was only eliciting little concurring noises from Elaine. It seemed that she'd become preoccupied and was having trouble working up enthusiasm for the local landmarks. Or maybe the problem was with the local tour guide. I thought I'd been forgiven for my absence at the airport, but maybe I was wrong. I decided to confront the issue. "So," I swallowed and kept going. "How did you get from O'Hare to Foxport on three dollars and fifty cents?"

"Twenty cents. Three dollars and twenty cents," she said but I could hear the smile in her voice. "I shouldn't tell you. Make you wonder." But I knew she would, and after a few seconds she did. "I went into one of those gift shops at the airport. You know, the ones that sell all kinds of practical items for the home. I stood near the register and waited until a woman came up to pay for two of these atrocious ornaments made out of, of all things, Mt. St. Helens' ash. Can you believe that? Anyway, she pulled forty some dollars out and I stepped in. I told her the truth. I was stranded at the airport and needed cab money, so could I pay for the ornaments on my charge card and take the cash she would have used to pay for them? Well, it took her and the clerk a few minutes to figure out that I wasn't trying to rip either one of them off. But the woman got a little piece of the mountain, the clerk got an American Express charge, and I got forty-two dollars and forty cents."

I smiled in frank admiration. "You're good."

"I know."

I pulled into the long, gravel driveway that ended adjacent to the gray wooden stairs leading to my second-floor apartment. About forty feet straight ahead, down the slope of the back yard, was the Fox River.

"End of the line," I announced, then in response to Elaine's frown, added, "This is where I live."

She nodded with the same detachment she'd shown for the police station and the 150-year-old cemetery. I didn't know whether she planned to spend the night at my place or elsewhere. Not that it was a problem, but damn, I had no idea what cards I held, let alone how to play the hand.

"On the river," she said as she got out of the car. "This is nice."

"I like it. Louise is my landlady. She lives on the first floor."

"She's from England, isn't she?"

I smiled. "How'd you guess? Cornwall."

This house, like many of the homes along the river, had been built about fifty years ago as a summer place. One of its previous owners had added insulation and an upstairs, turning it into a permanent residence. When Louise moved to Foxport, she decided she didn't want to take care of an entire house, so she had a kitchen added upstairs and a private entrance and began renting it.

We were at the bottom of the steps when Elaine stopped and said, "What are we doing here?"

"Two things," I said. "One, our dinner reservation isn't for another hour and two, I want you to meet my roommate."

She raised her eyebrows but said nothing.

"Wait here," I said and climbed the steps to my apartment.

My roommate burst out the door as soon as there was a space large enough for him to negotiate, hustled down the steps, stopping briefly to smell Elaine, then disappeared in the dusk near the river.

"That was Peanuts." I started to descend the steps. "Shall we join him?"

Elaine nodded and looked toward the river. "Peanuts?"

I told her how I'd gotten him at the animal shelter and held out on a name until I found one that suited him. One day he showed me how good he was at catching frisbees and I named him after Harry "Peanuts" Lowrey, an outfielder for the Cubs in '45 — the last time they'd been in the Series.

"People are always asking me if that's my favorite comic strip and sometimes I think I should have named him Spot or Walter. But then I see him shagging those Frisbees and I just know he's not a Walter."

Elaine was watching me with a curious expression, then she turned to look for Peanuts who was investigating a suspicious-looking rock near the water.

"What kind of dog is he?"

"He thinks he's a border collie, and he's close enough so I don't call him on it."

Peanuts joined us and Elaine crouched down to get eye level with him. I was pleased to see that she liked him. At least she seemed to. I could read Peanuts pretty well and he definitely thought Elaine was okay. But I could have told him that.

When we got back to my apartment, I poured Elaine a glass of wine and helped myself to a beer. And while she changed into a dress for dinner, I called Cal Maitlin. I'd neglected to mention to Julia that I'd done some work for him. And even though I'd tossed her suggestion back at her, I did want to see what Jeff's legal options were. Also, Cal had been practicing law in Foxport for forty years, he knew its people, and he loved to talk. Maybe he'd say something interesting.

As I suspected, Jeff's incarceration wasn't news to him. He chuckled a little and said, "They don't know Jeff Barlowe well if they think they're going to wear him down." I could picture him, horn-rimmed glasses dwarfing his small features, wearing a bolo tie and steel-tipped cowboy boots.

"How long can they keep him in jail?"

"Well, technically he's there until he either talks or someone else gives them what they want. The object isn't really to punish, merely coerce." He paused, then added, "But, between you and me, they'll hold onto him until they're convinced it's not doing them any good, that he's not ever going to tell them what they want to hear."

"It's sort of a 'who blinks first' deal?"

"That's right." Then I heard him sigh and he added, "But as bad as they want him to open up, it has the makings of a long standoff."

"There's nothing that can be done for him? Legally, that is?"

"Not unless he breaks out. Then he'll need a lawyer." He laughed, and when I didn't join in, he said in a more subdued tone, "You know, McCauley, I think he knows what he's doing. Think how much press coverage this is going to bring to Foxport and that industrial park they want to build." He paused. "Used to be that wetland was just another piece of nature another group was trying to protect. Now that group's got a martyr. No way to calculate the value of a martyr. Look what it did for Christianity."

"Well, let's hope nobody takes it to that extreme."

Elaine had come back into the living room and was watching me from the couch. Peanuts worked his nose under her hand until she got the hint and scratched his head.

"Well, listen I appreciate—"

"Quint," he hesitated, choosing his words carefully, "I don't know how involved you are in this, and I don't want you to tell me, but I'd be real closemouthed about what I knew if I were you. That cell Barlowe's in can hold two just as well as one."

24

"I get the picture. Cal, thanks a lot. Really."

I hung up the phone and considered our conversation while I stared at a coffee stain on the counter.

"Quint?" Elaine was standing next to me. "What was that all about? Who's the Fox?"

I told her what I could about the case, omitting the meeting with Julia, which was really most of it so far.

"Are you going to meet the Fox?"

I avoided her intense gaze and she caught right on. "You did. You did meet him, didn't you?"

Still looking away, I said, "I can't talk about that."

"Well, you can at least tell me if you met him." Elaine loved hearing about my cases. I think she used them to test her problem solving skills.

I finally looked at her and it was hard to resist the eagerness. But I did. "I'm sorry. This is real confidential."

"You did! You did meet him. What's he like?" She went pensive for a few moments. "I picture this middle-aged guy who looks kind of like Gene Hackman."

"Gene Hackman?"

"Am I close?"

I shook my head, then before she could interrupt I said, "I don't know. I mean, I couldn't say even if I did know. For all I know, it may be Gene Hackman."

"What else can you tell me?"

"Nothing. Elaine, I really shouldn't have brought it up. This is all really confidential."

She paused then nodded and as I watched her walk across the room to the window overlooking the river I could see that her buoyancy was gone. There was nothing I would have liked better than to tell Elaine everything I knew. Tell her about Julia, Cal Maitlin's doubts, everything. Not only did she have a good head for this stuff, but this was the first time since I'd seen her that just for a few minutes it had been just like before. Maybe we needed to work this out somewhere other than at my apartment.

"You hungry?"

"I'm starved," she said, continuing to stare into the darkness outside the window.

"God, you look nice." We were sharing a bottle of wine, which had cost more than I usually pay for a pair of shoes. Elaine wore a plum-colored dress and a silk scarf with the dreamy, muted pastels of an impressionist painting. Her auburn hair was longer than when I'd last seen her — just past her shoulders. It was thick and, depending on the weather, could be unmanageable. She was always threatening to cut it, and I was glad she resisted.

She accepted the compliment with a smile and let her gaze wander over the restaurant. A relatively large section of Foxport's population falls into the "quite comfortable" to "stinking rich" range. There are a few restaurants with white linen tablecloths, subdued lighting and small portions, which cater to this group. I had taken Elaine to one which was given four stars and as many dollar signs in *Chicago Magazine*. I'd asked for a corner table and told the waiter to give us plenty of time; a request that I'd backed up with what I considered a generous bribe, but which he had pocketed with irritating nonchalance. But it had been a good investment. I hadn't seen him in fifteen minutes and during that time, Elaine's mood seemed to have improved. I'd been talking about some of the people I knew in Foxport and some of the other cases I'd worked on. She was smiling, asking questions, making little jokes. I was feeling pretty comfortable and was setting in for a nice long evening with many possibilities when she changed the subject.

"How did you wind up owning part of an import shop?"

"I had a case about six months ago involving a woman who couldn't collect a substantial insurance policy on her husband because he had apparently committed suicide. Well, it turned out to be murder and I was able to prove it. She was a big tipper. Louise had been trying to find someone to buy out part of the Jaded Fox. It seemed like a good investment to me, so I did."

"And is it?"

"A good investment?" She nodded. "Yeah, it is. Though I really can't take any credit for it. It's built on Louise's reputation, which is a good one.

Elaine regarded me for a moment, frowning thoughtfully, then said, "You're putting roots down. That's not like you."

The waiter arrived and placed our entrees in front of us. Thinking I had successfully evaded a response, if one was expected, I dug into the salmon with dill sauce. As I chewed, I couldn't help but notice Elaine watching me, her brown eyes cool and amused. "That's not like you," she repeated.

I swallowed and continued to poke around the fish, avoiding her scrutiny. "They're roots, all right. But they're pretty shallow."

"You've got two businesses going simultaneously. If that's not getting in a little deep, I don't know what is." When I looked up at her, she was leaning on the table, her head cocked, waiting for more than a brush-off.

Shrugging, I said, "I could close down the P.I. business tomorrow if I wanted to. As for the shop, Louise really runs it. It doesn't tie me to Foxport. Not really."

Unconvinced, she nodded, "What about Peanuts?"

"Peanuts is portable."

"But he's still a responsibility."

"I can handle him."

"Well, I know you can. It's just that it isn't like you. You don't go out of your way to, you know, take things like that on."

Now she was eating her chicken while I waited for her to continue. I set my fork down. "No, I don't know. What do you mean?"

After a swallow of wine, she gave it a small shrug and said, "You don't accumulate things. You like your things disposable."

"Elaine, since when are you an expert on Quint McCauley?"

"I guess I'm not. We were only together for two months. Doesn't mean much at all, does it?" She ripped off a piece of bread and dabbed at the Madeira sauce.

"How much do you expect it to mean? Two months is barely enough time to find out what you like on your pizza."

She regarded me for several moments, then said, "You know, Quint, you can't blow everything off with a line."

Mercifully, the waiter appeared to ask if everything was all right. Elaine looked away and I managed a grim smile and a nod. He poured the remainder of the wine into our glasses. I wondered what it would take to rescind my earlier directive. Slip the guy a twenty and tell him to cut to the coffee? He'd probably seen stranger things. But I held on to my money and watched him disappear.

Sitting with my hands clasped and my elbows resting on the arms of the captain's chair, I tried to think. The food was sticking in my throat and Elaine wasn't helping. I drained my glass. "All this 'roots' stuff sounds kind of funny coming from someone who went tearing off to Santa Fe like they just discovered gold out there." The minute it was out of my mouth I was sorry.

She placed her knife and fork on her plate and pushed it back a couple inches. With her chin resting in the palm of her hand, it occurred to me for the first time that she looked tired. No, it was more than tired. She looked drained.

I leaned forward, "Elaine . . ."

Before I could start the sentence, she said, "I'd like to leave."

I'd pictured a lot of ways for this evening to end, but this wasn't one of them. Dropping my napkin on the table, I leaned back and tried to make eye contact with her. But it takes two, and after a while I figured it was time to make eye contact with the waiter.

"Is everything all right, sir?"

"Yes, fine. We'll take the check now."

He looked perplexed, almost sympathetic, but obeyed.

Before I had to ask, Elaine said, "Is there a reasonable hotel in this picturesque little town?"

The Fleetwood Inn is on the east edge of town. It's not anywhere near plush, but it's clean. And reasonable. There really wasn't much of a choice. When I'd first moved to Foxport, I'd stayed in another one that was a little farther east. It was called the Motor Inn and had the misfortune of being situated right next to a bar that had burned down right before the jello wrestlers got there. The marquee still stood, announcing their arrival on March 24 of some year gone by.

Before she checked in, I gave her forty dollars. "For the cab."

She hesitated, then took it, adding, "It was only thirty-two dollars so I owe you eight. I'll pay you later." She refused my offer to help her to her room.

I pulled my tie off, folded it, and tossed it in the back seat. Then, with the window rolled down, I lit a cigarette and stared at the sky. The moon was full and the night hazy, and it looked as though someone had tried to erase the big white disk and only succeeded in smudging it up.

Elaine had gone to Santa Fe with barely an explanation and had returned without one. Was that the sign of a committed person? What kind of person was that? Why was I the one being put through the third degree?

I was about to flick the half-finished cigarette out the window when I thought of Julia and smothered it in the ashtray.

It was ten fifteen — too early for bed, but I wasn't in the mood for a visit to the Tattersall Tavern. At some point it might require an exchange of pleasantries. I pulled out of the lot. Maybe it was a good night for watching someone else's life turn to muck.

I went home, cracked a beer, turned on the VCR and spent the next two hours telling Willy Loman how he could turn his life around. Easy for me to say.

Chapter 4

LEONARD NOVOTNY HAD NEVER aimed to impress clients with plush furniture and framed posters of defunct art exhibits. Someone was going to a lot of trouble to correct that. The smell of paint hit me the moment I walked into the office of Novotny and Associates, which was one in a row of connected, one-story stucco buildings. What furniture remained in the large outer office was covered with either plastic or canvas. At first I wasn't sure whether the walls were going from beige to peach or from peach to beige. A painter dressed in jeans and a red T-shirt turned as the heavy door fell shut behind me. He was husky with a ruddy complexion and wore a DeKalb Ag cap, which boasted their famous winged ear of corn. The brush in his hand dripped peach.

"Secretary's in there," he jerked his head toward one of the three doors I assumed opened to offices. A fourth was apparently a back entrance. A sheet of typing paper was taped to the door he indicated, and written on it in green highlighter were the words: Excuse our mess. I did, and knocked.

A pleasant-looking middle-aged woman pulled the door open, glanced at me, and peered into the large room, checking out the progress of the painter. Then she turned back to me and smiled. "Please forgive this awful mess." She was small and plump with gray hair lacquered into tight curls. Her dark red lipstick looked freshly applied. "We're in a state of transformation." From the tone of her voice, she wasn't too pleased.

I told her not to worry about it, introduced myself, and asked to see Rebecca Novotny.

"Why don't you come in here?" She stepped back a couple feet, allowing just enough room for me to sidle into the office. It was crammed with file cabinets, furniture, and a copying machine that probably belonged in the room getting the paint job.

She squeezed between a file cabinet and a bookcase to get to her desk, a cluttered island in a sea of chaos. Precariously balanced on the desk was a plastic woodgrain plate with white lettering, which read Mary Mulkey. She brushed past it, knocking it to the floor. I retrieved it and set it on top of an overflowing basket of files.

Taking a seat behind the desk, she said, "What was it you wanted to see Rebecca about?"

"Her father," I said and added, "I'm investigating his death for a client."

"I see." She wasn't through listening, but I kept my mouth shut and gave her my best lopsided grin.

After a few seconds, she said, "I'll just let Rebecca know you're here," then turned all her attention to the phone, picking up the receiver like it was a strange variety of shellfish someone had dared her to eat. She squinted at the dial and, after consulting a card taped to her desk, tentatively pressed three buttons. "Don't know what was wrong with the old phones either," she muttered. After a moment she said, "Yes, Rebecca, there's a gentleman here to see you. A Quint Mc-Cauley." She looked like she was about to go on but was cut off and closed her mouth, waiting. Then she said, "Well, he said he's here about your father's death." A pause. "Yes." Another pause. "Well, I don't know. Shall I ask? . . . All right." She might have been listening to the part of the weather forecast she didn't care about. "No, I haven't found it yet, but I'm sure it will turn up soon. What with all the confusion . . . yes, I will." She rolled her eyes and listened for few seconds, said, "All right" again and hung up.

"Rebecca's just finishing something up now. Would you mind waiting a few minutes?" I found an empty corner of a chair and eased myself into it.

I could feel her gaze on me as I studied an oil painting that was leaning against a wall. Its subject was a man in his fifties with heavy-browed eyes and a thick head of wavy hair that was just starting to gray. He had been a large man; probably just big when he was younger but had gone a little soft later in life. There was something about the way his chin thrust out that gave him a military bearing.

"You work for Mr. Novotny for very long?"

She nodded with a solemnity that was sort of touching and said, "I was his first secretary. His only one. Of course he had temporaries while I took some time off to have Billy, and then when God took Harold, but we'd been together for twenty-seven years." She swallowed and wrested a tissue from a plastic-covered box. Dabbing at her eyes, she sighed and said, "You'll have to forgive me. He was such a fine man. Hardworking and God-fearing."

"Did you find him?"

She didn't have to answer. Except for swatches of an unnatural shade of pink highlighting her cheekbones, her face lost all color. "I came in that afternoon to finish up some correspondence for Len. I often come in on Saturdays to do a few things, you know, get a head start on Monday."

"Did Mr. Novotny often work on Saturdays?"

"Sometimes. Never on a Sunday, but it wasn't unusual for him to come in on Saturdays. Maybe just for a few hours, but he often came in. I think he enjoyed it. He felt comfortable here." Glancing toward the door, she added, "I wonder what he'd think of all this."

"Probably not much. I'd bet that peach wasn't his favorite color." She rolled her eyes. "Nor mine."

"So you weren't surprised to see his car here that Saturday?"

Pausing, she cocked her head in another pigeon gesture. "Actually, like I told the police, I was surprised. He was supposed to go fishing that day. I don't know with who though. Perhaps alone. I just assumed he'd changed his mind."

"Was he in his office?"

She swallowed and closed her eyes. "Yes." The phone warbled. Starting, she placed a hand on her chest to calm herself, then answered.

When she hung up, she said, "Rebecca can see you now."

Rebecca's office was in stark contrast to her secretary's. Not only was it much larger, but there probably wasn't a piece of furniture that didn't belong. Even the computer had its own rosewood table. Seated at a large, pristine desk was the new head of Novotny and Associates.

Rebecca Novotny was her father's daughter with heavy brows and a square jaw that jutted out into a pointed chin. Her eyes were small and penetrating and if she was wearing makeup, you couldn't tell. Straight brown hair hung past her shoulders, reminding me of the ears on an Afghan hound. The jacket of her tan linen suit was draped over the back of her chair and the pink blouse she wore had flecks of tan in it. The look was conservative and expensive. She didn't get up.

"Are you with the police?" was the first thing she said after offering me a seat.

"No, I'm a private investigator." I showed her an ID. She nodded, unimpressed, and I went on. "I'm working for Jeff Barlowe, the reporter who . . ."

"I know Jeff Barlowe. I know all about him." From her expression I gathered Jeff wasn't high on her list of people she dropped down on her knees for every night.

Shifting in the chair, I returned the ID to my hip pocket. Rebecca's face, for all its shadows and angles, was difficult to read.

"He doesn't think the Fox did it."

She removed a cigarette from a slim, silver case, lit it and leaned back in her chair. Then she shot a stream of smoke up toward the ceiling and said, "I think he's wrong. You should have seen his office. There's no doubt in my mind it was the Fox's work."

"Yeah, I guess it doesn't look good for the Blue Fox, but I like to consider all the options before I get to my conclusions." There was no softening in her gaze, nor a glimmer of what was going on in her head. I went on. "Let me put it this way, if I'm convinced the Fox did it, that's what I'll tell my client. Then he can do what he pleases." I waited for a reaction, got none, then asked, "Were you in the office the Saturday your father was killed?"

"No. I wasn't." She studied me through a cloud of smoke. "You mentioned options. What are they?"

"Like maybe someone wanted to make it look like the Fox killed your father. Maybe there's someone else who wanted to see your father dead."

Again, the dispassionate stare. This woman belonged in a game of five card stud. "Who did you have in mind?"

I shrugged. "Nobody. Everybody. I'm going into this with an open mind."

Abruptly she leaned forward, crushed her half-smoked cigarette out in a marble ashtray, and said, "Well, it's not easy to have an open mind when it's your father who has been murdered. That damned Fox has become such a folk hero, he could blow up the National Oil Building with everyone in it and his followers would cheer." Just as the embers from her last cigarette were fading, she lit another. Her chair creaked slightly as she settled back. The corners of her mouth turned up in a mocking smile. I imagined she was conjuring up various ways to dismember the Fox. Finally, she said, "But I'm willing to bet there's at least one member of the flock who's got his or her priorities straight."

After a moment I realized that she expected prompting. "What do you mean?"

She pulled out the middle drawer of her desk and withdrew a folder, which she tossed across the desk to me. "That's running in the *Foxport Chronicle* tomorrow. I bought a quarter page."

The folder contained a message that didn't need a full quarter page. It read: "$10,000 Reward for the first person to give me the name of the

Blue Fox." In smaller letters it added, "All sources will remain confidential." Rebecca's name, address and phone number were included.

I tossed it back toward her. "I suppose you know you're going to get every crank in the county trying to collect."

Unfazed, she shrugged. "I don't care. As long as I get this guy."

"Who's going to follow up your leads?"

"You're not the only private investigator in town, McCauley." She had me there.

Rebecca was watching me closely. Oddly enough, I had the feeling she was waiting for my approval. I couldn't give it to her. Bounties make me real nervous.

"What if it turns out that the Fox didn't kill your father? What if he's got an airtight alibi?"

One elbow rested on the arm of her chair and her hand lay on her midriff. She began to fiddle with a button on her blouse. "It will still be worth it to me. I'd like to confront that character and show him that he's not the only one who cares about the environment. There are other ways of showing it."

I had the feeling there was a lecture coming and though I'd have to sit through it, I wasn't about to encourage it.

After an uncomfortable silence, she sat up and, propping her elbows on her desk, regarded me for a minute. Then she said, "People want progress, but they don't want to sacrifice anything for it. They want to be able to drive out to see unspoiled nature in their gas-guzzling cars, but they're ready to boycott any oil company that spills a drop in the ocean. They scream because taxes keep getting higher but they don't want to sacrifice any piece of land for industry, which would help keep taxes down. You know what I mean, don't you, McCauley?" She shook her head and scowled. "That stupid SOW group. What a bunch of cretins. What they don't understand is that they can get their tax relief and a better swamp to boot."

I decided I liked being lectured to by Julia Ellison better than by this woman and was about to try to change the subject, but she wasn't finished. "I'm as much a conservationist as any in that group. I refuse to wear fur. I drive a small, dull car that gets more than thirty miles to the gallon, and I recycle my trash. So I'm not going to let anyone call me a spoiler just because I'm trying to bring some jobs, tax relief and good industries to this area." She settled into her chair.

Before she got rolling again, I asked, "How did your father get into land development?"

Pushing a strand of hair behind her ear, Rebecca returned the folder to the drawer. "He was an early land speculator in some areas that paid off. Back in the mid-sixties, he got together enough money to buy up some land in DuPage County. Today that land is right in the middle of the high tech corridor. It's some of the hottest property in the country right now."

She shifted in her chair and examined the end of her cigarette before turning back to me. "After that, mother's family decided to let him handle all their holdings."

"Is that a lot of property?"

"Around here, yes."

"How long had you been working for your dad?"

"Three years now. Just after I graduated from the University of Chicago."

"Were you his only associate?"

"No, I wasn't. For several years he worked with a man named Nick Guthrie. He's had his own company for the last four or five years."

"Why the split?"

Shrugging, she drew deeply on the cigarette again. "I don't know. Why don't you bother Nick about that?"

I figured she did know, but decided that bothering this Guthrie guy couldn't be any more unpleasant than bothering her. I was only looking for a couple more answers, which I hoped to get as quickly as possible so I could leave. "Your father didn't own all the land he used in development?"

"No." She paused to push the cuff of her blouse up far enough to check the time. "As I said before, some of it belonged to my mother's family."

"Who besides your mother does that include?"

"Just her sister. Though Aunt Catherine is quite ill. She's not expected to be around much longer."

"The wetland area you want to develop. Who owns that?"

"Aunt Catherine."

"What about your brother?"

She didn't answer.

"Martin? Is that his name?"

"What about him?"

Before I could answer, we were interrupted by the sound of a door slamming followed by a shrill voice. "That's not the color I selected."

Rebecca rolled her eyes and closed them, pressing her thumb and forefinger to the bridge of her nose.

"Becky!" the voice demanded. "Becky, come look at this."

With deliberate slowness, Rebecca pushed her chair back from the desk and stood. She smoothed her skirt and, after ensuring that every ash from her cigarette had been reduced to soot, moved toward the door. I opened it for her.

The woman was tall, with a chiseled, somewhat harsh look to her features and blunt-cut hair that was a shade somewhere between blonde and gray. Her forearms protruded from slits in the flowing red cape she wore. She was in the middle of a heated argument with the painter.

"Yes, it is, ma'am," he was saying. "This is the color you ordered. Perfectly Peach." He pulled a work order from a paint-spattered jacket thrown over a plastic-covered chair. "See here," he pointed to an item on it, which the woman barely glanced at. "Perfectly Peach." Next he produced a sample card which he held up to the wall color. "This is going to fade a little as it dries. But it's the same color."

Ignoring the demonstration, she said, "Well, I'm sure it's not."

"If you'd like to pick out another color, that's fine, but I'm going to have to charge you for what I've done so far."

The caped woman stepped back, studying the painter as though he were a new form of insect, and said, "I'd like to speak to your higher-up."

"Ma'am," the painter's good nature seemed to be wearing thin, "I am the higher-up. I work for myself. Now I want you to be happy with this, but I've put in several hours of work here —"

"As if I don't have enough to do without supervising this simple job. Mary," she snapped, drawing the secretary from her office haven. "Find a better shade. Then let me see it."

Before Mary could respond, Rebecca stepped forward. "Mother, I like this color. It will be fine." She stood, arms crossed over her chest, several inches shorter than her mother.

Amelia looked around for another opinion and found me. "What do you think?"

"I think it looks fine," I lied, trying to picture this woman in a sixties coffeehouse.

"This color will be fine, Mother." Rebecca might have been speaking through clenched teeth.

"I don't think so, Becky." Amelia Novotny briefly regarded her daughter then turned back to me. "You really like it?"

"It's great. Very warm. Comfortable." She didn't look happy yet. "It's a 'let's do business' kind of color."

She heaved a sigh. "Well, maybe it is all right." Glancing at the painter, she added, "But I really don't think that's the color I selected."

"I like it, Mother."

"You know, I think I'll ask Martin. Yes, that's what I'll do." With that she turned and walked toward the door. "Be sure that's finished by Friday. Carpet layers are due then."

"Does that mean I should keep going?"

"Of course, it does. Just make sure it dries quickly."

Amelia missed the deep bow the painter graced her with as she swept out of the office. Rebecca didn't, but if I expected her to share the humor in the gesture, I was mistaken. She glowered at the door for a few moments, then said, "I really can't give you any more time, McCauley. I'm sure you can find your own way out." With that, she retreated to her office.

Mary just shook her head. I offered her my business card, and in response to her puzzled look, said, "In case you remember anything you think might be helpful. Just give me a call." After a glance at Rebecca's door, which remained closed, she took the card, then turned and went back to her clutter. That left me and the painter. He shook his head and spread more of the Perfectly Peach on his roller. I was half way out the door when he said, "Hey, buddy."

I stopped.

"Thanks." He began to roll the peach on the wall.

"For what?"

Looking at me over his shoulder, he continued to roll the paint on. "For lying."

Chapter 5

Aт ONE TIME CATHERINE Forrester's high cheekbones might have been her most striking feature. Now the skin hung loose and gray, emphasizing the hollows of her skull. The blue and purple scarf wrapped around her head like a turban and the silver dangling earrings made me think of ancient Gypsies and their curses. She leaned forward from the blue velvet cushions, grasped the arms of the chair in her claw-like hands, and, lowering her voice, said, "Have you got a cigarette?"

She saw my hesitation and added with a smile that was somewhere between bitter and amused, "I smoked two packs a day for forty-five years and the only part of this body that isn't diseased is my lungs." Her voice was clear, though weak, and had a mildly hypnotic singsong quality.

I withdrew a pack from my jacket and tapped up a couple cigarettes. She pulled one out using long sculpted nails which were shiny and red and waited for me to coax my reluctant lighter into producing a flame. After I lit it for her, she inhaled deeply and leaned back into the cushions, eyes closed, and released the smoke with a sigh. I placed the pack of cigarettes on the mahogany end table next to her chair and waited.

Catherine Forrester had been as easy to find as anyone listed in the Foxport phone book. I'd parted with tradition and called before coming and negotiated my visit through her live-in nurse. I guess I had expected to find a wraith of a woman hooked up to machines and IVs. But she was sitting up looking tired, but game, and didn't seem in any hurry to get rid of me. I decided to play the scene according to her timing.

She lived in a spacious, though not opulent, townhouse that overlooked a small, man-made lake — more like a large pond — which probably didn't yield much besides a nice view. We were sitting in an area that might have been intended as a bedroom, but which worked nicely as a sitting room. The late morning sun made checkered patches on the slate blue carpeting and a large gray tabby was curled up in the middle of one of them. At first I couldn't define the mild, pleasant smell that filled the room without overpowering it. Then I noticed several gardenias floating in a large crystal bowl filled with water. I'd been shown into the room by the nurse who, despite her pleasant features, seemed rather grim. A few minutes later she had materialized with a silver tea service and china cups and saucers. Catherine had introduced her as Gretchen Warren, her nurse and companion. After pouring for each of us, and telling Catherine not to tire herself, she disappeared.

Now I tried surreptitiously to study Catherine. I figured she was Amelia's older sister, though maybe not by as many years as it appeared. Hers was to be the kind of death that ate away at you.

Gesturing toward the cigarette, I said, "Does anyone try to stop you?"

She rolled her eyes toward the ceiling and shook her head. "They have fits," she added, then shrugged it off.

I nodded and waited for her to continue. It was several minutes and most of the cigarette before she said, "So, you want to talk to me about Leonard's death." She smiled and lifted the cigarette, "Before you leave, you're probably going to find that you've used up several of these and gotten little in return."

I shrugged. "Doesn't matter."

"I only know what they tell me. I was in the hospital when he died. Had been there for almost a week. I had what they euphemistically refer to as a bad spell." Pausing, she stared past me for a moment, then, slightly amused, said, "Imagine everyone's surprise. All of them standing around waiting for me to breathe my last, and then poor Leonard goes and steals the show." She turned away again and added, "I could have told them that wasn't my last trip to the hospital. I expect I'll know when it is."

She took the silver-rimmed teacup in both hands and, trembling slightly, lifted it to her lips as though she were taking the sacrament, then slowly set it down and said, "They told me he was killed by some crazed environmentalist." Her voice drifted off, then came back. "That's a shame."

"Why do you say that?"

"Senseless. When this whole wetland controversy started, I told Leonard to forget the area. Or offer some kind of compromise. No sense incurring the ill will of the community you've spent most of your life making better. People won't remember that. What's the line? 'The evil men do lives after them. The good is oft interred with their bones.'" Her smile was quick and apologetic as she added, "Did you ever have to memorize those words of Antony's?"

I smiled. "Those and a few others."

"They're so true, you know. The people of Foxport are going to recall how Leonard tried to fill in a damned marsh, but not how he made this community more than a town to pass through on the way to Iowa." She sighed and took another cigarette, which she waited for me to light.

"But he was stubborn. He said once the industrial park was bringing jobs and tax revenue to the community, once he'd developed new marshes and such, people would forget about the original wetland. People have short memories, he used to say."

"He may have been right. Politicians depend on it."

Smiling, she leaned toward me, leaving the hollows of her feather pillows, "I used to think that Leonard would have made a wonderful congressman. I could even have seen him as President." She settled back again, "But I hadn't known him long before I realized that he was entirely too ethical for politics. He lived according to inhumanly rigid guidelines that he expected everyone else to live up to as well." She noticed my untouched cup of tea, which seemed to distress her. "Don't you care for tea? I can have Gretchen bring you coffee or soda if you'd prefer."

"No, this is fine." I lifted the saucer and squeezed my finger into the cup's ear. Tea was okay, but I preferred the English traditions of stout and ale. And I always felt like I should cross my legs and spread a linen napkin over my knee when I was drinking the stuff. "Tell me more about Leonard," I prodded.

"Well, as I said, he was outrageously honorable. He had this strict code of ethics he expected the rest of the world to comply with. Yes, he was honorable, but not terribly realistic." She shook her head and took another sip of tea. "We spent many an hour arguing over that point. I told him that in an ideal world, his demands might be feasible, but this one is anything but. Still, he insisted."

"Was he religious?"

"Oh, yes." She paused, then said, "You know, I don't think Amelia's seen the inside of a church since she married Leonard. But Leonard would go weekly. When she was growing up, Rebecca used to go with him. It was kind of cute, this big man and his little girl. After a time she stopped going." Another pause, then a sigh. "Poor Rebecca." She didn't elaborate.

"Why poor Rebecca?"

"Well, she can be just as stubborn as Leonard, but she has none of his . . . oh what's the word . . . charisma? Also, she's just not as smart as Leonard was."

"Well, she's still quite young," I said, mildly surprised by my urge to defend her.

Catherine glanced at me. "Have you met Rebecca?"

I told her I had.

She studied me for a moment. "Some things can't be learned."

"I ran into Amelia at Leonard's office this morning. Looks like she doesn't have a whole lot of faith in her daughter either."

"Oh, what do you mean?"

"Well, she was redecorating and kept saying she needed Martin's opinion on everything. Practically ignored Rebecca."

Her eyebrows shot up and she leaned toward me. "Redecorating?"

"Yeah." I chuckled and added, "Hope the customers like peach."

She looked away and rested the tip of her chin on her curved fingers.

I gave her a minute, then said, "What about Martin?"

That brought her around and she even smiled. "Now, Martin has the Novotny charm. Yes, he does. Maybe he could stand a little more business sense, but that will come with time."

"Will he take over the business?"

"I suppose Rebecca will insist on sharing it, but Novotny and Associates needs someone with Martin's temperament."

"Martin has been gone for a while, hasn't he. How long?"

"Twelve years."

"Why did he move out west?"

"Oh, I think he was trying to find himself. Or perhaps prove he could succeed in something other than his father's business."

"There was no falling out or anything?"

She gave me an odd look. "Of course not. Where did you hear that?"

I shrugged. "Nowhere. Just seemed like a possibility. You know, fathers and sons being what they are." Pausing, I gave her the opportunity to interject. When she didn't, I continued. "What was he doing out there?"

"He's got quite a good job as manager at a restaurant called The Breakers. It's in Malibu or one of those areas." She straightened the folds in the afghan draped over her lap. It was a blue and white jacquard patchwork.

I tried to light my own cigarette with the recalcitrant lighter. Failing, I groped in my pockets for matches. "There's a book on the fireplace mantel," she said.

The matches were behind one of the dozen or so photographs assembled there. Several of them featured Catherine. "I was quite a looker, wasn't I?"

Shaking the flame from the match, I glanced at her and managed an awkward smile. What was I supposed to say? I returned my attention to the photos. "You were also quite the equestrian." In several of the photos she was astride an impressive-looking horse. Maybe the same one. I gestured toward one of the pictures. "This guy looks like he's got an attitude."

Her laugh was cut short by a wince of pain. She wrapped her arms around her midriff and held on for several seconds, before slowly releasing herself. "That's Beau James. He had every right to an attitude. One of the finest horses I ever sat. He's gone now too." There were other photos and I assumed some were family. One was of Catherine and Leonard. And there was one of Rebecca and a young man I guessed to be Martin. His light hair and eager smile contrasted with Rebecca's dark, brooding look. His arm was around her, and she looked like she wanted to squirm out of the picture. I only spotted one of Amelia and that was in a family photo. As I started to move back toward the chair, Catherine said, "Bring the matches with you."

Dropping them on the small table next to the cigarettes, I said, "Does Martin come home often?"

"Not as often as I'd like, of course. But travel from the West Coast can be expensive and he insists on paying his own way."

"Was he was here for his dad's funeral?"

"Of course he was." She gave me an odd look and added, "He came out when I went into the hospital. He's the one who told me ... about Leonard."

"Does he come by often?"

"Yes, he's been here several times. Martin is one of the few people who seems to enjoy visiting with me." I didn't respond, but she continued. "You see, people only like to visit sick people who are getting well. What else can you say to a sick person besides 'You're looking better,' and then catch them up on all the gossip? My friends know I'll never look any better than this, I'll only get worse." She paused and swallowed, wetting her lips before she added, "So now I don't get to hear the gossip anymore either." Then she managed a smile. "You don't have any good gossip, now do you?"

I shook my head. "I guess that's what I'm after too."

"Yes, well as you can see, you've come to the wrong place for it."

"Maybe you can just help me get a picture of a few things. All the land in the Forrester family. Is it all divided between you and your sister, Amelia?"

She nodded solemnly. "We're the only Forresters left."

"You don't have any children?"

She reacted as though I'd asked her if she'd ever considered walking on hot coals. "God no." Mellowing, she added, "I was married once, briefly. It only took me three months to decide I didn't care for the institution." She eyed me. "Are you?"

"Not anymore."

Nodding her approval, she continued, "Have you ever lived with a woman?"

"Yeah."

"More than one?"

"Not at the same time."

She laughed and winced again. Then she said, "You see. That's what I'd have done. I'm just sorry that custom didn't come into acceptance until it was too late to do me any good."

I smiled, then tried to get her back on the subject. "How much land does the Forrester family own?"

Waving a hand toward the wall behind me, she said, "Look for yourself. That map shows all our holdings in the Fox Valley area."

It was a large, black-framed map with streets and paths marked on it. There were two shaded areas, one in red and the other blue. The red area was larger, and included land north and northwest of developed Foxport. The blue area encompassed a few small sectors along the river and scattered patches due west of town. It included the wetland, standing out like a sapphire against the surrounding white of the map. "Blue is yours, right?" She murmured her assent. "Who owns the surrounding area?"

"I'm not sure. It may have more than one owner. Land around here changes hands so fast, it's hard to keep track."

I turned to her, not sure how to phrase the next question, but sure that she was expecting it. Finally I said, "Who are you leaving your land to?"

"I was leaving it to Leonard. He was smart. He'd know how to best develop the land. With the exception of that silly wetland, I usually agreed with him." She paused and added, "In fact, for the past couple years, since I've been ill, Leonard has been handling all my property matters. Of course he'd consult me, but I let him take care of it. I trusted

42

him." Her eyes filled with tears. She blinked and one welled over and slid down her face. "I miss him." She managed a smile and added, "Though, I suppose I won't miss him for long."

"Who will your property go to now?"

"I'm dividing it between Martin and Rebecca. I suppose I was tempted to leave it all to Martin. That just wouldn't be fair, though."

"Why would you want Martin to have it all?"

She chose her words carefully and proceeded with caution. "I don't pretend to know children well at all. It's like they're another species. I understand they're prone to mood swings. But as a child, Rebecca was so very moody. Quite unpleasant to be around much of the time. I can't say she has improved much with age either. There's a great deal of contact with the public in this business. Rebecca is the sort of person — bright but ill-natured — who would do better as a scientist, or something that doesn't require much personality. Martin on the other hand is a people person — handsome, charming, diplomatic."

"I noticed you didn't include smart in those adjectives." From the sour look she gave me, I might have put my toe over the line. "Who does the wetland go to?"

"Martin will handle that situation." She inhaled on the cigarette, already burned most of the way down.

I was about to ask her what kind of business savvy he would bring to the situation, when the door swung open and Catherine's nurse stepped in.

"Time for your eleven thirty pill, Cath—" she broke off when she saw Catherine pull the cigarette away from her lips.

Catherine sat, frozen for a moment, lungs full of smoke, then finally expelled it in a large white cloud. "Damn," she said without much emotion.

The nurse looked down at Catherine, disapproval registering in her posture and expression. Her blond hair was subdued into a thick braid and I noted again that she seemed to de-emphasize her beauty. But, because it was a natural beauty, it wasn't easy to hide.

Now Catherine sat, jaw set and eyes straight ahead, reminding me of a child who was going to deny complicity in whatever misadventure she was about to be accused of. The nurse turned and her glare settled on me. Finally she said, "Are you a physician?"

I shook my head.

"I didn't think so. You may think you're doing this woman a favor by giving her cigarettes, but you have no idea the extent of her illness. You don't know the effect those things can have on her. And secondary smoke isn't any better." I ventured a glance at Catherine who was still clutching the cigarette. When she caught my gaze, she rolled her eyes and turned away.

The nurse wasn't stopping. "It's easy to write her off, isn't it? Well, she's dying anyway so what difference can it make? Well, it can make a big difference in the quality of time she has left."

Catherine was extinguishing the cigarette during the lecture. Then she held her hand up, and the nurse stopped. "It's not Mr. McCauley's fault, Gretchen. It was the only way he was getting me to talk."

"Still, I'm going to have to ask you to leave. And," she reached in front of Catherine and snatched the half-full pack from the table, "take these damned things with you."

I pocketed them. "I'll show myself out."

"Mr. McCauley." I turned back to Catherine. "Stop by again. You don't even have to bring your cigarettes." Then, with a sideways glance to Gretchen, she added, "Unless, of course, you want to."

I was thinking about the chemistry in the Novotny family as I drove back into Foxport. Rebecca shut down at the mention of her brother, Martin, but apparently Amelia and Catherine thought he was right up there with Apollo. I had wanted to get a read on Catherine and Amelia's relationship, but was given the bum's rush before I could get at it. Still, the fact that there were no photos of the two of them suggested that they weren't real close. And it was apparent that Catherine thought a lot of her brother-in-law. Interesting.

I was sort of enjoying the mental exercises I was doing with the Novotnys, and I probably never would have noticed the car following me if it hadn't run a red light at the corner of Third and Main and then held back so it wasn't right on my tail. Still I wasn't sure. People do strange things. I was getting low on cigarettes, so I pulled into the Family Pantry to buy a pack and to see if the gray Chrysler would still show up in my rearview mirror. While I was in there, I bought a couple lottery tickets since the pot had rolled over the last couple weeks and was expected to hit forty million before the drawing. I'm one of those halfhearted players who doesn't buy tickets if the pot is a paltry six million. Weekly players probably hate it when guys like me win. Fact is, I always get a little nervous buying a ticket. I heard somewhere that the odds of your winning the lottery are about the same as the odds of your getting hit by lightning. I buy a ticket and until I find out I lost, I feel like I'm wearing a lightning rod.

When I left the store I didn't see anyone waiting outside for me, but I hadn't gotten a block down the street before I saw him in my mirror again. He'd pulled out of a side street. I'd barely begun my investigation, so it didn't seem likely that I'd stepped on too many toes yet. Unless Julia Ellison wanted to keep tabs on me. But she didn't seem the type to care much about what anyone besides herself did. The last, and most obvious possibility, was the police. Sure. If they knew I'd seen Jeff Barlowe, they might suspect that I'd talked to the Blue Fox. They might think I'd try to talk to her again. It's difficult to tail someone who stops for a drink or lunch, because you've got to be in there watching him in case there's something going on besides lunch. I smiled and turned down Gunderson. What the hell. I was hungry.

The small lot adjacent to the Tattersall Tavern was full so I parked on Wilson and walked a half block back to the bar. It wasn't crowded, and I had no trouble finding a table with a good view of the door. I had no idea how I was supposed to spot a tail once he got out of the car, but I'd just have to wait and see.

I ordered a turkey sandwich and a Guinness and by the time the waitress brought it, two possibilities had entered the tavern. The first was a man in his mid thirties wearing a lightweight sweater and jeans. He had dark hair and wore dark-framed glasses. He scanned the room's occupants before taking a seat a couple tables away from me. Less than a minute later another man came in, this one probably not thirty yet, wearing a sports coat over dark slacks. He also gave the room the once-over then sat behind me at the bar. I heard the guy at the table order a cheeseburger and a beer. After a minute I glanced behind me to see what the guy at the bar was drinking. Bingo. Nobody but a cop steps into a bar for a quick Coke. Nobody.

I ate my sandwich and finished the glass of stout as I decided what to do next. Once I left I could either go on my way, watch from a distance to verify my suspicion, or wait right outside the door and watch the look on his face as he practically stepped on me. Forcing his hand might be the best way to go. I was almost certain he was a cop, but maybe I could get him to prove it. And then maybe they'd give up on tailing me. Right. Police Chief Ed Carver would never miss the opportunity to harass me legally.

I waited outside. And as the seconds turned into minutes, I began to see myself as a paranoid. Before long I'd be checking my apartment for bugs and my food for traces of arsenic. Fish would speak to me in tongues. And then it was just a matter of time before I lined the windows with foil to keep the extraterrestials out. I decided it was time to move on.

It's funny how when something is wrong, your mind tends to come up with all kinds of outrageous explanations before hitting on the right one, which is usually unpleasant. My car is a late model Honda Accord so it's larger than some of the older models. But as I approached it, I was struck by the fact that it really was quite a bit smaller than the two domestic cars it was parked between. Then my mind rejected that notion when I recognized the models as being in the same size range as the Accord. So my mind leaped to the conclusion that I'd parked in a dip. A sudden, rather deep dip that made my car appear shorter than the other two. Only after I'd stepped up to the car and stared at the deflated tires for several seconds did it register. I wormed between cars and moved into the street to view the damage on the other side. It was just as bad. I stood in the middle of the street for several moments, hands sunk deep in my pockets, as I fought back the urge to shake my fist at the sky.

I was about to kick one of the tires when I heard a loud popping noise, and the rear window on the passenger side shattered. I hit the ground scrambling toward my car, realized there wasn't enough room for me to squeeze under it, and maneuvered into the space in front of it. I'd barely made the distance when I heard the squeal of tires and looked up just as a flash of gray tore past me.

▽

Chapter 6

THE KID FROM THE gas station dropped me off at my office on the way to the garage, my car in tow. He told me he could replace the tires that afternoon, but I'd have to take the car to a glass place for the window. He offered to call one for me.

"Thanks, but no. I think the window's going to have to wait a couple days."

"Suit yourself." He had a lopsided smile and a way of looking at me out of the corner of his eye as he drove, one arm draped over the steering wheel. "You know, mister, if I were you, I'd let the cops know."

Shrugging, I said without much enthusiasm, "What for? I didn't see anything."

"Yeah, but," he turned down the volume on the rock station, "somebody tried to kill you." His tone carried a mixture of disbelief at my lack of concern and excitement at the prospect of something like that happening to a customer of his.

"I doubt it. I suspect it was just a warning. I'd have been easier to hit than the window. Bigger target."

He dropped me off in front of the Jaded Fox, told me his name was Terry and to call him in a couple hours.

There was no message from Elaine, but one from Mary Mulkey, Novotny's secretary. I returned her call and she told me that she remembered Leonard always went fishing up at Lake Geneva and that was probably where he'd planned to go that Saturday. She wondered if that would help me in my investigation, adding that the police didn't seem to think it was very important and hadn't been very polite about it. I wondered if this wasn't the first time she'd called the police with a "clue," but thanked her and told her I'd look into it.

Now it was almost two o'clock and I wondered what Elaine had done for lunch. I tried calling her again. No luck. Although she hadn't checked out, there was no answer at her room. I left another message, wondering where she would go without a car. Where would I go without a car?

Sitting at my desk, forehead braced against the heel of my hand, I was drawing foxes on a yellow legal pad. The head-on sketches weren't too hot — they looked sort of like anteaters with whiskers — but the profiles showed promise. At the same time, I was debating whether I should find a member of the Save Our Wetlands group to talk to or go looking for Elaine. There was a light rapping at the door which I didn't have time to acknowledge before it creaked open and Louise stepped in.

After closing it behind her, she said, "Was that your car being towed past here?"

"I'm afraid so. I've got four flat tires and a shattered window. Apparently I've stepped on someone's toes."

"Well, if you need a car this afternoon, you're welcome to use mine."

"Thanks, Louise, I may take you up on that."

She didn't leave then, and I knew there was more coming. Finally she managed a tentative smile and said, "I know I'm being nosy, but I was just wondering how things went last night."

I shook my head, drawing a window around one of the foxes. "Not good, Louise. Not good."

Raising her eyebrows in disbelief, she said, "She didn't do that to your car, did she?"

I waved off her suspicions. "No, no, that's not Elaine's style." I sighed and added, "It just didn't go anywhere near like I planned."

"Oh," she drew the sound out with a sympathetic inflection and sat in one of the two chairs I'd purchased at a flea market. "She seems like such a nice girl."

I returned to my doodling and drew vertical bars on the window, didn't care for the look of it, and dropped my pencil on the pad. Lacing my fingers behind my neck, I gave Louise my full attention. "She is."

"Well, I wonder what happened."

I smiled as I watched Louise's features go into their high concentration mode. She drew her brows together, her forehead took on more wrinkles, and her mouth screwed up the way a kid's does when working a tough math problem. Louise was well into her sixties, but her gestures and dress might have belonged to a woman at least twenty years younger. "You know," she said, "I had the feeling . . . just from talking to her for a few minutes . . . I had the feeling that there was something troubling her."

"No kidding. I'd just left her stranded at the airport."

"Well, I know that." Her tone was abrupt, chiding. "It's just that there seemed to be something more." I waited for her to continue. "And frankly, I'm not surprised to hear things didn't go well for you two."

"What did she say?"

"Oh, it wasn't anything she said. Not really. It was more, I don't know, a way about her. Distracted almost. Pleasant, but distracted."

The way she'd sized up Elaine in fifteen minutes, when it had taken me all night, made me want to tell her to mind her own business. But I checked myself and waited for the advice I figured was coming next.

But all she said was, "She needs to talk to someone about it. If I were you, I'd be certain that someone was me."

"Well, I know that. How can I talk to her if I can't find her?"

"Find her."

"Don't suppose you've got a crystal ball I can use?"

She regarded me for a moment, then stood and, bracing both hands against the edge of my desk, said, "I think if you put your mind to it, you'd have no trouble finding her at all." She turned and left the room, closing the door gently behind her.

After staring at the door for a minute, I muttered, "Must be nice to have it all figured out."

I briefly debated whether to keep pushing on the Novotny investigation or trying to track down Elaine. What did she want me to do? Surely she'd call if she wanted to talk. Why the hell was she being so damned mysterious? She was stubborn — that I knew for a fact — revealing a piece of information only when she was good and ready. Revealing a piece of herself just when you thought it was closed off to you forever. I hadn't thought of myself as being tied down to Foxport. Not really. Not until she pointed it out to me. For the first time I thought of how much simpler my life would be right now if she hadn't come back. Why didn't she call?

The hell with her. At least I knew what Jeff's problem was.

I figured the SOW group wasn't big enough or organized enough to have its own office, and I was right. Fortunately, David Reaves was the type of politician who spent a lot of time in the district he represented. The fact that there was an election in less than two months didn't hurt either. He was a partner in a law practice with two other attorneys: Kendall and Phelps. Their office was on Second Street, just two blocks north of Main, in a half block of restored homes. Reaves had come to office in the last election, narrowly beating out the older, less photogenic incumbent, Barry Haller, who had voted for a tax increase once too often. Apparently Haller had also been involved with a young woman who worked for him. It seemed that the conservatives who could forgive the tax increase couldn't forgive the indiscretion and vice versa.

David Reaves was on the phone when I got there. He waved me into his office and motioned toward a chair. He was saying, "Look, Pete, I don't care what you have to do. Just handle it." He paused to listen, then said, "Isn't that what I pay you for?" Another pause. "Okay, then go earn some money for a change." He seemed to catch himself and, shaking his head, went on, "I'm sorry. Nerves are short today, I guess. Go ahead with your idea." He leaned back to listen.

The first thing that struck me about Reaves's appearance, was his beard. It's unusual for a politician to sport a beard these days. Some people think it makes a man look menacing, and the one thing a politician doesn't want to do is scare little kids and their parents. But on Reaves, the close-cropped beard made him look earnest, almost priestly. It wasn't long before I noticed he had a habit of stroking it as though it were a favored pet. Even sitting, he appeared to be a tall man—not massive, but tall—so that the large, campaign-style desk looked as though it were made to order. On one corner of this desk was a photo of the handsome blond politician, his lovely blond wife, and their three little towheaded offspring. No questioning that lineage.

The office was small and without the usual establishment trimmings. He had posters, not framed pictures, on the wall, and one was of a heroic-looking pig with its four feet planted in a pond. The pond's denizens flocked around him, seeking support. It reminded me of a Disney picture. "Save Our Wetlands" was printed across the top so that the first letter of each word was monstrous in proportion to the others.

In less than five minutes, Reaves and Pete, whoever he was, were back on better terms and the conversation over. He apologized for the wait. I introduced myself and said I was investigating the Novotny murder. His brow creased up. "May I ask who you're representing? I mean, the police are handling the investigation."

I smiled and nodded. "Yeah, they are. But they're convinced the Blue Fox is the murderer. My client believes otherwise."

"I see." He fondled his beard again. Maybe it stimulated brain cells. After a few moments, he lowered his hand and said, "Then you are either representing the Fox or Jeff Barlowe." Maybe it worked.

"Jeff Barlowe."

He nodded, apparently still chewing on it. "So, Barlowe's going to tough this one out." He frowned as though calculating how this was going to affect him, then said, "Knowing the identity of the Blue Fox could put you in the middle of a bad situation."

"I didn't say I knew."

Shrugging at the obvious conclusion, he said, "How can you investigate this and not know what Barlowe knows?"

"Easy." I decided it was okay to dispense with the truth. "I told Jeff I didn't want to know." Then I added, "Besides, what better way is there for me to conduct an objective investigation? If I don't know the identity of the Blue Fox, I won't be eliminating any possibilities before I start. You know, Jeff isn't serving time just to help a murderer stay at large. He thinks the investigation's taken a wrong turn. And he's willing to suffer some for the cause. On the other hand, if I can prove to him that this Fox character killed Novotny, he'll do the right thing."

"Which is?"

It seemed obvious to me. "He'll tell them what they want to know."

Reaves seemed to be busy in some other corner of his brain. After a minute he said, "All right. What can I do for you? Barlowe's a damn good reporter. I hate to see him in this situation."

"Don't suppose you could put in a word for him? For the sake of the First Amendment?"

Smiling, Reaves shook his head. "It wouldn't help." He gestured toward the pig poster. "My stand on this wetland issue is well known. My motives would be questioned." He paused. "And rightly so."

"Okay," I said, "Then let's start with this. What do you think? Are the cops right?"

Leaning back in the chair, Reaves propped his feet on an open desk drawer and clasped his hands against his blue pin-striped shirt. "Oh, I don't think so. The Fox has never hurt anyone. He's never even used tactics that might result in injury. No." He dismissed the notion with a wave of his hand. "I'm convinced that's the last thing he wants."

"I buy that. But what if he was trapped, cornered? What if Novotny walked in on the Fox while he was spray painting his office? The Fox panicked and shot him." I paused, then added, "I understand there was already bad blood between them."

Reaves frowned. "I don't know. I suppose it could have happened that way." Then he nodded. "I guess it's possible."

I locked my gaze onto his and, before he could stroke his beard, said, "Do you know who the Blue Fox is?" This might sound like a stupid question since it's the one thing I did know. But, I was real interested in learning who those few people were who Julia Ellison trusted with her life.

Smiling slowly, he shook his head. "But you're not the first to ask me that."

"Who beat me to it?"

"Ed Carver." Inwardly I sighed. I knew it was just a matter of time on this case before I got to tangle with Foxport's chief of police again.

"Okay, then do you have an educated guess as to who the Fox might be?"

"No names. But I'd say he's a supporter of environmental issues, who doesn't appear to be a zealot. He's probably a person who is careful not to draw attention to himself." He smiled. "Doesn't narrow it down much, does it? But the fact is, he's probably a very low-key person who's not going to be caught, unless it's with a can of paint in his hand."

"How old do you think he is?"

"That I don't know."

"Well, he was active in the early seventies, wasn't he?"

Reaves conceded the point.

"So, he'd have to be in his late thirties at least."

After a brief mental calculation, he said, "Yes. I guess that's true."

"But who's to say that the Fox has always been the same person? Easy enough to pull off the impersonation of someone who's never been identified."

Reaves frowned, then shrugged. "I suppose that might be the case." He played with the idea. "Or how about this. Maybe the Fox is a woman." I held his gaze and he added, "A mother-earth type. It's possible."

"Hasn't Jeff Barlowe always used the masculine pronoun when writing about the Blue Fox?"

He waved his hand as though brushing away a mosquito. "Could be his way of protecting her." He paused, then added, "*If* the Fox is a woman."

I nodded. "Interesting," then gestured toward the poster and asked, "What does Novotny and Associates have to go through to get a permit to fill in this wetland?"

"Well, first there has to be a study by the Army Corps of Engineers. That's already happened. Novotny has to convince the corps that the wetland will either remain untouched or he will create a new wetland that's as good or better than the existing one."

"And SOW's convinced that can't be done."

He got up and moved over to a coffee maker on the far corner of a wooden table. Picking up a mug that said World's Best Dad, he poured a cup. Before he returned the pot to its warmer, he held it toward me in a gesture of offering. I declined.

Back in his chair, elbows propped on its wooden arms, he continued, "Basically, you're right. We're talking a tremendous impact on the wildlife and surrounding area — the ecological impact. Some believe there are wetlands still developing in that area. Still growing." He drank from the mug, studying me over its rim. When he lowered it, he said, "Mr. McCauley, I don't mean to lecture here, so stop me if I do, but I don't know how environmentally aware you are." He'd hit a rhythm he was comfortable with now, and the earlier signs of stress had faded.

"You keep talking. It won't hurt me to listen."

His smile was a little thin, but he said, "All right." Then he cleared his throat and continued. "There may be species of fishes, fowl, insects, plants — you name it — that are unique or environmentally necessary to that area. Forty percent of Illinois' threatened and endangered species either live in wetlands or depend on them for part of their life. Then there's the fact that wetlands act as a flood plain. When you fill in an area like that, where is the water that would have been soaked up there going to surface?" He raised his eyebrows. I imagined my feet getting wet and made an appropriate face. Satisfied, he continued, "Wetlands are also a source of pollution control. It's fascinating. Their vegetation works along with microorganisms to filter and neutralize organic matter and chemicals. In addition to all this, we've got to consider the state of the wetlands in Illinois. Do you know how much of our wetlands we've lost since the early eighteen hundreds?" He gave me time to work out an answer. When I shrugged and told him I had no idea, he prodded. "Take a guess."

"Oh," I looked toward the ceiling for an answer. "Fifty percent," I said, figuring I'd guess low so he could impress me.

He smiled, pleased with the naivety of his pupil. "Try ninety-five percent."

I was impressed. He continued. "More than seven-point-six million acres. We've got to be very careful about what we've got left. And, personally, I don't believe that his industrial park is a good trade-off. Tax revenues and everything else considered, I just don't believe, in the long run, we're going to get more than we lose."

Reaves spoke with conviction all right, but there was a trace of something else there — maybe it was because, given his position, he'd had to give this speech so many times, he didn't think about the words anymore. Sort of like the national anthem. Who actually thinks about the bombs bursting in air when you're waiting for the home team to take the field. It was bound to get a little stale. Then I glanced at the pig poster. For every SOW supporter he wowed with his talk, there was bound to be at least one, probably more, who for financial reasons, would rather see the pig sliced into strips and frying in lard. Maybe Reaves was genuine.

"Getting back to the Fox," I said. Reaves nodded and steepled his hands, waiting. "Do you approve of his brand of protest? Assuming he didn't make the ultimate statement by killing Novotny."

He cocked his head and stared off in the direction of the coffee pot. "Yes and no. What he's done is illegal, but if you put it in terms of the ends justifying the means, then," he made a shaky boat movement with his hand, "maybe I'm willing to look the other way. Don't quote me, though. This eco-terrorism, monkeywrenching, or whatever they call it, makes the point in a dramatic way, and sometimes that's what's called for."

I took a moment to swallow all that. Reaves appeared confident in a fabricated way, as though he were running on some hidden reserve. "What's this industrial park going to do to your chances of reelection?"

"Depends on how it turns out."

I heard a door close and a voice that was familiar, but which I couldn't at once place. Then she stepped into Reaves's office and the mystery was solved.

"I'm starting to hear things that are worrying me." Julia Ellison was talking directly to David Reaves and hadn't noticed me, sitting to the left of the door. When she did, a flicker in her eyes was the only sign that she knew me from Adam. I played along. What was more interesting was the look of horror that slid across Reaves's face during the seconds before Julia spotted me.

Blandly, she turned her attentions on me. She wore her tan trench coat open, revealing a black and blue checked blouse and a black skirt that fit snugly and stopped a few inches above her knees. Reaves stood for introductions. "Julia, this is Quint McCauley. He's investigating Leonard Novotny's death in the interest of Jeff Barlowe. Quint, this is Julia Ellison." I started to stand, but she waved me off and, although there was another chair, she perched on the edge of the table in sort of a sidesaddle position, which added a few more inches between her knees and the edge of her skirt. I could see that wasn't lost on Reaves, either.

Concentrating on her eyes as I spoke, I asked her if she knew Jeff Barlowe.

She glanced at Reaves before answering. "Yes, I do."

Seated again, Reaves said, "Julia is familiar with Barlowe's plight. She's one of the SOW organizers. She also teaches sociology at Abel County College," he turned toward her and finished with, "where she is molding tomorrow's ecologists."

Julia was watching me with a slightly amused expression and didn't respond to Reaves. He continued. "I'm glad to see someone is trying to help Jeff Barlowe. None of this is his fault."

I returned Julia's gaze. "I know someone who could help him out."

"Who's that?" Reaves asked.

I turned and said, "The Blue Fox. He or she could turn him or herself in."

Reaves gave me an odd look, a look he shared with Julia as well. Then, summoning up some authority, he stated, "I don't know if that's the solution."

"Sure it is. It's the only one, because Barlowe's not going to do it, which is pretty commendable when you realize that he's not a person who handles confinement well. And I don't just mean that it cramps his style. He's got a real problem. Besides, if the Fox is innocent, what's he got to hide?"

"That's not the point."

"Sure it's the point. And it's a simple point. This heroic Fox character is really a garden variety coward." I smiled and added, "That's what I think."

"Perhaps it looks that way, but I don't believe that's the case." Reaves shook his head. "The good the Fox has done is immeasurable. You can't put a price on it. What good would it do for him to come forward? Maybe this thing with Barlowe is all a hoax. Maybe they're just trying to flush him out."

"Yeah, well, maybe it's time the Fox turned the spray paint over to a successor." I looked at Julia who didn't appear at all ruffled. What would it take? "What do you think the Fox is doing?"

She folded her arms over her chest and stared at me for a moment before she said, "I have no idea. I don't presume to know what other people are thinking. Even the simplest mind is difficult to read."

"Yes, maybe that explains it. He's simpleminded." I had a sudden and intense craving for a cigarette, but figured that lighting up in the presence of these two would be right up there with wearing a raccoon coat to an animal rights' benefit. So I resisted. After a few minutes, it was over anyway. And though I was real curious to know what business Reaves and Julia had to conduct, I had the distinct impression the meeting wasn't going to be called to order until I was out the door. It would have been interesting to be a fly on the wall in that room. I suspected that Reaves knew more about the Blue Fox than he let on.

I rolled down the window of Louise's Grand Prix, lit a cigarette, and inhaled deeply. Nasty habit, but damn it felt good. A woman once told me that I smoked because I hadn't been breast fed as an infant and was compensating as an adult. That might be true, though I never considered it an appropriate question to put to my mother. Some families talk about things like that; some don't. Mine never did. Maybe there were just too many of us, and there wasn't time to ask anything but essential questions. There are six kids in my family. I'm the fifth and final son. Then there is my sister. Mom always said Dad wanted a daughter so bad, he didn't care how many sons it took. I guess I'm glad it took at least five, though I used to think there was a little kid's soul floating around somewhere who would have been my little brother, but didn't make it because Patricia and Joe McCauley finally had a girl the sixth time out. Kids have weird thoughts.

I drove back to my office and called Elaine. She'd checked out an hour ago. No message. Then I got obnoxious, arguing with the desk clerk, and accusing her of not giving Elaine my messages. She insisted she had passed the message on and informed me that it wasn't her responsibility to force guests to return their calls. She cut me off before I could light into her again. I didn't blame her.

Without a car or cash, Elaine would have to be in Foxport, unless she called someone to come get her. But who? Why had I been such a bastard to the desk clerk? Well, I could grovel with the best. I called back. The same voice answered.

"Uh, hi, this is Quint McCauley. I spoke with you a minute ago and was rather unpleasant. I just wanted to apologize."

There was a long silence, then, "That was the only reason you called?" Still a bit of chill to the tone.

"Well, no. It's just that I'm real concerned about this person and I wondered if, when she left, did you notice anyone with her or waiting for her?"

Another long pause.

"It's very important."

A sigh and then, in a tone that implied a huge sacrifice on her part, she said, "Well, I saw her get into a car outside the hotel. But I didn't see who was driving."

"What kind of car was it?"

"I don't know. I don't know cars at all." A short pause. "I think it was black."

"Was it large or small?"

"Oh, one of those mid size cars, I guess. Not real big and not small. Definitely not small."

"Did it look fairly new?"

"Yeah. Yeah, I guess it did." She was showing some enthusiasm and quickly continued with, "It was kind of sleek, you know. And shiny. Like it had just been washed."

"That's good. Now you said you couldn't see who was driving. Could you tell whether it was a man or a woman?"

"No, sorry. The windows were tinted."

I thanked her, told her she'd been immensely helpful, and hung up. The rest would be easy. All I had to do was find a new, black, mid size car with tinted windows that could have come from anywhere and could be going anywhere.

Chapter 7

Wᴴᴇɴ I ꜰɪʀꜱᴛ ʜᴜɴɢ up, I was concerned. As I unlocked the car, I was getting ticked. I tried not to dwell on it, but I was fuming by the time I'd driven to the northwest corner of Foxport where Novotny's former partner, Nick Guthrie, operated his business. What did Elaine want me to do? I considered it from all angles and I couldn't believe she was still angry over the airport incident. That wasn't like Elaine. If she'd planned on never forgiving me for my absence, she'd have told me right away. So, what was the problem? And what was I supposed to do about it? Chase all over Chicago and its suburbs looking for bent twigs trying to pick up her trail? I didn't pick the fight in the restaurant. I didn't ignore a message to call. I didn't up and move to Santa Fe and return months later on three days' notice with no explanation for either act. So why should I feel like I'd let her down? Made a lot of sense.

By the time I arrived at Nick Guthrie's office, I was aching for the opportunity to beat a confession out of him. Nevermind that I'd never met the guy and had no reason to suspect him of jaywalking let alone murder. I slammed the Pontiac's door shut and mounted the stairs to his office, ready to do battle.

I don't feel good about myself when I hassle receptionists. Theirs is a tedious, usually low-paying job and they have to deal with morons who believe the telephone is their personal instrument of abuse. At least I planned on being abusive in person.

She was on the phone when I walked in, explaining to someone why Guthrie wasn't there to take the call. While I waited, I cooled off a bit and convinced myself that my attitude wasn't going to get me anywhere. She was under no obligation to tell me the time let alone the where-abouts of her boss. One thing a private investigator learns fast: nobody owes you anything.

I tucked my anger somewhere just out of reach and glanced around the room for a way to get my foot in. Nothing on the walls gave any of Nick Guthrie away. There were the usual innocuous paintings, a couple hanging plants, and several pictures of a residential development called Yorkshire Estates. One was an aerial shot before building started — flat, green Illinois plains. Another was a sketch of the proposed development—big homes, golf course, clubhouse, the works. The third was a palatial home, landscaped to the hilt. I wondered how much it cost to move into one of those places, and where the people were coming from who could afford it. I moved away from the wall and noticed, fanned out on a low table next to a carved mallard, about ten copies of *Archery World* with Nick Guthrie's name on the address label.

The receptionist hung up the phone and gave me a benign smile. "Can I help you?" She was plump and wore large-framed glasses which matched her pink suit.

I introduced myself and said, "Well, from the sound of it, I may be out of luck. I was hoping to get a minute of Mr. Guthrie's time."

"You're out of luck this afternoon. If you'd care to make an appointment for tomorrow morning, he'll be in then."

"Hmm," I said. I'm a firm believer in the element of surprise when questioning people, whether they're suspects for not. Once they know a P.I.'s going to talk to them, they have time to think about what they're going to say. I like to have the advantage. So, after a minute I added, "Can you tell me where I can reach him?"

"Sorry," she said, but I didn't believe her.

"I understand." Pausing, I tried hard for a look of anguish and continued with: "Here's the situation. I'm selling a custom made longbow by Earl Gilroy. It's one of only five of its kind. Gilroy passed away last year. And I heard from a friend at the NAA that Mr. Guthrie might be interested."

"Well, I'm sure he'll want to talk to you," as she spoke, she opened an elaborate appointment book. "Why don't you come by tomorrow at 9:30?" she asked, pencil poised over the cream-colored page.

I shook my head. "I'm only in town for the day."

"Oh. I'm sorry." Tapping the end of the pencil against the calendar, she studied me for a moment. Then, brightening, she said, "Why don't you tell me how Mr. Guthrie can reach you? If he's interested, he can get back to you."

I glanced at my watch and looked past her toward the wall. Tough decisions. I shook my head, looking down at her again. "I don't see how that's going to work. I'm seeing this guy tomorrow who's real interested in it. He's made me an offer already." Shifting slightly, I tried to look apologetic and a little ashamed. "Thing is, he's kind of a rich yahoo. You know, today his sport's archery; tomorrow it'll probably be white water rafting. He's not real serious about it. Hate to see a bow like that go to someone who, you know . . ." I finished with a shrug.

59

"Well," she hesitated, obviously torn. "He really is unavailable now, but . . ." I leaned forward in anticipation. "He usually goes to the country club after work. You might try there. About six."

I got directions to the country club, thanked her, and left, thinking that I'd have been better off going with the truth, but it was too late now. I had about an hour and a half so I called my office to check for messages. Once again, Elaine Kluszewski hadn't called but Mary Mulkey had. She wanted to know if I'd checked out the lead she'd given me and added another. Apparently the phone bill had just arrived and she wanted to share with me the numbers he'd called "without a reason that I know of." There were three—two in California and one in Arkansas. I dutifully wrote them down, promising to check them out when I was checking out Leonard's fishing hole. I hung up thinking perhaps I should be more discreet about handing out my business card.

Next, I headed over to the *Chronicle* offices, hoping that Jeff's notes were clearer than his head was right now.

Tim Skillman, a short, heavy man with a young face and a receding hairline, made me show some identification before he handed over Barlowe's notes—three spiral notebooks bound together by a rubber band. "I hope you have some experience as a cryptographer. You're going to need it to make sense out of Barlowe's shorthand system." A flip through the pages confirmed his statement. Well, I liked puzzles and it looked like I wouldn't have much else to do that night.

I had time to pick up Louise and drive by the gas station where my Honda, with its four virgin tires, awaited me. At no charge, they'd taped a piece of corrugated cardboard across the empty window. The makeshift windscreen wouldn't do much to keep the rain out, but it meant that Peanuts could still ride with me. It was just after six as I crossed the river at Main Street and turned north on Route 41 toward Foxport's only country club.

My family used to live four blocks from a country club that, for me, had been a source of speculation and awe. Back then, not so many people could afford to join one of those clubs, and I figured the members must all be gods or something and once I got in there I'd know what Mt. Olympus looked like. The club was surrounded by a hurricane fence, softened by the ivy that crawled in and out of its links. My brother, Mike, and I used to spend a couple hours a week combing the tall grass surrounding the fence for golf balls. Then we'd sell them back to the club's patrons at half their original price. We made a few bucks that way. When I was twelve and old enough to caddy, I figured I'd paid my dues and was ready for the big time. The thing was, you made more money if you were experienced. So when I applied, I told them, "Yeah, I've been doing this for years." They sent me out on the course with this twosome that carried in one of the golf bags, in addition to the requisite clubs, balls, and tees, a mason jar full of gin and a smaller one containing vermouth-soaked olives. They were a little perturbed over my lack of golf-club knowledge. Hell, I didn't know I was supposed to anticipate which club they wanted. Who was playing the game anyway? As the game progressed, my judgment improved and their ability to notice deteriorated rapidly. It was a blisteringly hot day, I recall, and somewhere near the twelfth hole one of the golfers lost his lunch, not to mention about four martinis. The thing was, he didn't want to puke on the manicured green where the next group would have to play through the unsightly mess, so he turned to the nearest golf bag. Unfortunately, it wasn't his. The bag's owner took exception, hauled off and belted the offender, and left him lying there on the green. I'll never forget the sight of this paunchy, red-faced guy, sprawled out next to the twelfth hole with blood and vomit dripping off his knit shirt. So much for Mt. Olympus.

The long, winding drive to Foxport Country Club's main building spilled out onto North 41 from between red brick walls, each bearing an ornately sculpted F. I wasn't sure how far I'd get, but hoped to make at least the entrance on my first assault. Unfortunately, there was a guard house twenty feet down the drive. I pulled right up like I knew what I was doing, nodded to the guard, and told him who I was and who I'd come to see. His badge said his name was Ramirez and he wore the khaki security uniform as though he took it all pretty seriously. As he moved away from the window, I pondered how far the upper class had come in all these years. Used to be only the top secret military installations placed a guard at the gate. I also wondered what I'd do once the guard told me to get lost. If I knew what Guthrie looked like, I could wait for him to leave, but I didn't have an inkling.

I was more than a little surprised when the guard leaned out of his box and said, "Go right in and park in the visitor's area." He pointed up the drive which curved past the big, white-brick building, spawning a parking lot just north of the clubhouse before winding back toward Route 41. "Mr. Guthrie is on the archery range." And he told me where to find it. This was bound to be interesting.

Foxport's country club, like the town itself, is an interesting mix of country charm and decadence. The clubhouse reminded me of a

French estate, and as I passed through it on my way to find Guthrie, I caught glimpses of a mirror-lined bar and a small restaurant with thick green carpeting and skylights.

The archery range was just north of the golf course, which brought to mind some interesting possibilities involving wayward arrows.

I was in luck. Only one person was taking target practice and I was going to assume he was Guthrie. As I approached from his rear, he was preparing to launch another arrow at the target, which was probably a hundred feet down the field. The bow itself was like none I remembered from my archery classes in high school. It was probably four feet from tip to tip, and the middle section, instead of consisting of a simple hand grip, made up a third of the bow's length. It appeared to be made of some material other than wood—a laminate maybe—and the grip portion was shaped so his hand fit it like an extension. In all, it reminded me of some futuristic weapon which might turn up in a Road Warrior movie. I stopped a few yards back as he nocked an arrow and drew one string back with three fingers—the first above and the second and third below the arrow. After taking aim, he released the arrow. I could hear it cut through the air on its course to the black heart of the target.

Guthrie lowered the bow, and after looking in the direction of the target for several seconds, slowly turned toward me, pulling another arrow from a quiver hanging from his belt like a holster. He regarded me for several seconds. "A bow made by Earl Gilroy? Where the hell did you get that name?"

I shrugged. "My seventh-grade shop teacher." Guthrie didn't respond. He stood watching me, not sharing the humor, waiting, a bow in one hand and an arrow in the other. Though he was not a big man, five ten at the most, I could tell even through the knit shirt he wore that his upper torso was powerfully built. His hair was dark and coarse, with traces of gray, and he wore a pair of metal-framed aviator glasses.

"Why'd you let me in here?"

"Curious, I guess. I figured anyone desperate enough to come up with a story like that must have important business." He paused and added, "Besides, it'd be easier than you would believe for me to get you thrown out of here."

I took a step closer. "Well, I do have important business. I'm trying to find out who killed your former partner."

"Len?" He looked genuinely puzzled. "Don't they know who killed him?"

"Not to my client's satisfaction."

"Who's that?"

"Jeff Barlowe."

He nodded slowly and turned back to the target. I stepped up next to him. As he nocked the arrow and drew the string back, I could see the movement of muscle beneath his shirt.

"Jeff Barlowe?" He took sight and released the arrow. It hit just off center. He turned to me. "Isn't he that reporter they locked up?"

"That's him."

He drew out another arrow. "You ever try this?"

"Some," I said, then asked, "You watch a lot of Robin Hood when you were a kid?"

He smiled as he took aim. "As a matter of fact, I did. I must have seen Errol Flynn's Robin Hood a couple dozen times. After the first I was hooked. That's when I took up the sport. What about you?" There was something about the way he drew out the word *I* that reminded me of a drawl, but maybe he just liked the way it sounded.

"I've only seen it a couple times."

He released the arrow, which found the other two near the target's center. Didn't this get monotonous for him?

"You shoot anything besides targets?"

"Sure. I use it to hunt. Deer mostly." He continued as he nocked a new arrow and drew it back, "Though it's not the only weapon I use when hunting." He released it and, without noting that he'd made another bull's-eye, turned to me. "The bow and arrow is a graceful weapon. The gun is an efficient weapon."

"Yeah," I said, "I don't guess I'd care to go eyeball to eyeball with a charging bull elephant armed with one of those," I gestured toward the bow.

"A good crossbow can take down an elephant."

"Yeah, but what if you miss?"

"You don't."

"You ever done it?"

"No. Seems like these days safaris are for wimps with cameras."

"Pity," I murmured.

"Here." He held the bow out. "You like to take a shot at it?"

"No, thanks."

"C'mon, give it a try." I shook my head and he added, "It'll make you feel like Errol Flynn."

For a lot of reasons I didn't care for the idea. But in the end, it wasn't so much what he said as the way he said it—more an order than a coaxing — that helped me figure out that I'd have to do this if I wanted to ask more questions. Reluctantly, I removed my jacket and took the bow from him. I was grateful for the hours I'd spent tossing the Frisbee for Peanuts, because that was about all the workout my arms and shoulders got. I drew the arrow back ever so slowly, feeling my arms tremble with the pressure. The veins in my left forearm bulged, my shoulder hurt so badly it burned, and I could feel my forehead getting moist.

"Now, take aim. Use both eyes. Take your time."

Seeing as how I felt like a tension trap about to be sprung, I didn't feel like doing any of those things and was only interested in relieving my pain. I released the arrow and staggered backward, recovering fast enough so that I didn't land on my ass. When I had the opportunity to see how I'd done, I saw that the arrow had hit the farthest ring from the center then sort of flopped down. Even though it was just a flesh wound, I was elated.

"Thanks, that was great." Guthrie held my gaze as I handed the bow back to him, looking as though he'd just been amused. "How long did you work with Novotny?"

Somewhere nearby a bird chirped and I heard voices from the golf course. Guthrie took the bow from me and shifted his attention to it as he said, "Oh, let's see. It must have been, what, ten years ago that we first got together. Yeah, that's about right. I learned a lot from him and I think he sort of took me under his wing. I think maybe I reminded him of himself when he was my age. I'd worked my way up the hard way too. And I guess he knew that Martin wasn't going to follow in his footsteps, so he was in the market for a successor."

"Why did Martin leave Foxport?"

Guthrie frowned. "That's probably a good question. Apparently they had some kind of falling out and it must have been a bad one. One day Martin was coming around the office, helping out when his dad would let him and the next day you say the kid's name and it's like he doesn't hear you."

"Is that when Martin moved out to the Coast?"

"Think so. And I also don't think it's a coincidence that in the time he's been gone — at least ten years — Martin's only been home two or three times, and I guess it's always been when Leonard was away."

"Didn't all this happen before you and Leonard became partners?"

"Yeah, I heard it all second hand. Mary Mulkey, you know, Len's secretary. When I was working with Len I'd take her out for her birthday. Still do. She's a sweet lady. She likes to talk."

"She know what the falling out was about?"

"Nope. Who's to say?" He shook his head. "The whole family's a strange lot."

"Anything to do with the reason you and Len split up?"

"Indirectly I guess. A lot of the property we were handling belonged to his wife's family. Maybe you knew that," he added. "Well, that's one family I don't care to deal with. Catherine — the one who's dying — she's all right. But Amelia," he shook his head. "She's a winner. Len was married to her so he had to put up with her, but I didn't. Thank God." The sun was just touching the tops of a ridge of trees in the west. Guthrie squinted in that direction and added, "But I guess in the end it was the falling out we had over a choice little piece of property we'd been trying to sell. Wasn't big enough for the kind of developing we were interested in. Got a nice offer for it, then Len got a whiff of some plans to turn the adjoining area into a landfill. Just a rumor and I figured if Len heard it, this buyer, who was no babe in the woods, would have heard it too. I said go ahead and sell, but Len made a big deal out of this landfill rumor and scared the guy off." He shrugged. "Five years later and they're still arguing about the landfill. It'll never happen. Well, between the two of them — Amelia and Len — I'd had enough."

"Mind if I ask how you financed your own business?"

"Yeah, I kind of mind. Don't know what you're trying to get at."

I shrugged. "I'm not sure myself, so I tend to ask a lot of questions."

"Well, it's on public record anyway." He pulled his gloves off. "Len bought out my part of the business and I used that money to make a couple purchases, then I managed to get a few investors interested in my vision of this area. So far they're not complaining. Once you've got a track record, some bank will come through for the really big loans."

"How well do you know Rebecca Novotny?"

He bent to open a large case, which turned out to be lined in felt with recesses molded for the bow. "Little Rebecca. She's not so little anymore. Used to come around the office all the time." He fit the bow into its case, gently lowered the lid, and snapped it shut. "She's okay. She'll do all right by Len." He paused and added, "Poor kid, she got stuck with her father's looks. Now Martin's his mother's son. He's got her good looks and her attitude."

"Have you seen him since he's been back?"

Guthrie had unbuckled his belt and was drawing the quiver off it. He stopped. "Yeah, I ran into Martin at O'Hare a few days before the shooting. I was flying in from a meeting in Boston."

"Did you talk to him?"

He shrugged and said, "Sure. Just to say hello." Guthrie buckled his belt and gestured toward the target. "I've got to collect my arrows." I walked with him.

We were halfway there when I asked him about Leonard and Amelia's marriage. "I don't think it was much of a marriage. Though I heard it got worse after Martin split. I think they both just went their separate ways."

"Why'd they stay together?"

We had gotten to the target. "You'd have to ask Amelia." Bracing his open palm against the target, with his other hand he twisted and pulled an aluminum arrow out, repeating the procedure for each of the others. The one I'd inflicted on the target didn't require much effort to extricate. Finally Guthrie continued. "Though my guess would be there were benefits in that marriage for both of them. Len got all that land to play with and Amelia had someone people respected to take her to social functions. Her older sister, Catherine, had a pretty high opinion of Len. I got the feeling she preferred Len to her own sister. Though who could blame her?"

Guthrie picked up the bow case as we walked back toward the clubhouse.

"Do you think Novotny might have been seeing anyone?" I asked.

His laugh was unforced. "That'll be the day. You're talking about Mr. Self-righteous himself. Not only that, the guy was a workaholic, so I don't know where he'd find the time. I don't know. I guess I like my free time too much. What's the use of making all kinds of money if you don't take the time to enjoy it?"

"That's exactly how I feel."

As we walked through the clubhouse I asked him about Yorkshire Estates. He smiled as a proud father might. "That's the development I've always wanted to build. Full of dream homes. The one in the photo in my office is the top of the line. It's featured in the Fall Festival of Homes this year."

"What does it sell for?"

"Six fifty."

I whistled softly. "At some point, when I wasn't looking, a monarchy must have evolved."

He chuckled. "You're right. And, you know, they're willing to pay that kind of money and more so their wealth shows."

We suspended our conversation as Guthrie greeted several country clubbers. He seemed to know everyone. Then we descended the clubhouse steps and Guthrie stopped next to the circular drive. "You know," he said, "I've got to hand it to Barlowe. Takes guts to stick that kind of thing out." He looked down the curve of the drive, as if watching for something. "I'd hate to be the one to tell him his loyalties are misplaced."

"You think it was the Fox?"

He shrugged. "Those two had been clashing for a while. Something was bound to happen." He watched a silver Mercedes convertible make its way up the drive. "Too bad Len didn't get the last word. He really wanted it." The Mercedes came to a stop in front of us. Its driver, what I could see of her, had long, blond hair. She wore a red and black scarf draped around her neck, a black jacket, and dark sunglasses. For all I knew it was Faye Dunaway. She kept her gaze straight ahead, not acknowledging either one of us. Even when Guthrie said good-bye, inserted his bow and quiver into the small back seat, and climbed into the front, she moved the car forward without checking to make sure she'd picked up the right guy.

I watched them disappear onto Route 41, then got into my Honda, started its engine, and sat for a few minutes. When I first take a case, I like to question as many people as I can without making any judgments, shuffle together what I've got and see what kind of hand I come up with. Right now it was looking a lot like fifty-two pick up. Then I recalled how Elaine liked to help me puzzle things out, and how good she was at it. And it occurred to me how hurt she must have been when I completely shut her out of this one. Not that I'd had much of a choice. Still, there were other aspects I could have discussed without revealing the identity of the Fox. Maybe it was worth one more attempt to find her. It's amazing how a few minutes on the archery range can cool you off. I pulled out of the lot and down the drive, waving at the security guard as I passed him.

I wasn't having much luck at figuring out who killed Leonard Novotny, so why not set my deductive abilities to work on finding out where Elaine Kluszewski had gone? The clerk at the Fleetwood hadn't mentioned anything about her being forcibly thrown into the car, so wherever she was and whoever she was with, it was of her own doing. Most of Elaine's friends were in Chicago. Then there was her father and two brothers. One brother was a lawyer and the other taught high school — computer science or one of those subjects they hadn't even thought of when I was in school. Though Elaine got along with both her brothers, she didn't much care for the lawyer's wife — she'd been bitten early in life by the Phyllis Schlafly bug and never missed the opportunity to tell Elaine she should settle down, marry a six-figure professional, and have children (in that order). Her other brother's wife was another story. In fact, she might have been a friend of Elaine's before she met Jack. But where did they live? We'd had dinner with them once, but met them at Ed Debevic's on the north side. Jack was a sucker for their fries and gravy. It showed too.

It seemed to me that they lived in one of the northwest suburbs but, for the life of me, I couldn't recall which one. What I needed was a phone book. How many Jack Kluszewskis could there be in the northwest suburbs?

Chapter 8

I'M ALSO A FIRM believer in the element of surprise when confronting women who might turn on me. I guess work has rubbed off on the rest of my life. That was why I was driving northeast toward the "land beyond O'Hare" with Peanuts in the back and a song in my heart. Or something like that.

There was a Jack Kluszewski living in Schaumburg. I didn't even want to think about the very real possibility that he wasn't *the* Jack Kluszewski. I'd hit the end of rush hour—which in that area tends to conjure up new images of eternal damnation—and it was more than an hour before I got to Schaumburg. It also took the directions of two gas station attendants—one of them confused—before I found Jack's street.

Sommerset Place was lined with homes that looked like they'd been cut out of the same mold and given slightly different window treatments. Every fifth house seemed to be painted the same color.

Before I saw the number of Jack's house, one of the gray ones, I saw his car—a late model black Oldsmobile with shaded windows. I pulled up behind it in the driveway and before I could change my mind, told Peanuts to hold down the fort, and walked up to the door. I drew in a deep breath, said a brief prayer, and just as my finger hovered over the doorbell like an indecisive bumblebee, the door opened and a small person wearing a sweatshirt and a baseball cap came hurtling out, ramming me on the way. Staggering back, I groped for something to hold onto, but those houses don't come with porches or anything like that. By the time I'd found steady ground, the kid was looking up at me from behind dark-framed glasses. He reminded me of a raccoon staring into a pair of headlights. Then two more figures emerged from the door. One of them said, "Nathan, watch where you're going. Say excuse me."

" 'Scuse me," he said, mouth agape. I noticed his sweatshirt bore the Chicago White Sox' logo and his cap the Cubs'. No wonder he looked bewildered. I turned to the woman who'd spoken and, recognizing her as Jack's wife, was elated.

"Hi, Judy. I'm Quint McCauley. Elaine's friend." Her eyes shifted away for a half second, but I was watching for it. "I was wondering if she might be here." Judy was a small woman, not much taller than her son who was still gaping at me. She wore her hair short and her jeans tight. Both looks worked on her. As she glanced back into the doorway, Jack stepped out.

"Hey, Quint," he extended his hand. "Long time no see." It really hadn't been that long. It just seemed that way. "You remember Quint, Judy. Where was it we ate?" He stepped down and pulled the door shut behind him.

"Ed Debevic's."

"That's right. Gravy and fries. Great stuff." Judy was smiling now, nodding. Both gestures seemed forced. Jack looked the same — a little on the heavy side with thinning hair and an infectious smile. I noticed they both had jackets on and Judy carried a purse.

Placing her hands on her son's shoulders, Judy turned to her husband. "He's looking for Elaine," she said as though he might not have heard. I could tell from the way he wouldn't make eye contact with me that either Elaine was there or he knew where she was. And he wasn't used to lying.

"Gosh, Quint. I don't know where she is. I thought she was still in Santa Fe."

Nathan turned his little uplifted chin in his father's direction. "Dad, Elaine's —" he stopped short, possibly due to the pressure Judy was exerting on his shoulders.

Playing along, I shook my head. "No. She flew in yesterday."

"That's odd." He tried to look distressed. "Wonder why she didn't let us know."

I returned his look. So this was how it was to be. "I don't know either." I let the conversation lapse. After a few seconds, Nathan looked up at his mother. "Mom, I'm hungry. What are we waiting for?" Judy loosened her grip on him.

Holding up my hands, I said, "Won't keep you folks any longer. If you do see Elaine, just ask her to call me."

"Sure, Quint." Jack said. "Nice to see you again."

As I retreated to my car, he yelled after me. "You should have called first. Saved yourself the trip."

"Just felt like a drive tonight," I called back and got into my car. Peanuts's nose was pressed to the window, trying to get a better look at the Kluszewskis. "Let me know if you see her," I said.

I backed out of the drive, waved, and drove around the block. The blocks were long and I drove slowly, but by the time I'd made the circuit, their car was still in the drive. I circled again and saw the three of them climbing into the Olds. On my third circuit, they were gone and I pulled right up in front of the Kluszewskis' house, parked my car, and began the wait. I knew she was in there. If I sat here, she'd be forced to play her hand. She'd either come out and talk or call the police and have them chase me out of the neighborhood. Either way, I wasn't leaving without an answer.

A half hour went by and I was beginning to worry about one of the neighbors calling the police before Elaine did. I kept an eye on the windows. If she was spying out of them, she was doing a good job. I saw no shadows or movement in the curtains. But as the windows gaped at me, dark and uninviting, I had the feeling I was being observed. Finally, after almost an hour, the front door of the Kluszewski house opened and Elaine stepped out. I told Peanuts to get into the back seat, which he did with some grumbling, reached across the passenger seat, and rolled down the window.

She wore a bulky white sweater and her arms were folded across her chest as though she were trying to keep the warmth in, even though it wasn't very cold. Stopping a couple feet from the car, she studied me through the window. Peanuts was emitting soft whines from the back seat. I felt the same way only I was quiet about it. Elaine looked more puzzled or confused than angry. After staring at me for a full minute, she said, "How'd you know I was here?"

"Hey, remember, I'm a P.I. I earn a living doing stuff like this." Her expression didn't change. I looked out over the steering wheel, then back to her. "I figured Jack was my best shot. I guess you could say I'm here on a hunch and a hope."

By now, Peanuts was going crazy with his whining and pacing, and I was beginning to think that bringing him along wasn't such a hot idea. Just then Elaine bent at the waist and peered into the back seat, placing her hands on the door.

"You brought Peanuts," she said and almost smiled. What a dog.

"He likes to ride with me. I say car, and he acts like it's Christmas."

She squinted at the makeshift window. "What happened to your window?"

"Long story," I said, adding, "and not of major concern to me right now."

When she turned back to me, I said, "Why don't you get in for a minute?"

"Why'd you try to find me?"

"Get in and I'll tell you." There was something in the situation—Elaine on the curb and me in the car trying to get her to climb in—that seemed real awkward.

She straightened up again and looked down the street; maybe expecting Jack and his family to return. Maybe hoping. Then she opened the door and got in. Once she was situated, Peanuts began licking her ear. She laughed a little and stroked the white ruff around his neck. So far, he was doing a lot better than me. "That's enough, Peanuts," I gently pushed him back into the seat. He snorted, but otherwise played along. Finally it was just Elaine and me in the front seat.

"Why did you come looking for me?"

"I guess I don't much care for loose ends. You want to end this, you tell me that." I paused, then went ahead. "Maybe we weren't together long enough to know what we like on our pizza, but it was long enough for me to know when you're troubled about something. And right now the trouble detector is going way off the scale."

She didn't respond but pulled her elbow in and rolled up the window part way.

"You hungry?" I asked.

"Yes. No. I don't know." She laughed a little. "Always the decisive one, aren't I?"

"I'll take that as a yes." I started the car and eased it away from the curb. "We'll have to make it a drive-in. Peanuts has got lousy table manners."

"When you get to the corner, turn left 'til you get to the light. That's Golf Road. There's got to be a million fast food places."

Neither of us spoke as I drove. I was tempted to turn on the radio, but that seemed too obvious a way to fill the sound gap. Fortunately, it was less than five minutes before I turned onto Golf, and her estimate of the number of fast food establishments hadn't been far off. I pulled into a place that advertised beef, chicken, and fish. Something for everyone. There were about six cars lined up for the drive-in and it seemed like a potentially awkward wait, so I pulled into a parking space. "What do you have a taste for?"

"Um, I don't know. Beef, I guess."

"With cheese?"

"No."

"Fries?"

She hesitated. "Yeah, fries sound good."

As I walked across the parking lot toward the door, I heard her call my name. When I turned, she said, "If they have chocolate shakes, would you get me one? If not, I'll have a Diet Coke."

Ed's Express was a tiny place with four small formica tables crammed into it. The smell of grease almost knocked me over as I stepped in. As I purchased the three beefs, one with cheese, a couple orders of fries, one Coke, and one chocolate shake, I tried not to think about my arteries or how I was going to get Elaine to open up. As I pushed the door open, I wondered if she might have used the opportunity to escape again.

But she was still there, scratching Peanuts where he liked it most—right behind the ears. She took the bag from me and set it on the open glove compartment. "The one with the cheese is for Peanuts," I said. "He loves cheese."

Elaine quickly located Peanuts's meal, which was pretty easy seeing as cheese was seeping out of the wrapper. "How does he eat it?" Peanuts was whining and pacing in the back seat. He was probably drooling too, but I didn't look. Dogs just don't know how to be cool.

Settling into the seat, I said, "I have to tear it up for him. Otherwise he'll eat it whole. It's not a pretty sight." She peeled back the white paper wrapping the sandwich and proceeded to tear it into dog-sized bites. As she bent to her task, her hair fell forward. With her hands full of grease, she tried to shake it out of her face and had no success. I reached out and secured it behind her ear. Her hair is thick and usually somewhat unruly, and I'm always surprised at how soft it is. She smiled as I moved my hand away. I watched her finish shredding the sandwich and said, "I warn you, he'll gobble that down in two seconds and come begging for yours. You've got to be strong. As a last resort, he'll hit on me."

I keep newspaper on the floor for these occasions, and I spread one out on the seat and took the sandwich-laden paper from Elaine. Before it hit the newspaper, Peanuts's nose was buried in it. When I turned back, Elaine was wiping the grease from her fingers with a white paper napkin. Now we could get on with it.

I was working on my beef and searching for a way to start when Elaine said, "I've been a real bitch. I'm sorry."

"That's okay."

"No, it's not. Don't go absolving me. I don't deserve it."

I swallowed a bite and washed it down with a swig of Coke. "I guess I figured you wouldn't be acting like that without good reason."

"Jack thinks I'm pregnant." Then she stabbed me with a look that said my response here was real important.

"I guess I thought of that too, but I rejected it." Her gaze softened, but she waited. After a minute, I said, "Whether you believe it or not, you are pretty decisive. You'd decide whether to abort or go through with it, and you'd live with your decision." I shook my head. "No. Whatever's bothering you, you haven't come anywhere near resolving. Maybe it's too big." She looked away. "But I don't know what it is." She sucked on the straw, making it go dark with chocolate.

"How's the shake?"

"Delicious. Sinful, but delicious. I can feel it going right to my hips."

It was time to take the gloves off. "Elaine, why did you go to Santa Fe?"

I felt her turn toward me, but kept my eyes on the reflection of the lights from Ed's Express in the windows of the Pizza Hut next door. After a moment, she said, "I told you. Ginny had set up a catering business. She wanted me to go in with her."

"That's it?" I looked at her now, waiting.

With a little shrug she said, "Though sometimes I wonder what I would have done if you'd asked me to stay."

"We'll never know." And then, because that seemed cold, I added, "That's not me, Elaine. I don't ever make people's decisions for them. Not ever. Not anymore." I hadn't intended for those last two words to slip out, inviting clarification.

"What do you mean 'not anymore'?"

I rolled the window down and lit a cigarette, searching for a way to change the subject. Then I figured communication was supposed to go both ways. I blew a cloud of smoke out the window and said, "My wife, Joan. When I asked her to marry me she'd just been offered some kind of music scholarship in New York. I guess that's why I asked her there and then. I figured I'd lose her if she went." I glanced at Elaine and couldn't tell what she was thinking. Only that she was interested. I tapped an ash off the cigarette. "She stayed. We got married. She never forgave me. Said she'd be first oboe in the Chicago Symphony if she'd gone to New York." I shrugged. "Maybe she was right. So, I asked her to stay because I thought I'd lose her if she went. She stayed and I lost her anyway."

The silence grew and I tried to fill it by listening to the traffic on Golf. Finally Elaine said, "Did she go back to the oboe?"

"Last I heard she'd married some stockbroker. They already had two kids and a pool and were living in Winnetka."

"Sounds like she never really believed she could do it." She spoke as though that was the only logical conclusion. I'd tried to convince myself of the same, but without as much success.

"Or maybe the time was never right again," I said.

She sighed and settled back, an ankle crossed over her knee. After a long drag on the straw, she said, "Do you ever wish you'd stayed with the minor leagues? Like maybe you were just about to peak, but now you'll never know?"

That caught me off guard, but I gave it a minute and said, "I had a lot of peaking to do to get out of the minors." The fact was I used to think about it, especially in the spring, but had come to terms with it. "Besides, even if I had gotten to the majors, I'd be out by now. I'm a little old, even for a pitcher. I figure I'd be worth, what? Maybe me and two utility infielders would get you one Ron Santo in a baseball card trade."

"Yes, but at least you'd be on a baseball card. You know what I mean?" Then, in a familiar gesture, she pulled her hair back and released it with a shake of her head. "I'm sorry. That came out all wrong. I don't want to make you feel lousy. It's just that I've been thinking a lot about this lately. You know, when you're young you have all these dreams, these possibilities. There's no way you're going to be like everyone else. But then one day you wake up and you're thirty-three and you realize that not only are you not exceptional, you're not even above average."

She didn't want to hear that I thought she was exceptional and had from the moment I first saw her. She wasn't measuring herself by my ruler. Hers had a lot more inches on it. "What would it take to make you exceptional?"

She sniffed and chuckled, her half-eaten sandwich abandoned, holding a French fry. "That's the hell of it. I don't have the slightest idea." I heard her take in a deep breath and release it. "I guess I thought that by working for myself I could prove something to myself. You know? I don't need the backing of a major corporation to be a success. I mean, I realize that running a catering business isn't like running IBM, but it would be something I could, you know, be proud of." She ate the fry.

"What happened?"

"Everything."

"You go under?"

"Worse."

I waited.

Finally she said, "I've known Ginny forever. Since kindergarten. Best friends through high school. Even when she went to college, we were still in touch. I'd go down to see her in Macomb at least once a month. This catering idea of hers was a good one. She was keeping the books—she'd been an accountant—and we were doing fine. I put money into the business, but so did she. More even. We'd invested in supplies, equipment, lots of things. Once a month we went over the books together. She wanted me to know what was going on. I trusted her completely. And we were doing fine. Building up regular clients. Getting some good jobs." She paused, folding her legs under her on the car seat. "Then this guy starts showing up. Richard. They met at one of the dinner parties we catered. She started seeing a lot of him. I used to wonder what he did for a living. You know, he'd show up at the store at odd times during the day. Not like he was on lunch or anything. Ginny said he was in investments." She looked heavenward and shook her head. "I should have known then."

Peanuts was trying to worm his way into the front seat. I pushed him back.

"Anyway," she continued, "I show up at work one day and there's no Ginny. She hadn't come home the night before, but it was getting so that wasn't at all unusual. But we had a big luncheon that day, and I was really worried. I tried calling Richard. No answer. God knows how, but I managed to pull the luncheon off myself. When I got back to the store, the cops were waiting for me." Shaking her head slowly, she said, "How dumb can one person be? It seems that Richard, Mr. Investor, was busted trying to sell an ounce of cocaine to an undercover cop. Ginny had split." She looked at me, blinking back tears. "You'll never guess what they used to finance this investment."

"Your money?"

"All of it."

"Did the cops think you were involved?"

That sent her groping for her purse, which she hadn't brought. "There's Kleenex in the glove box," I said.

She nodded her thanks and took the box out, holding it in her lap. After she'd wiped her eyes and blown her nose, she said, "Yeah, they did. At first. They'd been staking out the store for a couple months. They thought we were all in on it together. I got printed, mug shot, the works." She pulled out more tissue. "Fortunately, the next day they found Ginny. She told them I wasn't involved and they couldn't prove otherwise, so they let me go. I've got to go back to testify." She turned to me. "Do you know what she said to me? Do you know what her excuse was for turning our little catering business into a money-laundering operation?" I shook my head. "She said she was afraid Richard would leave her if she didn't go along. Shit. What an idiot! She was my friend and she did this to me. Just to keep this louse for a boyfriend. I mean, he was using her and our money and she never saw it. The hell of it is, if he hadn't been caught, this could have gone on for years. And then I found out that some of our best clients were referred to us not because of our great culinary skills, but because we could supply them with drugs. There I was, happily stuffing manicotti shells while everyone's waiting for me to turn my back so they can get down to business." She pounded a fist against her knee. "What a sap!"

"Elaine, if you had no reason to suspect something was going on, why would you even look for it? And it's not like they were doing this for a long time. Just a few months, right?"

She nodded. "Still, I shouldn't have been so trusting." After a minute, she said in a soft voice, "I'm broke, Quint."

"You mean broke as in no disposable money or broke as in not a penny to my name?"

"The second one."

"The condo?"

I barely heard her say, "That's gone too."

"You sold it?"

She sniffed and cleared her throat. "So I'd have something to invest in the business. It turned out that we had a lot of debts we had to pay off too. Debts I never knew about." Sighing, she shook her head. "I just don't know what to do." Each word was an effort. "I feel frozen. I can't do anything. I just want to curl up under a blanket somewhere and never come out." Her shoulders began to rise and fall with her sobs. I tried to move over next to her. Damn the gear shift anyway. I managed as best I could and held her for a while as she released some of her grief. Losing your money was one thing; losing your ability to trust someone was another. After a few minutes, her tears abated and she wiped her eyes and face with a couple tissues. She forced a little laugh and said, "Thanks. I needed that."

I moved slightly so the gear shift pierced another part of my rib cage. "You want a little advice?"

I felt her head nod against my chest.

"You're broke, you start over. You learn. You don't make the same mistake twice. And, you let your friends and family help you through it."

Abruptly, she pulled away from me, shaking her head. "No. I can't do that."

"Your family doesn't know about any of this, do they?"

"No. And I'd like it to stay that way."

"Elaine, your brother's a lawyer."

"Yeah, and he's married to a bitch who blames women who work outside the home for everything from child abuse to the high cost of designer clothes."

"Screw her. Who cares what she thinks? He might be able to help you. You may have legal options. You've got to let him." Before she could argue, I went on. "How do you think he'll feel when he finds out about all this and you never asked for help. And he will find out. You know that."

She sighed. "I suppose that's true. It's just . . ."

"I know." I pulled her closer. Neither of us spoke for a minute. Then I took her hand and gave it a small squeeze. It was still damp with her tears. "Hey, I've got an idea. Why don't you come back to Foxport with me?" I gestured toward Ed's Express. "We don't have quite the selection of fast food, but it's not a bad place. Give yourself a couple weeks. Talk to your family. Give yourself time to decide what you want to do."

Pulling her hand away, she said, "I don't . . ."

Interrupting, I said, "You can stay at my place. You take the bedroom, I'll be fine on the couch."

"I couldn't."

"Yes, you could. Half the time I fall asleep on the couch anyway." Pausing, I added, "Your next decision is going to be an important one. Give yourself some time. Don't rush into it." With that, the defense rested.

Sighing, she wiped her face with a Kleenex. She seemed calmer, more self-contained, and after a few minutes she said, "Maybe we could try it for a day or two."

We stopped at Jack's so Elaine could get her things. She gave him a cursory explanation, one which would probably drive him crazy guessing. But she promised to call him in a day or so and explain everything. By the time we got back to my apartment, it was almost eleven. I took Peanuts down by the river while Elaine got settled in. I felt both relieved and a little ashamed. Now that I understood what was eating at Elaine, I could deal with it. I almost wished that her only problem was that she'd come back to find that I wasn't what she wanted at all and just didn't know how to tell me.

78

When we got back, Elaine was standing at the sink, drinking a glass of water. I was surprised to find that I'd missed seeing her in that ratty blue robe. "I'm pretty tired," she said. She looked as though caught between two thoughts. Then she asked, "You've got blankets and everything for that couch?"

"Yeah. Don't worry."

Setting the glass down, she walked around the counter to where I was standing. "Well, I'll see you in the morning." Tilting her chin up, she gave me a quick kiss on the cheek. "Thanks." Then she turned, and walked down the short hallway into the bedroom, closing the door behind her.

I looked at Peanuts. "Well, I guess it's you and me, kid. Roughing it."

Peanuts sat in the middle of the living room, watching as I made the couch up into a reasonable excuse for a bed. After I settled under the blanket, he gave me one last look, turned, and trotted down the hall. Then I heard him scratching at the bedroom door. The door opened. I heard Elaine coo something at Peanuts. The door shut and there was silence. Just wait until seven in the morning when the furry little turncoat wanted to go out. I turned off the light.

Chapter 9

W HEN PEANUTS AND I returned from our morning run at nine, Elaine wasn't up yet. He trotted down the hall, on his way to letting her know we were back, and I stopped him just short of the closed door, ordering him into the living room. This must have posed quite a dilemma for him, because he stood in the hall, tail slowly wagging, possibly considering the consequences of outright disobedience. He finally went with my suggestion, curling up in a mistreated ball under the coffee table. I told him to stay put and, miraculously, he was still there after I'd showered and shaved and put on a pair of old jeans and a red NIU T-shirt. I started the coffee and called my office. There were no messages so I gathered up Jeff's notes and settled on the couch, with my feet up on the low table. Even though the light wasn't real good, I chose the end nearest the kitchen, which gave me a view of the hall and the bedroom door so I could keep Peanuts from sneaking past me.

Jeff's handwriting was bad. Not that it mattered. Most of his notes appeared to be in some sort of code. At nine fifteen I had deciphered two of his symbols and I celebrated with a second cup of coffee. Leaning against the formica counter, I sipped from the mug and tried again. No good. I was too far away from it and the coffee was making me hungry.

I eat out a lot and, as a rule, I skip breakfast, but if I get an urge to cook, it's usually bacon and eggs. I guess it runs in the family. Dad always made Sunday breakfast with a flourish and a lot of commotion. Poor Mom cooked the other twenty meals and we barely noticed. I put on three strips of bacon, hesitated, then added three more. Maybe I'd give them to Peanuts.

They were three quarters of the way to being well done when Elaine padded into the kitchen wearing her robe and argyle socks, her hair a mass of red curls and tangles. Finishing a yawn, she said, "God, that smells good."

"Want some?"

"I'd love some."

"Eggs too?"

"Yeah, one. Over easy." She opened the refrigerator. "Do you have bread?"

"It's out." I pointed with the fork toward the counter and watched as she removed a small stack and dropped two slices into the toaster. "How'd you sleep?"

Yawning again, she drew up the collar of her robe and tightened its tie. Then she looked at me, a smile pulling at the corners of her mouth. "Your dog snores."

I glanced at Peanuts who was in the middle of the small kitchen having trouble standing still what with all the good smells. "You hear that?" He licked his chops.

Once breakfast was ready, we moved into the living room, setting the food on the coffee table. Elaine sat on the floor, her legs crossed beneath her.

"You're not big on furniture, are you?"

She was right. Aside from the couch, a canvas director's chair, a lawn chair, and the coffee table, the room was empty except for the stereo, TV, and a floor lamp. I wondered why that surprised her, then remembered that she'd never seen a place I lived in alone. Our time together had been at her place and I recalled in particular the small dining room table and its chairs with the purple seat covers stitched in crewel. Were they gone too? "It's tough," I said. "Just can't make up my mind. Am I traditional, contemporary, or old-fashioned? Hell of a quandary."

As we ate, I watched her, trying not to be obvious about it. But there was something different and I couldn't place it. She'd poured herself a cup of coffee and now she blew on it before sipping. Her glasses steamed up. That was it.

"You get new glasses?" I asked. Although Elaine usually wore contact lenses, they never went in until after her makeup was on.

Smiling as her glasses began to clear, she said, "Yeah. They're part of my new image. What do you think?"

Her other glasses had been a pale tortoiseshell and they brought out the traces of gold in her brown eyes. These were either dark brown or black and seemed harsh against the fairness of her skin. I finally said, "They make you look serious."

Biting off a piece of bacon, she said, "I don't like them either," and smiled. We ate in silence and Peanuts managed to con us out of a couple pieces of bacon and a half slice of toast.

When she finished, Elaine moved onto the couch. "That was good," she sighed. Then, noticing the notes on the floor, she gestured toward them. "What's all this?"

"These are Jeff Barlowe's notes. You remember, he's that reporter who's locked up?" Elaine nodded and I continued. "I hoped maybe I could get an idea of who he might have made nervous with all his questions. Who knows? Maybe whoever it was had enough clout to get him out of their hair by locking him up."

"How's it look?"

"Hard to tell. I'm spending more time deciphering them than anything else. And not doing a very good job of it either."

She studied one of the notebooks for a moment. "Some of this is in note hand. Though he's customized it some." She pointed to an obscure mark. "I don't know what this '2' followed by a check mark is supposed to mean."

"Ah," I said, "that one I've figured out. It means double check. He uses it a lot. Very skeptical."

Elaine nodded. "Yeah, I see. That's clever."

An idea occurred to me. "You know note hand?"

She shrugged, "I took it in high school. It was supposed to make me a super note-taker and once I got it down I'd breeze through American History."

"Did it work?"

"I don't think so. I found the note hand helpful, I still use it occasionally, but I never pulled my history grade above a low C." She continued to study the page from Jeff's notebook.

I watched her for a minute. "Would you do something for me? It would qualify as a big favor."

She looked up from the notes, eyebrows raised. "What's that?"

"Would you translate those notes? What you can. It'd take me hours and I might never come close." Glancing at my watch, I added, "And I want to see if I can talk to Leonard Novotny's widow and his son this morning."

She hesitated, then gave a half shrug and said "Sure," without much enthusiasm.

"You'd really be helping me out."

"I know. I'd like to. Really."

"Thanks," I said, watching her as she flipped past a few pages. After a minute, she looked up and, behind the dark-framed glasses, one eyebrow arched. "Am I going to learn the identity of the Fox?"

Both my knees cracked as I pushed myself up from the floor. "I don't think so. Looks like whenever he refers to her, he just uses an *F*." I knew the second it was out I'd made a mistake, but I picked up my half-filled mug and walked into the kitchen like nothing was wrong.

"Her?" Elaine said as I rinsed the mug out under the tap, pretending to be lost in the process.

"Her? You said her." Elaine was right behind me, impossible to ignore. "The Blue Fox is a woman, isn't she?"

Shaking the water out of the mug, I said, "She? Did I say 'she'?"

"Her. You said her." She waited until I turned. "Don't try to weasel out of this. I won't let you."

"I know you won't." I knew I'd revealed a piece of confidential information, but it had slipped out. And seeing the way Elaine had latched onto it like it was the map to a buried treasure, I wasn't sorry. I sighed and said, "You've got to promise me you'll keep that to yourself."

"Of course I will." She said, almost insulted. But she allowed herself a brief smile of victory. "Why does everyone think she's a he?"

I couldn't see any harm in telling her that much. "When Jeff first began to report on her escapades, she hadn't contacted him, and Jeff, being the chauvinist that he is, assumed the Fox was a male. After she contacted him, he kept it up to help conceal her identity."

"Quint, who is she?"

I shook my head. "Sorry. I can't."

"You can tell me. You know I won't say a word."

"I know you won't, but I promised."

"Promises are something to share." She was smiling, as though she knew I wouldn't budge, but still wanted to get in some goading.

I looked up at the ceiling for a moment, then back to Elaine. We shared a long look, then, placing my hands on her shoulders, I said, "You've got to swear this will never go beyond these walls."

"Cross my heart and hope to die." She crossed her heart but probably didn't think much about the rest.

Squeezing her shoulders slightly, I said, "I mean it. Dead serious here. We're talking lives at stake."

"I swear." Clasping her hands at her chest, she whispered, "Who is she?"

I locked onto her gaze, swallowed, and said, "Jane Fonda."

For a fraction of a second, the look of anticipation remained, hanging there like a fly ball before it succumbs to gravity. Then she scowled, called me shithead, and dealt me a quick jab in the ribs. It was almost like the old days.

The Novotnys lived northeast of town, off a little gravel road called Derry Lane. The estate's entrance was marked by an unassuming mailbox. Then it turned into the rabbit hole from *Alice in Wonderland.* Here was this simple hedge, obscuring the view into the place, and two gravel ribbons for a driveway. But if you followed the ribbons, down a lane bordered with maples, all of a sudden the view opened up and you were looking at the five acres in Abel County least likely to become a landfill. The house itself was enormous and, like the property, sprawling. Most of it appeared to be one floor, though it was built on a hill so there might have been a lower level in the back. I drove past a duck pond and a flower garden splashy with fall colors, both of which were bordered by precisely trimmed hedges. A small, red-faced man wearing a wide-brimmed hat and holding a pair of shears, straightened up from one of the hedges and watched me drive past. I pulled my car right up to the house and parked it.

The Novotnys' maid was a tall, somewhat gawky young woman with eyes that seemed disproportionately large for her face. But she had a smile that engaged and I figured if I was going to get grief for my efforts to interview Martin and Amelia Novotny, it wouldn't come from her. She told me Amelia was out but Martin was home, then she disappeared for a minute. When she returned the pleasant expression had been replaced by one that lingered somewhere between puzzled and upset. She led me down one of the two hallways that branched off from the foyer, opened a door at the end and motioned for me to enter. But her look said, Do so at your own risk. I went ahead.

Despite the eastern exposure, the late morning sun had a hard time seeping through the cracks in the shutters that enveloped the two windows. I had to take it on the maid's word that Martin was in there, but when she closed the door behind me, I didn't see any sign of life. Then I heard a faint sound that slowly evolved into a tune I thought I recognized, but it wasn't until the performer moved on to the chorus that I realized I was hearing a really bad rendition of "Waltzing Matilda."

" 'And he sang as he sat and waited while his billy boiled ...' " the disembodied voice got hung up on the last two words and kept repeating them, sort of like a broken record only without the precision.

As my eyes adjusted to the dimness, I saw that the song was

coming from a large leather chair facing one of the shuttered windows.

The heir to the Novotny fortune wasn't so much sitting in the chair as he was draped on it. One leg hung over one of the chair's massive arms and the other connected him to the floor. One hand led the invisible orchestra accompanying him, while the other grasped the bowl of a brandy snifter, filled past the level of decorum. Within easy reach on a small table was a leather-bound decanter.

"Martin Novotny?"

Slowly he opened his eyes, squinting. "At your service," he attempted a salute, but his elbow slid off the arm of the chair and he almost lost his brandy.

"That's all right," I said. "Don't get up." I glanced behind me for a chair and, finding none, went with the leather hassock that Martin didn't seem to be using.

"Where are my manners? I've got company and here I sit around singing." He made a slurred tsking sound, and I was mildly surprised that his speech was still relatively precise. "Think I was born in a barn." He grabbed the decanter by its neck and held it up. For a moment I thought he was going to take a swig, but instead he extended his arm toward me. "Have some?"

I didn't want any. The idea of a drink before lunch made my stomach queasy. I can't think of many things less appealing than a hangover before the soap operas are over. But one way to keep a drunk talking is to drink with him. Martin was trying to sit up and having little success at it.

"I'll pour my own, thanks." I took the decanter from him and poured an inch into a snifter. Then I breathed in the captured fragrance — a wonderful smell anytime of day. "Cheers," I said, lifting the glass.

Martin seemed to like that. We clicked glasses and while he took a swallow, I managed to barely draw up a drop.

He squinted at me again, blond hair hanging just above his eyes. A grin came easily to him. "So you're the guy's making a pest of himself."

I shrugged. "Could be."

"Well, go ahead, have at me." He giggled.

I glanced around the room, noticing the dark wood paneled walls, the gun rack, the massive wood desk, and framed maps of ancient continents. Amelia's touch was definitely missing from this room.

"This was your dad's place?"

"How'd you guess." It wasn't a question.

Sitting there, pretending to drink brandy with him, it didn't seem right to start in immediately with the grilling. But I couldn't think of another topic and Martin didn't seem in any hurry to move the conversation along.

"What did you hear about me?"

"Oh, just that you're sniffing around hoping to find some crazy plot behind the old guy's death," he paused long enough for a drink, then said, "instead of the obvious."

"You think it's likely that the Fox is the one who killed him?"

"Shit yes. Dad was always pissing those people off."

I gave him a moment to elaborate. When he didn't, I said, "Those people? The environmentalists?"

"Yeah, them. Whoever." He smiled and stared into the bottom of the snifter. "You know how some people think of that poem about trees whenever they see one? Well, Leonard Novotny, all he could think of was how much more the land would be worth once they cut 'em all down. Only good tree's a stump." He giggled again.

"I talked to your aunt yesterday."

"Ah, Aunt Catherine." He nodded his approval. "Too bad she's not gonna last long."

"Why'd you come back here?"

"Auntie, of course. Knocking at death's door as they say." Smiling, he shook his head in admiration. "Old girl keeps foolin' them. Cheatin' the old bastard."

"She told me you'll be inheriting some of her property."

His eyes widened and his mouth dropped open. "I am? Why this is wonderful news." Struck by the hilarity of his response, Martin was overtaken by an attack of giggles. One of the worst things about drinking too much is that even the most macho specimens tend to giggle rather than guffaw, and Martin wasn't anywhere near macho. He was slim, probably tall once he unfolded himself, and his aquiline features were definitely from the Forrester rather than the Novotny side.

Once he'd gathered himself, I asked, "What are you going to do with all this land?"

"Beats me," he said without a trace of amusement and took another drink.

"You know the land business at all?"

"Shit no. Find someone who does." Another swallow and he nodded in agreement with himself. "Yeah, that's what I'll do."

"That area where your dad wanted the industrial park. The one with all the wetlands. That's going to you, isn't it?"

"So I hear."

"If it were yours right now, what would you do with it?"

After staring off into space for several moments, he said, "Don't ask me. I just drink here."

"Would you start building before you got a permit for the rest?"

He shrugged as though it wasn't of any interest to him.

"Tell me about Rebecca."

His expression changed and he blinked, trying to clear his vision. "Poor Rebecca. Got stuck looking like the old man. Acts like him too." He shook his head and took another drink, apparently oblivious to the fact that the snifter was empty. "Used to be cute when it was baby fat. But it never went away. Used to eat in her room with the door shut. Hid shit under her bed. Behind books." He poured himself another helping of brandy.

"You going to stay in Foxport?"

He shrugged. "Yeah, I guess. Maybe. I don't know. Kind of a dull little place."

"Now that your dad's gone, no one will stop you from staying."

He didn't respond for a minute, then turned to me, and said, "You got a father?"

"Yeah."

"What's he do?"

"Well, he's retired now, but he used to own an auto body repair shop."

"What's he like?"

"He's a good guy." Still watching me, Martin wanted more. "Seemed more comfortable with me and my brothers and sister after we grew up."

"You're lucky, you know?"

"I guess I am."

"There's lots of sons of bitches out there passing themselves off as fathers."

"What was Leonard like?"

He opened his mouth to respond and a female voice came out. "What are you doing here, Mr. McCauley?"

Amelia Novotny stood in the doorway, illuminated by the hall light. I could only make out her silhouette, but could see that she was wearing her trademark cape and a fedora.

Without moving, Martin said, "Ah, lighten up, Mom, he's just having a drink with me."

The figure in the door didn't move for several seconds, then abruptly entered the room and marched right up to Martin and with one swipe, sent the half-filled brandy snifter flying. It smashed to the hardwood floor and the thick, sweet liquor spread with the languid consistency of blood. Something besides inebriation flashed in Martin's eyes, but he stayed rooted in the chair. She turned her back on him so she stood between us. By this time I was standing too, so Amelia had to look up in order to turn the force of her anger on me. Still, it was effective.

"Who do you think you are, invading our privacy? If I'd known who you were yesterday, I would have had you ejected from our office. Now I'll have the pleasure of ejecting you from our home."

Finding no convenient place to put the glass of brandy I still held, I handed it to Amelia who took it before she thought to react differently. I shook my head. "You know, I don't understand why you'd want to eject me from anywhere. I'm just trying to find out who killed your husband."

Her eyes narrowed and it occurred to me that I'd handed her a loaded glass. "Don't you take that tone with me. I know exactly what's going on here."

"Then tell me. I'd really like to know."

She glared at me, "Don't underestimate me, Mr. McCauley. That would be a mistake."

I tried to see past her to get a look at how Martin was taking all this, but she moved with me, blocking the attempt. "Thanks for the drink, Martin," I said anyway. To Amelia, I said, "I'll find my way out, thanks."

As I walked to the door, I caught a little Australian slang from "Waltzing Matilda," discordant, but there was no mistaking it. I had hoped to listen through the door to the exchange between mother and son, but the maid was there as my escort.

As I drove back into Foxport, I searched for a logical reason for Amelia to entrust the family business to Martin rather than Rebecca. Martin admitted knowing next to nothing about land management. And at the rate he was consuming brandy, if he wasn't presently an alcoholic, he was well on his way. Catherine had also preferred Martin to Rebecca. What was I missing? Rebecca wasn't exactly a joy to be around, but she had experience, knew her dad's business, and had some sort of degree to back it up. Maybe I needed to run this by someone who hadn't met any of them. Yeah, that's what I needed — an objective opinion.

On my way to the apartment, I stopped at Dominick's to pick up a few groceries. I didn't mind looking at an almost empty refrigerator and cupboards containing nothing but dog food (which the dog refused to eat). But if Elaine was staying with me for any length of time, I felt obliged to offer options other than fast food and pizza. Knowing that Elaine craved chocolate with a passion she otherwise reserved for books by Ray Bradbury, I picked up a quart of frozen yogurt in that flavor. She'd either be elated or horrified, depending on whether she thought she had to lose weight. She looked fine to me, but I wasn't exactly calling them right these days.

As I pulled onto 35, I was a little surprised at how anxious I was to see her again. Hell, it had only been a couple hours. But my anticipation dissolved into dismay when I turned into the driveway and saw the squad car parked there. I wanted to believe that Louise was the one entertaining Foxport's finest, but I knew better.

Chapter 10

I HAD A SUDDEN attack of territorial proprietorship when, laden with groceries, I stumbled into my apartment and found Ed Carver sitting on the couch with Elaine, looking like he'd just stopped by for coffee. They watched as I staggered into the kitchen and dumped the brown sacks on the counter. I shouldn't have tried to carry two and a half bags at the same time, but I knew once I confronted Carver, I wasn't going out the door again until after he did. And I didn't know which bag the frozen yogurt was in.

Peanuts greeted me with more than the usual enthusiasm and kept bumping against my legs as I put the groceries away. Carver spooked Peanuts. Peanuts had once growled at him, and Carver responded by threatening to kick his furry butt down the river. Although Peanuts would never follow through on a verbal threat, apparently he sensed that Carver might. I noticed that Jeff's notebooks were out of sight and hoped that didn't mean they were in Carver's pocket.

Elaine had changed into a pair of pants and a T-shirt with a coyote howling at the moon on it and was sitting on the opposite end of the couch from Carver with her legs crossed beneath her. Her contacts were in and she'd brushed her auburn hair so it shone. They were both drinking from red mugs and I wondered how long ago he'd arrived. Elaine set her mug on the table and unfolded her legs. "Let me do that, Quint." Carver's gaze followed her as she crossed the room.

"Chief Carver and I were just talking about Santa Fe. Did you know he used to live in Albuquerque?" She took two cans of soup from my hands and a couple more from the bag. "But he didn't come here to see me and, besides, he's probably tired of hearing about the catering business, so I'll give him a break."

"Not at all, Elaine," Carver spoke for the first time. "Sounds like you had quite a business going there. Why'd you come back here?"

Elaine shrugged and looked away from him as she answered. "Oh, you know, things happen." She opened a couple cupboards which were, for the most part, empty. "Do you care where any of this goes?"

"No. Just don't move the coffee." I poured myself a cup and stepped around the counter and into the living room, trying to place what was wrong with this picture.

Carver and I had gotten off on the wrong foot when I'd first come to Foxport. Since then, I'd won a modicum of respect from him, and we'd found a gray area where we could coexist, but I wasn't about to ask him to start writing references for me. And in his moments of wishful thinking, I was sure Carver had me in another town. He watched me now, his gray eyes intent but calm. I guess that was what threw me. Carver was a lean, angular man who made the most of his six feet three inches, usually carrying himself as though he had a steel pipe up the back of his shirt. Or somewhere else. But here in my apartment, certainly not his favorite place in the world, he looked almost relaxed — ankle crossed over his knee, elbow resting on the arm of the couch. All I could think of was what he might possibly have on me. I couldn't imagine what would prompt this sort of bliss in Ed Carver other than a warrant for my arrest.

"Well, I think that hell probably hasn't frozen over, so I guess this isn't a social call," I said, leaning against the counter.

His eyes narrowed, but just for a second. "Good guess," he said with a brief smile. Carver is one of those people who should forget about smiling. The expression looked about as natural on him as it would on a bird of prey.

I shrugged and waited, listening to cupboards open and close as Elaine unpacked the groceries. Totally uncertain about the direction Carver was headed in, I decided to let him lead.

After a noisy slurp of coffee, he said, "I'm bothered by some things I've been hearing."

"Oh?"

"Yeah. Real bothered." He paused, reflecting for a moment, then continued, "First I hear you're the first phone call Jeff Barlowe makes. And then I hear you're poking around making a nuisance of yourself. So I put two and two together, and I came up with something that smells pretty bad."

"Yeah? What's that?"

"You know you could get your licence yanked for interfering with an ongoing investigation?" His voice remained impassive as he elaborated. "Let's say I'm just trying to warn you. What you *do* know can hurt you."

I frowned. "I'm just asking a few questions. Shouldn't bother anyone unless they've got something to hide."

"I'm not talking about that. I'm talking about concealing the name of a suspect."

As he waited for my reaction, Elaine let a little sound of pleasure escape. Carver and I turned toward the kitchen and I saw that she was holding the carton of chocolate yogurt like it was a solid chunk of gold. When she saw us watching her, she stammered something unintelligible, then held the carton up, and said, "Anyone care for some frozen yogurt? Chocolate?"

I told her no and Carver just shook his head, but, again, I thought I noticed a trace of a smile.

Before I had a chance to regroup, Carver said, "I think you know who we're looking for and I'm here to offer you a deal."

"Why should I know who you're looking for?"

"How else could you be helping Barlowe?"

"I don't need to know the identity of the Blue Fox to prove he didn't do it."

Carver uncrossed his leg and leaned forward, elbows on his knees. His change of position made it harder for him to look up at me, but he did. "Whatever. Here's my offer. I'll only make it once. When I leave, I'm taking it with me."

I shrugged and waited.

"You tell me who the Blue Fox is, and I'll forget where I heard it."

I guess I knew what was coming, but I still couldn't believe it came out of Ed Carver's mouth. I shook my head. "Can't help you."

"You can't or you won't?"

Elaine returned to the couch with a dish of chocolate yogurt. She savored her first bite, rolling it around in her mouth like it was a ten-year-old cabernet. When she saw us watching her, she raised her eyebrows and said, a bit defensively, "I asked if you two wanted any."

Carver turned back to me. "You know you're throwing it all away just to protect the identity of a murderer. How much sense does that make?"

"Well, I'm not convinced the Blue Fox is your killer anyway."

"You got anything to back up your theory?"

"No, but I've got reason to believe I'm making someone nervous."

"Let's hear about it."

From her seat on the end of the couch, Elaine was watching the exchange as if we were competitors in a tennis match.

"Try this on. Yesterday someone slashed my tires and shot out the back window on my car. So go ahead and tell me that's not a nervous person. Go ahead."

"Ever occur to you that maybe the Blue Fox paid you a visit?"

"I thought of that. But it's not his style. Not a drop of spray paint."

"Well, if you think that's so damned important, why the hell didn't you file a police report?" His tone was approaching dangerous and I heard the clink of Peanuts's collar as he moved from the kitchen into the hall toward my bedroom. Carver's gaze settled on me and darkened. "You're trying to run the goddamned show. Aren't you? What else are you keeping to yourself? I'll say this again, my offer leaves when I do. And I advise you to take it. You think you know so goddamned much. You know, maybe you're not the only one who's been doing some digging."

"How's that?"

"Well," Carver sat back, spanning the arm of the couch with one long, narrow hand, "I'm not telling you anything you won't be reading in the paper tomorrow, but it looks like it happened just the way we thought. Novotny came in, surprised the Fox who was in the process of spray painting a message on the wall. Looks like the message wasn't completed. The drawing of the fox's head was only a partial." I shrugged, unimpressed. He continued, "And then, because your reporter friend and his editor needed to be convinced, we autopsied the dead ducks."

"You what?"

"That's right, we autopsied the ducks. What do you think they died of?"

"Carver, how the hell am I supposed to know what ducks die of? And why should I give a —" I broke off, realizing I was about to be had.

"They died of natural causes. Now do you think someone pretending to be the Blue Fox would bother to find ducks that had died of old age? When there are so many healthy ones just waiting to have their necks wrung?"

Frowning, I tried to think. Finally I said, "I don't know. Have you ever tried to catch one? They can fly, you know?" Carver gave me a sour look. "Is that all you've got? A partial drawing and a couple old ducks?"

He smiled, holding on to my gaze, and I knew there was more. "It also looks like," he turned toward Elaine as he was talking, "the Blue Fox is a woman." Elaine hesitated, the spoon of yogurt inches from her open mouth, then followed through. It was only a moment's hesitation. You wouldn't have noticed if you hadn't been watching for it. Unfortunately, Carver had.

I moved away from my place at the counter and sat in the director's chair across from him. "How do you know that?"

Carver took another drink of coffee, then said, "Apparently there was a fight between Novotny and the Blue Fox. The physical kind." The amused look on his face was his way of letting me know that I had no secrets. "We found strands of hair caught in the button on one of his shirtsleeves." He gave that a minute to sink in before adding, "After analysis, we've determined it's a woman's hair."

"Isn't that amazing?" Elaine was dragging the bottom of her dish for melted yogurt. "You can actually tell the sex of a person by hair samples. I mean, it can't just be from the length, can it? Lots of men have long hair these days."

Carver regarded her for a moment, then said, "Length and width. Women's hair tends to be thicker."

She set the empty bowl on the coffee table. "Interesting. What color was it?"

"Brunette."

"Well, I guess I'm off the hook."

Carver's gaze lingered on Elaine's auburn hair, then he turned back to me, waiting.

"Gee," I said after a few seconds, "I can't think of any other reason for a strand of a woman's hair to be caught in a guy's button. What else could it be besides murder?" I shrugged. "That's gotta be it."

The muscles in his jaw flexed and he said, "McCauley, we're not idiots. I don't care what you think. If Leonard Novotny was running his sleeves through some woman's hair, he didn't give it away to anyone. And I don't care how discreet you are, someone always knows." He paused and added, "Right, McCauley?"

I conceded the point, then said, "Rebecca Novotny's a brunette."

"She never saw him that Saturday, but someone did. You got any idea who that might be?"

I shook my head. "I can't help you. Sorry."

Carver set his coffee mug down and, grabbing the arm of the couch, pushed himself up. The calm look to his eyes was gone; the chill was back. I braced myself. After twenty minutes of keeping a lid on his animosity, he was about to blow. But, his voice was quiet like the eye of a hurricane, "You *will* be sorry." Then he turned to Elaine. "Nice meeting you, Miss Kluszewski. Thanks for the coffee."

Elaine gave him a thin smile and nodded.

After he left, neither Elaine nor I spoke for a few minutes. She was scraping a drop of frozen yogurt off her T-shirt. She gave it one final brush and said, "I really blew it, didn't I?"

"No, you didn't. He can't prove anything."

"No, but he knows that we know the Fox is a woman. He saw that I knew."

I took the coffee mugs and Elaine's empty dish into the kitchen where Peanuts had been hiding out. "I've got a hunch he knew that anyway. But, like I said, he can't prove a thing."

She followed me into the kitchen, "Can he really do that? Take away your license?"

I opened a box of dog bones and offered one to Peanuts. He took it gently, like I'd taught him, and went into the living room to eat it on the carpet. "Maybe, but I keep telling you, he's got to prove it." I put my hands on her shoulders and looked into her serious eyes. "Don't worry about it. It's not going to happen." When her expression didn't change, I added, "Besides, is a little import shop going to be enough for a guy like me who craves excitement and life in the fast lane? It'll never happen."

"If I show up here and wind up helping turn your business into a ruin, I don't know what I'll do." Her shoulders sagged and I drew her to me. Her head fit just under my chin and I held her and breathed the clean smell of her hair.

"It's not going to happen," I repeated. "And Carver knows it as well as I do. Who's he going to have to kick around if I become a respectable merchant?" I hoped she bought all that but the truth was I couldn't get a read on Carver today. He'd been so contained — so painfully contained. I had to go along with Peanuts. He spooked me.

Wrapping her arms around my back, Elaine stayed in my embrace. I could have held the position for hours but Peanuts decided what was going on in the kitchen was lots more exciting than his dog bone, and he began circling our legs, making little attention-getting snorts. It worked. Elaine pulled away first and smiled at the wriggling beast. "He wants to be hugged too."

"No," I said, reluctantly releasing Elaine, "he just can't stand it when he's not the center of the universe."

Elaine squatted on the floor to give Peanuts the attention he craved. "How'd you do with Jeff's notes?"

"Okay. I was just about done when Carver showed up. I hid them under the sofa cushion before I answered the door."

As I paged through the notes' translation, Elaine switched on the radio and began to straighten the kitchen.

According to Jeff, Reaves stood to lose a lot of voter support if Novotny had his way with the wetland. It might not cost him the election, but it would be enough to make it an interesting race. Then there was something about Martin that Jeff hadn't been able to follow up. Apparently he no longer worked at The Breakers, and was now employed by a place called Pasadena Pete's, a name which didn't exactly have a high class ring to it.

"Quint, are you listening to this?" Elaine turned the radio volume up.

The newscaster was finishing with, "Coincidentally, the Save Our Wetlands group, is holding its first fund-raiser tonight." Elaine lowered the volume and turned to me. "Did you hear that?"

"Not all of it."

"The army engineers, or something like that, just approved Novotny and Associate's request to fill in the wetlands. They're expected to start building soon."

"That's going to make for a lot of mixed feelings."

"I guess," Elaine mused, then added, "That SOW fund-raiser tonight. There might be some interesting things going on there." She eyed me. "What does it take to get into a fund-raiser?"

"Funds. Sometimes lots of them." Peanuts was looking at the door as though he were expecting someone. Then he glanced over his shoulder at me. Some days, when the weather's lousy, I play dumb with him. But the sun was shining and the leaves were turning, and I couldn't think of a reason to stay inside. "Let's take the spoiled one for a walk."

Peanuts raced down the bank to the river so fast I wondered how he kept his legs from tangling in a knot. "Wait'll you see the command he's got over these ducks." And true to my word, Peanuts began to herd a group of them that had been minding their own business doing whatever it is that ducks do.

As we watched him, Elaine said, "What Carver said, you know, about Novotny's killer being a woman and all, does that change anything for you?"

"Not really. You see, I never actually eliminated her as a suspect. Jeff did, but I'm not so sure he's one hundred percent objective about all this."

"What do you mean? Is he in love with her?"

"It's not that." I paused, trying to put words to my thoughts. "It's more like he's so caught up in the rightness of her cause — the environment — that he has trouble seeing past it."

"You don't agree with her methods? Is that what you're saying?"

"You know, at first I thought that was it. But it's not. I mean, I look at what she's done and I can't help but think, you know, 'way to go,' that kind of thing. I don't have the balls to dump a bucket of sludge on the carpet of some oil company that's just polluted a big chunk of coastline with a spill. But I think it's great that someone else does. I see those pictures of half-dead, oil-smeared birds and otters, and like everyone else, I feel someone ought to pay for that. And my boycotting a gas station is really only going to hurt the poor slob who owns the station, who's got nothing to do with oil tankers and spills. So, yeah, I say go for it. Stick it to them."

I stopped and Elaine waited. Finally she said, "So, what does bother you about this Blue Fox?"

"How can someone be so concerned about the fish and the ducks and the trees and the land and care so little about a human being — supposedly a friend, or at least an ally — who's suffering? And she knows he's hurting. I don't buy this higher cause crap. She knows she can get Jeff out of jail. But she's not doing it. That's what bothers me."

"Sounds to me like she's guilty."

"I don't know." I wasn't convinced, but I wasn't sure why.

We walked north up the bank toward one of several parks that flank the river. I was carrying Peanuts's Frisbee, and Elaine walked with her hands in the pockets of her baggy cotton pants. She walked slightly ahead of me, watching Peanuts working the ducks, and it occurred to me that from the back, with her long legs and slim, almost boyish figure, she looked like an eighteen- or nineteen-year-old instead of a woman in her early thirties. And there was something in her movements and gestures — the way she'd shake the hair from her face or put her hand to her mouth when she laughed — that was both unsophisticated and incredibly sensual. I sighed and looked across the river at the west bank with its rows of trees reflected in the calm water.

"What's this?"

I looked up and Elaine had turned and was walking backwards, watching me, smiling. "You're brooding," she said.

"How could you tell?" I caught up with her and she turned to walk with me.

"You look like Hamlet when you brood. Hamlet with dark hair. Your face gets all dusky and shadowy and your eyes sink even deeper."

"Hamlet, you say. Sure you don't mean I look like Olivier or Mel Gibson?"

"No. You look like Quint McCauley, only darker. Melancholy." After a few steps she added, "I'm not complaining."

I glanced at her and saw that her hands were no longer in her pockets and one was almost brushing mine as it swung at her side. I hesitated one moment, then another. Then I heard a child squeal. We both looked and saw about thirty feet up the river a boy of maybe five getting a kite-flying lesson. His dad was doing most of the steering of the blue, black, and gray Batman kite. When I turned back to Elaine I saw that the moment was gone. I swore at myself and wondered how many of them I'd get.

"So," she said, "Who do you think is trying to do your car in?"

We talked for a while about the possibilities. I'd ruled out only Catherine Forrester, though it might have been someone acting on her orders. Guthrie knew his way around weapons, but how much skill did it take to blow out the window of a car? It was good going over all of it with Elaine. I'd forgotten what an agile mind she had, and how she didn't feel the need to censor her thoughts and ideas.

Once we got to the park, we exercised Peanuts with the Frisbee for about a half hour. He was patient with Elaine as she mastered the art of tossing one. Afterwards, we sat on a picnic table while Peanuts lay in the sun getting his second wind.

Then from out of nowhere, Elaine asked, "What does Carver have against you anyway? He seems like a reasonable enough guy."

I managed only a dry chuckle. "Oh, yeah, when he wants to, he can come across like Andy of Mayberry."

"Really, Quint. What's going on?"

Truth be told, I suppose I would have said, 'Oh, he just hates all us guys in private practice' had I thought the truth was out there circling Mars or something, and would never come back and bite me on the ass one day.

"It's a long story," I said, bracing my elbows on my knees and twirling the red Frisbee. As I talked, I could feel Elaine watching me, but I trained my gaze across the river. "When I first moved out here, I was at a bar on the east end of town. Kind of a divey little place. I don't know." I shrugged and added, "I guess I was lonely. That was before I got Peanuts." Pausing, I searched for the right way to word this. Realizing there was no other way, I went ahead, "I met this woman who was real friendly and seemed nice enough. We were both feeling pretty good. I was living out of a motel. She went back there with me. Before anything really happened, there's a knock at the door. Three off-duty cops come busting in. Turns out my friend was married to the chief himself."

When I stopped, I felt the silence. I was afraid to press it by looking at Elaine. Let her work it out first. I was watching a drake waddle his way into the river when I heard something that sounded like sobs. Shit. Did she expect me to turn into a monk? This whole Santa Fe experience had made her so volatile, I didn't know how to handle it. Was I supposed to humor her? Tell her how sorry I was? Who was it who moved, anyway? I turned to her, prepared to defend myself, and it was a moment before I realized that these weren't the sounds of devastation. Her eyes were squeezed shut and her face screwed up all right, but not in grief. She wasn't sobbing, she was doubled over laughing so hard she couldn't breathe. I stopped fooling around with the Frisbee and watched her.

After a minute, I said, "Get a grip on yourself, Elaine."

She waved my attentions off, shaking her head. Finally she sat up, took a deep breath, and said, "Quint, that's priceless. That could only happen to you." More laughter, only it was louder now. She faked a pretty bad Bogart impression, "Of all the women in all the gin joints . . ." and trailed off into giggles.

I had to laugh then. Not as hard, but I laughed. As she wiped the moisture from her eyes, I had to admit that it was better knowing these were tears of laughter she was drying. Then she sort of collapsed against my shoulder, still laughing, and before I shot another moment to hell, I maneuvered my arm around her shoulders and pulled her closer.

Chapter 11

WHEN WE GOT BACK to the apartment, I called my office for messages. Mary Mulkey had another possible clue. This one, she insisted, was *really* important.

"This woman," I said as I hung up the phone. "She worked for Novotny and I asked her to call me if she thought of anything that might be important, but I think our definitions of the word vary somewhat. I've created a little gray-haired monster. I think she's trying to tell the cops all this too, only they're not calling her back."

"Are you going to call her back?" Elaine had discovered the stash of books in the corner of my bedroom and was curled up on the couch with the *The Little Drummer Girl*.

"I don't know."

She opened the book and turned to the first chapter. "What's it going to cost you besides a few minutes?"

I glanced at my watch. I still had time to get over to the jail to check up on Jeff. Wouldn't hurt to humor the woman. Besides, you never knew. As I punched in her office number, Elaine bent down to the book, smiling.

Mary thanked me profusely for returning her call, then said, "Something's come up, but I'm just not sure . . . I don't want to get anyone in trouble who shouldn't be."

"Nobody's going to get in trouble who shouldn't be. Remember we're trying to catch Leonard's killer."

"I suppose I owe it to him."

"I think you do."

"Yes, that's right."

"What happened?"

"Well, you know how Rebecca told the police that she was home on that Saturday Leonard was killed."

"Yes?"

"She told them she didn't come to the office that day at all. I know that's what she said."

"And?"

She took a deep breath and expelled it. "Well, she lied."

"You're saying Rebecca was at the office the day he was killed? How do you know?" Elaine wasn't even trying to get into the book now.

"Well, you know that diskette she was asking me for? The one she wanted to make some changes to before I ran it off?" When I didn't answer immediately, she elaborated, "You know, that day you were at the office Rebecca asked me about it. She said she put it on my desk that Friday. What with the tragedy and all, well, I mislaid it. She was most upset and I told her I'd keep looking for it."

"And?"

"I found it." Her voice rose in triumph on the last two words. "You know how things, thin things like those computer disks, you know how they can slide into drawers and places so you hardly notice, well that's what happened. But I found it. Today. And I know it's from that Saturday." She paused. "You know how I know?"

"Tell me."

"A computer will tell you the last time a file has been updated." I wasn't very computer savvy but I grunted in agreement. "Well, it does. And this file—the one she wanted me to run off—was updated on Saturday the 14th. The day Leonard was killed. The day Rebecca said she wasn't in the office. But she was. She must have been."

I crossed my fingers. "It doesn't by any chance give you the time, does it?"

She lowered her voice. "This is what's so frightening. It was 1:46."

That fit. Novotny's estimated time of death was between one and three.

When I didn't respond, she said, "I don't want to make it seem like she's guilty or anything, but I just can't ignore this. Can I? I mean I owe this to Leonard."

"Sure you do. Besides, this doesn't mean that she did anything." A picture of Ed Carver flashed in my head. "Did you call the police with this?"

"Well, yes, but they haven't called me back. Do you think I should keep trying?"

After a moment's thought, I said, "No. Just wait for them this time. They'll get back to you." Then I said, "The file she'd worked on. Was it anything unusual?"

"No, not really. It was just one of our standard proposals for a client she'd been working with. For something like this, she just goes in and inserts the names and makes any changes to the proposal and then I run it off on the printer on the special stock. That's all."

When I didn't say anything, she continued, "Do you think this is important?"

"Well, it sure could be. It proves she lied. Though her reason for lying might not have been murder." I paused. Elaine was watching me. "How did Rebecca and her father get along?"

"All right, I suppose . . ." she broke off.

"Did they fight?" She didn't answer. "Mary? Did the two of them argue loudly?"

"Well," she drew the word out, "that was odd. You know how families always argue, fight. It's part of being a family, isn't it?"

"Yeah."

"Well, they hardly ever fought, but then I hardly ever heard them speak if it wasn't something about the business. But there was that one time, not very long ago, that he was quite upset with her. And for the strangest reason."

"What was that?"

"Well, for a time there, Rebecca was in a decidedly better mood. Almost cheerful. Then one day . . . well, she's such a plain girl, you know. Never does anything to accentuate her qualities. One day she wore some makeup. And she'd done something with her hair. Curled it. She looked quite nice. I even said something to her about how nice she looked. But then when Leonard came in and saw her, well, you'd have thought she was parading around the office in one of those short skirts and a halter top."

"What did he say?"

"Oh, he called her a tart and then he said, what was it?" I held my breath. "Oh, yes, he said, and I think these were just about the words he used, 'You brought ruin to this family. I won't have you doing the same to this business.' That's what he said."

"Do you know what he meant by that?"

"I have no idea. But she never wore make up again."

"I don't blame her. Well, thank you, Mary. Was there anything else?"

"Why no." She sounded slightly affronted. "Isn't that enough?"

"Oh, yes. Yes it is. I appreciate your letting me know about that. You think of anything else, you call me back, okay?"

Mary Mulkey promised to do just that and we hung up.

I moved over to the couch. Elaine was still watching me, her knees pulled up and I noticed that her purple socks matched her T-shirt. I told her what Mary had said. She reflected on it for a minute, then said, "That's weird about the makeup. Does Amelia wear any?"

"It's probably what holds her face together." Elaine gave me a sour look and picked up the translation of Jeff's notes. I saw that Elaine had added her own annotations to them. Jottings such as "there's no way" followed by a few of Jeff's more outrageous hypotheses.

"But what would Rebecca wearing makeup have to do with the family's ruin?"

It took me a second to switch tracks. "Got me."

"Wouldn't he want her to look nice? For the business? And then there's the other thing." She stopped.

"What other thing?"

"Well, he's lost a son, hasn't he? You'd think he'd like a shot at a son-in-law. Especially if part of his problem with Rebecca is that she's a woman, therefore not what he had in mind for a replacement."

"Good questions. Got any more?"

"What's Rebecca like?"

"I don't know. Really, she is kind of an unpleasant person. But there's something sad about her too."

"Do you think she might have killed her father?"

"Who knows? I feel farther away from knowing than when I started. Maybe that's why I keep trying to link it back to the Fox. It's just easier."

"Maybe it's easier because it's right."

"I don't know," I repeated and, without thinking, grabbed Elaine's ankle and pulled her leg straight. Once I had her foot in my lap, I didn't know what to do with it, so I just left it there and went back to something in Jeff's notes. Jeff had also been interested in that property adjacent to the wetland Novotny wanted to develop. Apparently he had been curious enough about the area to check into it. He'd come up against a brick wall though, because the property was in a blind trust.

I must have muttered something out loud because Elaine tickled the notes with her toes to get my attention. "What's a blind trust?"

She was watching me intently and the foot that wasn't in my lap was resting against my thigh. I swallowed and cleared my throat. "Um, I think it's when the ownership of property is concealed. For whatever reason, it's not a public record."

She thought for a moment. "Seems to me there ought to be some way to find out who owns it. Don't you think? Why do you care, anyway?"

"Well, the value of that property is going to be affected by what's next to it. Unless whoever owns it doesn't plan to do anything with it."

"That's promising."

"Could be. I think I'll go see if Jeff knows anything about this." I shook my head. "I feel like I should be doing more to get him out of there."

"It's not like you haven't been busy, you know."

There was no arguing the point. Elaine was at her best when defending someone else. A born advocate. She didn't cut herself much slack though.

"While I'm seeing Jeff, could you find out about that fund-raiser tonight?" I paused, wondering where a group like that would hold one. "Maybe you could call the . . ." She stopped me with a mild jab in the leg.

"I'll figure it out. You go see your friend."

I gave her ankle a squeeze as I returned her foot to her, briefly marvelling at the courting rituals of the modern American male.

When I first saw Jeff, it took me a minute to figure out what was wrong. He wasn't as fidgety and his movements were fluid, almost restrained. I wondered if they were sedating him.

"No," he said when I asked. Slumped down in the chair with his elbow resting on the long table, he looked like he'd just stopped at the coffee shop on a lazy Sunday morning. Then he looked at me, and with a sheepish grin said, "I'm meditating."

In response to my blank look, he elaborated, "Remember when everyone was into transcendental meditation?"

"Not everyone," I corrected him.

"Yeah, maybe not. Well, I used to do it every day for twenty minutes. Felt great. I'm trying it again here, and it really helps. Focuses me." Right now he seemed mostly focused on the chipped ash tray. "But it's been a while. I don't even remember my mantra."

"Is that important?"

He shrugged. "It's supposed to be. That's what you paid the hundred and fifty bucks for. To get this little word to use." With a little laugh he added, "They say you're not supposed to speak your mantra out loud. I think they tell you that so someone else can't use it without paying for it."

"Well, you don't seem as uptight so I guess it must be doing you some good."

"Yeah, maybe. They gave me a notebook too. I'm taking notes on all this. Who knows? Maybe when it's all over I'll write a book."

"Speaking of your notes . . ."

"Can you make anything out of them?"

"I'm managing. I've got a couple questions though."

"Go ahead." He folded his hands over his chest, waiting.

"What about this area next to Novotny's? You said it's in a blind trust, but you couldn't track down its owner."

"Yeah, when I'm tracking one of those down, I check to see where the tax bills are mailed. Sometimes a person will go to all the trouble of putting their property in one of those things, cloaking their identity, then they have the tax bills sent to their home anyway. So it's easy to figure. Not in this case though. It goes to a post office box."

"Why would someone put property in a blind trust? Why hide the fact that they own it?"

"It's real common in the city. The landlord doesn't want tenants calling and bugging him about the plumbing backing up."

"What if there's no buildings, just property?"

"Well," he shrugged, "I think it's got something to do with probate being simpler if you live in one state and own land in another." He sat up in the chair, propping his elbows on the table. "You got a line on this?"

I lit a cigarette. Jeff made a face. "No, just fishing, really. But if I owned this piece of property, I'd have a real stake in what was next door."

Jeff nodded.

"I just have to figure out who owns it."

"You'll think of something."

"Thanks," I said and abruptly switched gears. "I just found out that Rebecca Novotny was at the office that Saturday."

Jeff's eyes widened, magnified by the lenses of his wire rims. "How'd you get that?"

"The secretary found a disk Rebecca had used that day. The file even noted the date and time last updated."

He smiled. "Yeah, that's right."

I told Jeff what Mary Mulkey had said about the disk and Leonard and Rebecca's relationship.

"What's Rebecca say about this?"

"Haven't brought it up yet."

Jeff stared at an invisible spot on the wall and drumming his fingers on the table. "She's kind of a strange one, all right." He nodded to himself. "Yeah, I think you're on to something there. I think so."

"Saying you weren't there when you were could be pretty incriminating."

"I'd say so." A smile was playing at the corners of Jeff's mouth as his meticulous reporter's mind sifted through the facts. "She wants more control. She knows she's smart. Maybe smarter than her old man; for sure smarter than her brother. But for whatever reason, Novotny doesn't let her take the reins. Maybe he knows there's more to it than brains. She doesn't want to wait around for him to die the natural way. Yeah, this could work."

I helped him along. "You fit a convincing motive with opportunity and it's hard to resist a scenario like that."

I let Jeff savor his theory for a minute. Then I said, "You know, Rebecca Novotny's not the only one who might have lied about being there."

He turned to me slowly, his smile fading. "Who else?"

"They found strands of a woman's hair caught in the button of Novotny's cuff. Long, dark hair."

"Rebecca's got long, dark hair."

"That's not all. They also say the Blue Fox's signature—the fox's head—wasn't complete. Like someone was interrupted in the middle of it. If it was a frame, whoever was doing the framing would have completed the picture."

Jeff leaned back into the chair, lacing his fingers behind his neck. "What're you getting at?"

"I'm saying that, at this point, anyone who rules out the Blue Fox has lost his objectivity somewhere."

He stood slowly, easing the chair back. "You think she did it. Don't you?"

Nodding, I said, "It wouldn't take much to convince me that you're sitting in here, meditating or whatever you're doing to keep going, to protect the identity of a murderer."

He took a deep breath and squared his shoulders. But all he said was, "You're full of shit, McCauley."

Now I stood. "What does this woman have over you, anyway?"

"Nothing. Not a damned thing. I just happen to believe in what she's doing and I know her well enough to know that she's not capable of murder."

"You know that, do you?" He looked away briefly. "Just how well do you know this woman?"

"N-not that well." He began to pace the small room, his right hand thrust into his back pocket, gesturing with the left. "Enough to do the stories. That's all."

I watched him pacing and wondered if I could get away with what I wanted to say. Then, figuring there was only one way to find out, I said, "How far will you go for a story? How far will she go for good press?"

He stopped and whirled on me. "I don't like what I'm hearing, man. You can just forget it. I don't need people like you on my side."

"Then you should have told me you only wanted the truth if you were going to like it."

"Oh yeah? I suppose you know the truth?"

"Mine's as good a guess as yours. And probably a hell of a lot more objective. You see her as some kind of Joan of Arc leading the ignorant away from the brink of ecological disaster. Well, I happen to think that she's a self-serving woman who doesn't really care what happens to you. And I have a hard time believing she's that sincere about the environment when she's willing to write off a human being so fast." He stared at me, shaking his head in disbelief. "And she's sure as hell not going to burn at the stake if she's got someone else to do it for her."

"Oh, God, man." Raking his fingers through his hair, he turned away. "I can't believe what a cynic you are. I can't fucking believe it." He began pacing again.

"Yeah, well, you used to be one. What happened to that old news bureau quote you're so fond of. What is it? 'If your mother says she loves you, check it out' " I fell into step with him. "What can she do now as the Blue Fox? She's wanted for murder. What kind of statement can she make for the environment with that label?"

"What are you saying?"

"I'm saying you'd be doing a lot more for the cause if you'd stop protecting someone who isn't doing it any favors right now. What is it you care about? The message or the messenger?"

He stopped suddenly and I almost ran into him. "That's not a choice. Don't you understand?" Jeff never let his stature stop him from getting in someone's face, which was where he was now. I didn't move. When he continued, his voice was low and measured. "Even if I thought she was as full of shit as you are I couldn't give her up. What about the next guy who has to trust me. Is he going to?" He shook his head. "I doubt it. I wouldn't."

We stared at each other for a half minute. Finally I said, "Is that all there is to it?"

"That's all there has to be."

Sometimes things were that simple. I backed away from him, knocking on the door for the guard.

Jeff was watching me. "What're you going to do?"

I shrugged. "What you asked me to do."

Chapter 12

THE FACT THAT Save Our Wetlands had become a popular cause among Foxport's upper strata was evidenced by the caliber of the automobiles parked in the lot of the cultural arts building where the fund-raiser was being held. The building was the pride of Foxport with its domed roof and windows of green glass. It rose up out of the cornfields like some futuristic version of Oz.

When I'd told Elaine that all we needed were funds to get into the event, I'd figured fifty bucks a plate, tops. But SOW aimed high—to the tune of a hundred bucks a person. Elaine had offered not to go, but I'd insisted, telling her I'd look less conspicuous if I had a date.

Part of our "donation" was going to the parking attendant who had been hired for the occasion. Figuring we might as well do this up right, I handed over the keys to my Honda, customized window and all.

It had turned into a cool fall evening and Elaine wore a turquoise shawl over a plain black dress and dangling earrings that brushed the curve of her jaw. And even though she complained about the heels she wore, they did wonderful things to the shape of her calves. Looking like she did, she could have been going to the races or a coronation. I wore a gray tweed sports jacket over black slacks and hoped that the rest of the guys weren't wearing their tuxedos.

As we stepped into the small banquet room, Elaine was giggling over her suggestion that SOW highlight their event with a pig roast. I was trying not to encourage her. Giggling just didn't seem appropriate at a funeral and that's what this was like. At first glance it seemed as though more than the usual number of people wore black. To that extent, Elaine and I fit right in. A couple people gave us curious looks as though they were trying to place us and, failing, returned to their groups. I surveyed the room, which held close to a hundred people. I rounded up and placed the take at around ten thousand less whatever the sweet and sour meatballs cost. With a cash bar going too, SOW was going to do all right.

"Is she here?" Elaine whispered.

"Is who here?"

"You know who. The Blue Fox."

"I don't know." The fact was, more than anyone else I'd met during this investigation, Julia was the person I was interested in seeing. In my first scan of the room, I hadn't spotted her and I wondered if she bothered with these events. As I pulled at the knot on my tie, I wondered if anyone actually enjoyed them. A young woman wearing a short black skirt and white blouse, carrying a plate of hors d'oeuvres, stopped by us as she worked her way around the room. The tray was filled with circles of white bread, each spread with cream cheese and topped with either a half inch square of lox or a black olive slice. I took one of the lox pieces and so did Elaine. As I chewed, I realized it wasn't going all the way down without some help. Elaine licked a smudge of cream cheese off her thumb. "Outrageously original hors d'oeuvre," she muttered.

"Maybe you should try to get the next SOW contract. You could feature delicacies like water chestnuts wrapped in bacon, barbecued pork rinds . . ." as I searched for other possibilities, Elaine suggested Rocky Mountain oysters.

"Ouch," I said.

Elaine was giggling and I was looking for the bar when a middle-aged woman wearing a green silk dress swirled up to us, greeting us like we were guests in her home. Her hair was steel gray and sculpted around her head like a tight bathing cap, and judging from her coloring, she spent a lot of time outside. "We're so pleased to see you. I'm Mrs. Eugene Graham." She shook both our hands, then cocked her head, and raised her eyebrows in anticipation. I introduced myself and Elaine, but she still seemed to be waiting for something. I didn't know how to help her, so I waited too.

Finally she cocked her head the other way and said, "Have we met somewhere?"

"I don't think so. This is our first time at a SOW function." I glanced at Elaine then back to Mrs. Graham. "We decided now was a good time to get involved. What with the industrial park and all."

She sighed as though I'd referred to a dearly departed friend. "We're so disappointed. We can't let it happen again. We just can't. It's so good to see some new faces. Perhaps I can introduce you to a few of our more active members," she added, but before she could follow through, someone coming up behind me said, "Why, Quint McCauley, you've decided to take sides."

Cal Maitlin, lawyer and occasional client, came up to us. He gave Elaine a blatantly appreciative once-over and Elaine responded with a smile. I suppose it was hard to be offended by Maitlin. A small, wiry man in his late sixties, he was bald except for a meager amount of fringe circling his head. He dressed as if he'd just stepped off the set of "Dallas": jacket with western piping, cowboy boots. He must have checked his hat at the door.

Mrs. Graham seemed eminently relieved that we knew someone and she could leave us with him in good conscience.

"C'mon," he said, taking Elaine's arm and moving us across the room to the bar. "What're you having?"

He paid for my beer, his own, and Elaine's glass of chardonnay. "So, how's our young friend Jeff Barlowe doing?"

The beer tasted good and washed down the cream cheese that was clinging to my tonsils. But the reference to Jeff brought a stab of guilt. "I guess he's hanging in there. I wish I could say I'm close to getting him out, but I'm not.

"The only clue I've got that I'm breathing down someone's neck is four slashed tires and a shot-out window." I took another drink of the beer and shrugged. "But hell, that could've been anyone who's not especially fond of me."

Maitlin nodded to a man balancing three drinks as he threaded his way through the crowd. "You talk to Catherine Forrester?"

"Yeah, a couple days ago."

"How is she?"

"Well, considering she was on her death bed less than two weeks ago, I guess she's doing all right. Though I don't suppose she's far away from it."

He stood with his drink in one hand and the other behind his back, talking to us, but, at the same time, aware of his surroundings. "Yes, that's a shame. More's the pity. Catherine was really something in her time. Still is. Too bad she sat around waiting for someone like Leonard." He took a couple long swallows of beer.

Elaine and I exchanged looks. "Did she have something going with Novotny?"

"Oh, my no." He smiled and shook his head, licking a bit of foam from his upper lip. "Leonard was too straight an arrow for that. No, that never would have done. But I'm sure she thought about it. Len probably did too. I know for a fact that she and her sister never got along." He peered into his glass, swirling the white foam, possibly wondering where half the beer had gone. He lowered his voice and added, "Though I don't think Amelia's anyone's favorite person. Sure isn't mine."

"You know anything about Martin? Like what drove him out of town twelve years ago?"

"Well, if you hear the family tell it, he just wanted to get out on his own." In an exaggerated aside, he added, "You know how boys are." With a small shake of his head, he lapsed back to his usual delivery, dry and slightly amused. "My guess is Leonard gave him some kind of ultimatum and Martin decided he'd better go while the going was good." He broke off as he looked past me at someone approaching. Transferring his beer to his left hand, he extended his right. "Well, it's good to see you , David. You know Quint McCauley?"

As Reaves turned to me I heard Cal addressing someone just behind him. "My, you're looking lovely tonight, Pamela."

David Reaves shook my hand, "Why, Quint, I'm glad to see you here. A little surprised, but glad."

"That's quite a convincing spiel you have. Thought I'd check out the movement." I introduced him to Elaine.

"And this is my wife, Pamela." He reached around her waist and drew her up to us. She was tall and slim with eyes the color of the pale blue linen dress she wore.

He took his arm from around his wife and accepted the drink his advisor handed him. Perhaps "advisor" wasn't the right word. He was a burly man who looked like he'd had his nose broken and set by the same person.

Reaves was addressing me again. "Well, Quint, you getting any answers to your questions?"

"I've got to admit they're hard to come by, but I think I've made some progress."

His grin wavered but he covered quickly with, "That's good to hear. I've been doing some thinking about that myself. A few thoughts that might be worth sharing. Can you stop by my office Monday? Ten o'clock."

"Sure thing."

I heard Elaine asking Pamela Reaves if these fund-raisers ever got tedious, and Pamela was responding with lines like, "This cause is so important to my husband and me that any time we devote to it is . . ." As they talked, Pamela occasionally pushed a lock of her long blond hair back from her face. All the while she kept smiling.

We got about three minutes with Reaves and his wife before they were pulled away by Mrs. Graham to the accompaniment of her profuse apologies. Elaine drifted off toward the hors d'oeuvre table. "Research" she called it.

Cal Maitlin regarded me with narrowed eyes, a smile pulling at the corners of his mouth. "What are you going to tell him on Monday?"

"Beats me. Maybe he's bothered by the possibility that I'm on to something. He might want to talk."

"I'd say he's bothered. Though you're going to have to come up with something to keep him bothered."

I poked my chin in the direction Reaves had gone. "You think he knows who the Blue Fox is?"

Cal looked after him. "Don't know. If he does, he knows his butt's in the ringer."

We watched Reaves as he smiled and chatted with his constituents. In his light-colored suit and a shirt that matched his wife's dress, he looked like a cross between a college professor and a young executive.

The conversation in the room died down and I saw that Mrs. Graham had taken the dais. Standing next to her was a lean young man with a guitar.

After the usual "Is this working?" with the microphone, and the screech of feedback that got everyone's attention, she laughed a little and said, "First I want to thank each and every one of you for coming tonight. It's especially gratifying to see new faces here. Perhaps our failure to save the wetlands north of town has rekindled our sense of purpose. There are other wetlands out there that need saving."

The crowd responded with a cheer and raised hands, some holding glasses. "I'd like you all to listen to Randy Allyn, who happens to be the son of Roger and Marjorie Allyn. He's going to do a few songs for us — I know you'll enjoy them — and I'd like you all to welcome him."

We did, and I was prepared to be embarrassed for the slightly built kid with the guitar that seemed to dwarf him, but was pleasantly surprised to find his voice clear and strong and the accompanying guitar sweet. The discomfort he felt at Mrs. Graham's introduction evaporated into a confidence you only see with someone who is doing something well and knows it. His first song was one he'd written called "I Remember the Day." One of the lines went "when the power of your voice was worth more than the silver in your hand." The audience loved it. He moved on to a second song without more than a quick smile before the applause from the first died down.

I saw Nick Guthrie approaching the bar. He was with a blond woman, probably the one I'd seen pick him up at the country club. There was something familiar about the way she tilted her head, though I couldn't place her. She stopped to talk to another couple as Guthrie came up to me. "How's the sleuthing business?"

"Not bad," I offered.

The bar is the best place to hang out at one of these things. Not only are you an arm's reach from another drink, but sooner or later everyone migrates there. As Guthrie and I made small talk, I noticed that, just as at the country club, Guthrie seemed to know a lot of people. I guess that's what being a joiner is all about. There was something puzzling, however. While I had no trouble fitting him in with the country club set, it wasn't so easy to make him out as a conservationist. I don't know, maybe it was the image of him nailing wide-eyed does that spoiled the picture.

Then I saw that Julia Ellison had arrived, looking low key in a navy dress, her hair caught back in a knot. She hesitated in her visual sweep of the room when she got to me, then kept going. I turned back to Guthrie who had acquired a glass of bourbon. "I suppose you've heard what the police are releasing," he said as he joined me.

"What's that?"

He smiled as if he knew I was putting him on, but said, "The Blue Fox is a woman. And she was there when Novotny showed up."

"Who needs the media?"

"Still think she didn't do it?"

"Guess it doesn't look good, but there are other things that could've happened."

"Like what?"

"Like maybe someone came in right after she left. Killed Novotny. Perfect cover."

He shrugged, "Perfect timing, anyway."

"That too."

"Oh, Nick," Mrs. Graham came up to Guthrie and gave me an odd look, possibly wondering how I knew all the people she knew. Her consternation quickly passed and she said to him. "We walked through Bob and Linda's house. It's going to be grand." Turning to me, she explained, "Nick is building a home for my daughter and son-in-law in Yorkshire Estates. It's breathtaking." Then she asked Guthrie if he'd seen David Reaves.

"When I first got here, but not since then."

As a last resort, she turned to me. "You haven't seen him, have you, Mr. McCauley?"

I told her I was sorry and she shook her head. "There's a reporter and a cameraman here from the *Chronicle*. We need him." She paused then, and eyed me. "What is it you do for a living, Mr. McCauley?"

"Private investigator." Her eyebrows shot up and she looked at Guthrie for confirmation. He nodded and she gave me a thin smile, then continued her search for Reaves.

I watched her move through the crowd, light on her feet but heavy on the histrionics. "Her daughter can't be very old," I commented to Guthrie.

Smiling, he shook his head. "This is one hell of a starter home."

"Mrs. Graham had better find Reaves soon or she's going to flutter herself to death."

"That woman's at the forefront of every environmental issue in this town. Don't let her flakiness fool you. She's incredibly organized and, when it comes to wearing down the opposition, quite effective."

"Too bad she doesn't have a first name."

He smiled. "Maybe she figures it doesn't make much difference. Her name's Eugenia. Her husband's Eugene."

I tried to find the logic in his statement and, failing, said, "I suppose that's what brought them together."

He took a swallow of the bourbon and grimaced. "That plus his millions."

"Is SOW her brainchild?"

"Yes, it is. She approached David about it, and he saw it as a good move."

"One that wouldn't hurt his campaign either."

Turning to me, more amused than surprised, Guthrie said, "My my, you're the cynic, aren't you?"

I shrugged. "I guess he could be the real thing. Maybe I just don't know what the real thing is anymore."

We listened to the folk singer go into his fourth song, apparently a request from Mrs. Graham to fill some time. Still no sign of Reaves, though Pamela was surrounded by a small cluster of people and was engaging them in conversation. As I watched her, I noticed that her smile, for all its endurance, was the kind you see on a beauty contestant who's just learned she's first runner-up.

I glanced at Guthrie who appeared slightly distracted. "What's a developer like you doing involved with SOW?"

He turned to me slowly and took a long drink before he said, his words measured, "Just because I develop land doesn't mean I don't have a reverence for it."

"Quint." It was Elaine, who I'd forgotten to miss for the last ten minutes. "Guess what . . ." then she saw Guthrie watching her and she finished in a less enthusiastic tone, "this is being catered by one of the biggest outfits in town. I may have a future here."

I introduced her to Guthrie. "You in the catering business?"

"I used to be," she answered and left it at that.

Then I saw Reaves working his way through the crowd, his arm around Mrs. Graham, and his advisor in tow. Mrs. Graham was obviously distressed, and he was laughing and trying to joke her out of it. By the time they neared the dais, she was starting to smile.

The young guitarist seemed relieved to relinquish his position, practically running from the platform. Mrs. Graham stepped up and pulled Reaves up behind her.

"Thank you so much, Randy. Let's all show him how much we enjoyed that." Randy had almost made it out of the room when the applause started and he turned and backed out the last couple feet. Once it quieted down, Mrs. Graham began, "As it happens, today isn't a red letter day for Save Our Wetlands. It's a black letter day. As you know, we lost our fight to preserve a part of our community. And we've been told that appeals won't be heard. But this is a show of force, and a fine one at that. We've all been disappointed by this setback, but as long as we have someone like Representative David Reaves on our side, we know that, ultimately, we will win most of the battles." I imagined that Mrs. Eugene Graham had made a pretty fair cheerleader in her day.

Reaves thanked her and gave her a kiss on the cheek, which she accepted graciously, his earlier disappearance apparently forgiven. He looked casual and at ease in front of the group. But then why wouldn't he be? They were all on his side. "We're here today, not to mourn a defeat, but to commit ourselves to the future. Not to dwell on yesterday's failure, but to define tomorrow's agenda. Mrs. Graham used the word 'battle' and it is, indeed, a war. We can't expect to win all the battles. But we can win most of them. SOW is growing. I am so encouraged by the turnout today. And especially by the new faces. People don't join a cause that is dying. They join one that has hope and committed people and one that has the power of right on its side."

The crowd cheered and its more refined members applauded.

"I believe the way to encourage the growth of this organization is to reach out beyond the wetlands, to all the issues that threaten our open spaces in Abel County. It's not right that the few people who own large parcels of land in this county can dictate what our town will become." This was followed by murmurs of assent and a few whistles.

"Furthermore, as we grow and as Illinois' resources dwindle, we're going to get the attention we need . . ."

I became aware of the voice raised above the crowd, responding to Reaves's comments not with cheers, but with words of derision. It had asked a question, which I hadn't caught. The voice got louder and I looked behind me and saw Rebecca Novotny standing there, less than five feet away, looking up at Reaves on the dais, her hands clenched in fists and her little eyes filled with loathing. People backed away from her. As Reaves tried to continue, she repeated her last question.

"Isn't that right?" She stood, head lifted toward the man on the small platform, and thrust her fists into the pockets of her brown jacket. "SOW doesn't know how to lose gracefully. Isn't that right, Mr. Reaves?"

Reaves looked genuinely perplexed as he scanned the crowd, trying to connect the voice with a body. When he finally found her, she continued. "SOW also underestimates its adversary. If you think that sabotaging the hydraulic systems of heavy equipment with sugar is going to stop progress, you'd better think again. You think you're the only people in town who are committed. Well, you're not."

"Miss Novotny, I don't know anything—"

"Oh, don't play ignorant, Mr. Reaves." Rebecca cut him off. Her face shone with sweat, which settled in gray pools beneath her eyes. "You'll stop at nothing to have your own way. Maybe you should have tried sabotage before murder."

"Now wait a minute." Reaves had the microphone, but Rebecca had everyone's attention. He stepped down from the dais and motioned his advisor to stay put. As Reaves approached her, Rebecca continued, "And never mind who owns the land. Never mind that there are families who own these parcels of land who have done so for the last hundred years, when Abel County wasn't the mecca of the suburbs." A few of the people standing near her were starting to snap back, first telling her to be quiet, then being less polite about it. Most of them just looked embarrassed. But when she said, "And never mind that we're going to improve the land," she put her toe over the line.

I heard Cal Maitlin's voice above the flood of retorts. "And you presume to do a better job of it than God?"

She ignored them and kept going. "The love for this land goes back a long way with my family. And what kind of movement is this that supports murderers? Is that how we protect our resources, Mr. Reaves? Is it? What about our human resources? What about Leonard Novotny?"

Just as the crowd parted to let Reaves through, Mrs. Graham materialized and grabbed Rebecca's arm. In a low voice, sharp as a razor, she said, "You're going to have to leave, Miss Novotny." Rebecca snatched her arm from the other woman's grip and they glared at each other. Rebecca, heavy and rumpled, versus Mrs. Eugene Graham, trim and polished. Mrs. Graham repeated her request. "You'll have to leave."

Rebecca's eyes narrowed to slits and her jaw set. Mrs. Graham allowed herself a quick glance, searching for her supporters. No one had moved. Everyone was watching, including Reaves. "Don't tell me what I have to do," Rebecca said. "My family donated the land this building's on. I have every right to be here." Turning to the crowd, she added, "And someone's got to hear the truth."

Mrs. Graham made another grab, this time taking both of Rebecca's wrists. Once again, Rebecca pulled away, and this time she pulled herself up and announced to the group, "It takes more than a rich do-gooder to shut a Novotny up." She was appealing to the group I was standing with. Some looked like they wanted to hit her, most just looked away. And Elaine was looking at me as if I should be doing something.

"There's a first time for everything, sweetheart." Reaves's advisor took her by the arm and hauled her toward the door. She kicked him in the shins with the pointed toe of her shoe. He winced, but didn't loosen his grip.

"I've done nothing wrong. Why can't I express my own opinion? Are you afraid of it? Are you afraid of what I know?" She turned her glare from Mrs. Graham to Reaves. "Well, you should be afraid. I know things. I know things that should make all of you," she paused to sweep the crowd with her gaze, "very uncomfortable."

"Rebecca." Reaves stepped toward her. "We can have a discussion. We can—"

"I don't have discussions with murderers." She punctuated her statement with a long, hard look at him. Then her gaze dropped from Reaves to take in those around her again. "You're all responsible. All of you. You know who killed my father and yet you revere him, or rather her, like she's some kind of Robin Hood. You think I'm going to sit quietly while you undermine everything we're trying to do for Foxport?" The burly man began to drag her out. "Let go of me. I can leave on my own. I've said what I came here to say." He released her, cautiously. Straightening the lapels on her suit, she gave the crowd one last, long disdainful look and said, "We start excavation on Monday."

I grabbed Elaine's hand and we followed Rebecca out. By the time we made it out of the room and into the hallway, she was pushing open the big green doors to the main entrance. "She's kind of crazy," Elaine warned, but kept right up with me.

"Rebecca! Wait a second!" She kept going.

I took the steps two at a time, heard Elaine stumble, then pick herself up, cursing. She waved me on.

Rebecca was at the door of a Honda Civic that was parked in the fire lane, but she wasn't getting in yet.

"Rebecca, I just want to talk to you for a minute."

As I neared the car, I saw that she was fumbling through her purse and trying to keep an eye on me at the same time. I held my hands up. I wasn't surrendering, it just seemed the thing to do. I gestured toward the building. "How did you get past the valet parking?"

"I paid him off, what do you think?"

"Ah," I said, "I see." When I got within five feet of her, I stopped and put my hands down. And then because I saw no signs of recognition, I said "I'm Quint McCauley. You remember, we spoke the other —"

"I know who you are," she cut me off and with one decisive yank, pulled a set of keys from her purse.

"I'm the guy who's not taking sides. I just want to know who killed your father."

"I know who killed him," she jammed a key into the car's lock.

"Maybe. But what if you're wrong?" Rebecca looked past me and I could hear Elaine behind me.

"I'm not." She opened the door and tossed her purse in.

"Rebecca, this is Elaine Kluszewski." Elaine smiled and said hi and Rebecca stared at what Elaine was holding in her hand.

"You broke your heel," she said.

"Yeah," Elaine placed her hand on my shoulder for balance and removed both her shoes. "You know, sometimes I think it's amazing when they *don't* break. I mean, what a stupid thing to do to your feet." I failed to see where Elaine was going with this, but Rebecca hadn't gotten in her car yet. "Yep," Elaine continued, "I'll bet some guy designed them." Rebecca almost smiled and rested her arm on the car's open door. Then she looked at me, waiting.

I ran with it. "Back in there, you said you knew something, something Reaves should be afraid of."

"I don't think I mentioned Reaves specifically."

"But you looked at him when you said it."

"So? More than anyone, except maybe that silly woman, Reaves represents SOW. If SOW gets hurt, so does Reaves." She bounced the keys in her hand. "No, what I know should make them all afraid. They're going to lose their symbol. Their figurehead. I know who the Blue Fox is." She held the pause, savoring it, then added, "And I'm telling."

"Who is it?"

She smiled and shook her head.

"Why haven't you told anyone yet?"

"Because by tomorrow, I'll have proof."

"Why didn't you tell them what you just told me? I mean, instead of these obscure threats, why didn't you just say you were going to rat on the Fox?"

"I didn't intend to say that much, it just came out. Mrs. Graham makes me crazy. I don't know. I wanted her to be worried. By not being specific, I was covering my ass. If it falls through, I won't lose face." She climbed into the car and started the engine.

I knocked on her window and, with a disgusted look, she rolled it down a couple inches.

"Why did you lie to the police?"

With barely a hesitation, she said, "I didn't."

"You were at the office on the Saturday your father was killed. At around the time he was killed too."

Her eyes narrowed. "That's bullshit."

"Is it? There's a computer disk with the date and time on it. Saturday, one forty. It's your disk."

Her laugh was brittle. "Anyone could have used that disk."

"Maybe," I said. "But I don't think so."

After a moment, the window glided up and we watched her pull away.

"Really, Quint. Did you expect her to say 'Sure, I was there'?"

"No. I just wanted to see her reaction. I don't know whether I should feel sorry for that woman or dislike her intensely."

"I feel sorry for her," Elaine said, and I wasn't surprised. Then her face began to light with mischief. When her smile reached its zenith, she said, "I know who the Blue Fox is too."

Chapter 13

LOOKING OUT OVER THE seventy-five acres that would soon be Forrester Prairie Industrial Park, I was reminded of growing up in DuPage County. My brothers and I spent a lot of time trekking through the marshes. Mom would yell at us when we came home with our dungarees soaked to the knees. Sometimes, to the delight of our mother, we brought home frogs or snakes. Actually, my brothers brought home the snakes. I never warmed up to them. And now, as then, marshes reminded me of a primeval landscape. It's like slipping back via a time machine and getting a glimpse of the world a few billion years ago. And a million years from now, the buildings will be gone, the land reclaimed by the marshes. Like nothing had ever changed. The morning fog was burning off, but it was still hazy, and the marsh smelled of water and growing things. A shadow passed overhead and I looked up to see two Canada geese swooping in for a landing. I'd half-expected to see one of those pterodactyls gliding by. Maybe half-hoping. Yep, I'm the kind of guy who would sit all day on the banks of Loch Ness, waiting for the monster to pop his head up out of the water and wink at me.

"Penny for your thoughts."

I shrugged and slid my hands into my jeans pockets, feeling the cool morning breeze on my bare arms. "Oh, I was just wondering what this is going to look like in a year."

Elaine nodded, suddenly distracted by Peanuts. She was trying to convince him that being on a leash was not the worst thing that could happen to a dog. But he wasn't buying it and kept trying to back his way out of the collar. "Have you ever considered obedience school?"

I looked at Peanuts whose eyes were imploring me to put a stop to this nonsense. "Not really. I don't want to break his spirit."

Elaine muttered something about maybe bending his spirit, and I turned to look out across the marsh again. No, it wasn't the Grand Canyon or even the Ozarks. If you were looking for spectacular, you'd be disappointed. It was so distinctively Illinois. The one thing that continued to amaze me about the state was its flatness. Looking straight west I could believe there was nothing between me and the Mississippi River.

We had ignored the No Trespassing sign posted by Novotny and Associates and ventured into the controversial wetland. It was north of town, occupying a portion of the land between Route 41 and Ridgeland Road, Foxport's far western boundary. There were other things I should have been doing, and I figured pretty soon my curiosity would be satisfied and I'd start doing them. But I was having trouble leaving, as though I were waiting for something, afraid that I'd just miss it.

It was a Saturday and it looked like no one was around. The bottoms of my jeans were wet and I could feel the water squishing in my shoes when I curled my toes.

After a minute, Elaine said, "So this is why they call Illinois the prairie state." Before I could ask where she'd been all her life, she added, "Remember, I'm a city kid. My idea of a prairie is a vacant lot." I didn't respond and she continued, "It's pretty. In a quiet sort of way. You know, I guess I was expecting the water to be more, well, visible." She lifted a shoe that was also soaked. It wasn't always easy to tell where the water was. "This is really just a wet prairie, isn't it? I'll bet the mosquitoes love it here." She made a face and glanced around, as if worried that they might have overheard her.

"I guess I just wanted to see for myself."

Peanuts had his nose buried in the long grass, scratching and making soft growling sounds. A small frog jumped straight up, probably hitting Peanuts's nose on the way. He leaped back, head up, ears perked. Elaine and I laughed at the look of utter shock that came over his doggie features. Then, to save face, he crouched, front legs splayed, and barked at the little green creature. It didn't move from the blade of grass — an act of either incredible bravery or overconfidence in his camouflage.

"Have you seen enough, yet? Your dog is being a brat."

As we walked the half mile back to my car, I wondered what Julia Ellison would do now that the Army Corps of Engineers had handed down the sentence to these wetlands. I hadn't spoken to her last night. Figuring we'd seen the best part of the show, Elaine and I had decided not to go back to the fund-raiser. Instead she told me how she'd witnessed a scene between David Reaves and a woman with dark hair wearing a navy dress who I was certain had to be Julia Ellison. Julia had been upset and Reaves was trying to comfort her — "without laying a hand on her, but still being very effective" — was how Elaine put it. As soon as Elaine was within earshot, Julia had shut up and given her a "what in the hell are you doing here" look.

I'd played dumb when Elaine said she thought the woman with Reaves was the Blue Fox, telling her that I saw any number of dark-haired women with dark dresses at the fund-raiser. "Name one," she said and I countered by asking how Julia Ellison could have been terrorizing polluters twenty years ago. She admitted that had stumped her, but plastic surgery was a possible explanation. I admired her perception, still, I wasn't about to tell her that she'd guessed right, based solely on one of those "feelings" she gets.

As I opened the car's back door for Peanuts, I made a mental note to make time to stop at Valley Glass and Mirror and get the new window put in.

On the way back to the apartment, I didn't feel like talking. The morning had burned a bad mood into me and I was wallowing in it. Elaine tried to start a conversation or two, then gave up. I kept thinking about the marshes.

We were driving down Ridgeland, coming into Foxport from the west, when Elaine tried again. "Quint?" I responded with a grunt.

"Quint," she spoke sharper this time and I glanced at her.

"What?"

"Are you scared of snakes?"

I shrugged, not wanting to admit that I went along with Indiana Jones when it came to the snakes, but wanting to be honest. "What sane person isn't? Why?"

"I don't know. That place reminded me of snakes." After a few seconds she said, "There's a Convenience Mart up ahead. Could you pull in there? I need something."

I was in a hurry to get home and out of my wet shoes. "Can it wait?"

"I need tampons," she snapped, and I felt like a clod.

"Sorry." I slowed and switched on the left turn signal. In the middle of the turn, I reached down to scratch my thigh and heard Elaine moan. Instead of feeling the denim, what my hand touched was cool, dry, and slender like a rubber tube. And it was moving. I gripped the steering wheel, glanced down, and saw that its eyes were looking into mine and its forked ribbon of a tongue was draped over its open jaw. "Holy Shit!" I think I screamed. I know I slammed my foot down on the accelerator instead of the brake because we lurched forward, crashing into something. The shoulder restraint jerked me back into the seat. Peanuts tumbled over the arm rest and I grabbed him before he hit the dashboard, pulling him to my chest. That was when he saw the snake trying to burrow down somewhere under my seat. He tried to follow it under

123

the steering wheel, which would have been all right, except parts of me were in the way. I groped for the release on my seat belt and Elaine was yelling for me to grab Peanuts. His front half was under the dashboard and his butt was on the driver's side of the steering wheel, back legs delivering a series of sharp kicks to my crotch. With all his squirming and kicking, I couldn't get a grip on his haunches. "Push him all the way!" Using both hands, Elaine pushed his back half down with his front half. I found the release on my seat belt and bailed out.

Elaine came around the car with Peanuts's leash. He was still barking and clawing at the carpeting under the seat. I decided it was time to take control of the situation and took the leash from Elaine, hoping she didn't notice my hand shaking. "C'mon, kiddo. Fun's over." Peanuts continued to bark as I clipped the leash to his collar and hauled him out of the car, closing the door behind him.

We'd missed the Convenience Mart's entrance by only about four feet and had been stopped dead in our tracks by a steel guard rail. As I stepped to the front of the car, I saw that the Honda's fender had taken most of the impact and the guard rail looked pretty good.

"What in the hell happened?" I looked up and saw that the incident had attracted a small crowd, maybe seven people. A big guy with a beer gut that strained at his black "Born to kick ass" T-shirt had stepped forward. A small blond woman who might or might not have been with him was standing a couple feet behind him. "You were turning in here normal-like and then you go nuts."

Before I could answer, a skinny kid with acne came out of the store and told us the police were on their way. I didn't thank him, but turned to the big guy. "It was a snake. I'm making the turn and there's this big snake on my leg."

He shot a look at the woman behind him. Then he turned back to me, smiled slowly and completely before he said, "You sure it was a snake?"

Everyone except the blond woman, whose lips seemed in a perpetual pout, had a good laugh. When it was quiet again, I said, "Yeah, I'm sure."

"It had sort of a ribbon or a stripe down its back," Elaine said.

"Where'd he go?"

"Under the seat, I think."

He made a face and shrugged but didn't move. The blond's pout had blossomed into a taunting smile and she stepped up to the big man. "Go ahead, Mickey. Get the snake out of the guy's car."

He looked at her, then at the car.

"Hey," I said, "why don't we wait for the cops. They're good at stuff like this."

Mickey looked relieved until he turned back to his little friend who was still smiling, her arms crossed over her chest. With a burst of resolution, he threw his hands up and said, "Ah, what the hell, sounds like one of them garter snakes. Let me at it."

I moved in front of him. "I don't think that's a good idea. You see, no one knows if it's harmless. Two days ago someone tried to shoot me and did shoot the back window out on my car." I gestured toward the cardboard as proof. "Now, I don't know how a snake would get in my car unless someone put it there. So, I don't know that we can assume it's a garter snake."

He stared at me for a moment and backed off. Apparently an attempt on my life moved me up in his estimation. Turning to the woman, he said, "We'll wait for the cops." Her smile dwindled back into a pout.

The police were there within five minutes and while one officer wrote up a citation an animal control officer arrived and pulled the garter snake out from under the driver's seat. Just about everyone was disappointed that it wasn't some kind of Asian viper that might have left me dead and bloated.

It was almost noon before we drove back to my apartment and by then I'd decided that I didn't mind the fact that I wouldn't be around in a million years. There was no way I'd fit in.

As we pulled into the driveway, Elaine and I were arguing about whether the snake had been planted or not. I wanted to believe it had just crawled into the car, through one of those secret openings that only snakes know about. Elaine said that was ridiculous and, besides, why would a snake want to get in a car? I suggested that perhaps he was trying to evolve.

"Try another one, McCauley. And, by the way, why didn't you tell me someone was trying to kill you?"

"Well, we've been so busy it just didn't come up. You know, if someone were trying to kill me, why did they use a garter snake instead of some obscure viper who comes without an antiserum?" I kept Peanuts on the leash, much to his disappointment, because I didn't want to take him down to the river right then. "When's the last time a garter snake killed someone?"

Without hesitation, she said, "Probably when it surprised some guy driving seventy-five miles per hour, wedged between two semis."

We were about to climb the stairs to my apartment when Louise came around the side of the house. I was grateful for her interruption.

Peanuts was greeting her and she leaned down to pat him, then stopped and wrinkled her nose up. "Nothing like the smell of a wet dog."

"Going to the shop?"

"Yes, then I saw you. I just heard the most horrible news and I thought, well, you'd want to know, seeing as you're involved in this investigation and all."

My head flooded with images that ranged from Jeff Barlowe hanging himself to Julia Ellison throwing herself in front of a back hoe.

But when she said, "David Reaves was murdered last night," I was not prepared.

After a beat I said, "State Rep. David Reaves?"

Louise murmured a confirmation. The clouds closed in on me for a second. Somewhere a lawn mower whined and something shifted imperceptibly. I tried to focus on it, but couldn't quite make it.

Louise lowered her voice and said, "You're not going to believe where they found him."

"Where?"

She glanced at Elaine, then back to me. "The Cedar Street Inn."

I wasn't sure I'd heard right. "No."

"What's the Cedar Street Inn?" It was Elaine.

Louise gave me a solemn nod. "Yes."

"How'd it happen?"

"Shot. Twice."

"What's the Cedar Street Inn?"

"Well, one thing you pay for at Cedar Street is discretion." Then I quickly added, "Or so I've heard."

Louise confided to Elaine, "It's rumored to be the base for a call girl operation."

"No kidding." Her eyes widened. "Here in Foxport?"

"Actually," I said, "it's in an unincorporated area. Sort of a mini sin strip. There's a drive-in that shows movies like *Ninja Chainsaw Massacre* and a couple porn shops that morally outraged citizens are always trying to close down." My mind was charging ahead with possibilities. "When did you hear?"

"Only a half hour ago." Then she added, "They're holding a press conference this afternoon at two."

"Do you know where?"

"The police station, I believe."

"We may give it a try."

Louise glanced at her watch. "Well, I hate to drop a piece of news like that and leave, but I do have to be getting to the shop. Joleen has to leave early today. Again!"

As soon as Elaine and I got into the apartment, I turned on the radio, moving the dial to the local station, and stood there, waiting. I learned there was a cold front aimed right at us that would start by dumping some rain on the area, and that Pollack Ford was offering five-hundred-dollar rebates. Then the news announcer came back on, recapping the story and saying little was known at this time, but there were leads.

Elaine had liberated Peanuts from his leash and was sitting in the director's chair. "That press conference should be interesting."

I glanced at her out of the corner of my eye. She was watching me like a kid waiting to hear it was time to leave for the zoo.

"Why don't you change into something that will make you look like a reporter?"

She jumped up, startling Peanuts who seemed oblivious to the situation from his station beneath the coffee table. He had taken to sleeping under things — the coffee table, the bed — the way someone in an earthquake-prone area might. Maybe his instincts were better than ours.

If Elaine was going to pull this off, she'd need more than a convincing costume. I called Tim Skillman, Jeff's editor, to see if he'd come through with a press pass for us. He hesitated, and I didn't blame him.

"Who's going to use it?"

I told him Elaine was.

Another pause. "What makes you think there's a connection between Novotny's death and Reaves's?" he asked.

"I guess I don't know that right now, but they were two people who were on opposite sides of the wetland issue."

"Yeah," he sighed, and I figured he'd already thought of that. I reminded him that it was his reporter we were trying to get out of jail and he finally agreed to supply us with a press pass, though I had to swear it would be Elaine, not me, who used it. I told him we'd stop by within the hour.

I called my office and there were two messages from Julia Ellison. In both recordings she sounded upset and impatient with me for not being there. But, of course, she didn't leave a number. I tried to find her phone number but realized that all I knew about Ms. Ellison was the fact that she taught at Abel County College, tended bar part-time at The Den, and was an environmental terrorist. I called the college. Then I remembered it was Saturday. Well, it wouldn't hurt her to wait. I gathered Elaine's translation of Jeff's notes, folded, and slipped it into my jacket pocket. Not that I wanted to wait. Julia was so indifferent about my involvement, if she was trying to contact me, it must be big. And given the timing of her calls, I had to believe it had something to do with Reaves. I managed to come up with one place where I might be able to get in touch with her. Fortunately, you could eat lunch there too.

Elaine emerged from the hall wearing a tan jacket over a black skirt. She'd pulled her hair back and secured it with combs. "No matter how authentic I look, I'm not getting in anywhere without a press pass."

"We've got that handled."

She held up her empty hands. "I'll need something to write in. A notebook."

I gave her one of Jeff's that wasn't full. She hesitated, then took it. "He's going to hate me for this. I've never met the guy and I've invaded his code and his notebook."

"You help me get him out of there and he won't complain."

She dropped the notebook into her black leather shoulder bag. "You got a pencil?" I asked.

"I use a pen."

"Don't be silly. All reporters use pencils." She didn't respond so I added, "Don't they?"

"I don't care." I held the door open for her. "I don't like the feel of a pencil." As she walked past me onto the porch, she added, "I even do crosswords in pen."

A moment later I followed. "I didn't know that."

Stopping on the third step down, Elaine turned to look up at me. "When I'm feeling really dangerous, I use a red pen."

"How do you correct mistakes?"

"I don't make them. Either that or I write over."

"What a reckless woman."

I stopped at the *Foxport Chronicle* and got the press pass for Elaine. Skillman made me swear again that I wouldn't use it. I promised. He gave me a skeptical look. "If you're lying, do me one favor. Leave me gagged and tied to a chair so I can say it's not my fault." When I got out to the car, where Elaine was waiting, she asked where mine was.

"I can't go. There's people who will be there who know I'm a P.I. and not a reporter."

She looked puzzled. "Ed Carver knows who I am. Won't he be there?"

"Yeah, but I'm betting on him being so busy he's not going to take the time to hassle you." I paused and added, "If he asks what you're doing there, just tell him you're freelancing."

The waitress at The Den put us next to a window. The wind had picked up and somewhere a cloud was blocking the sun. From where Elaine sat she could see the river spilling over a small dam. "This is pretty," she said, and I watched her adjust one of her combs. I had to agree.

After we ordered, I went into the bar. I didn't hold out much hope that Julia would be working, but maybe someone could tell me how to get in touch with her.

Even though it was almost one o'clock, the bar was practically empty. Just the bartender and a woman perched on a stool at the far end. The bartender was the same guy who'd relieved Julia that day I talked to her. Rob. He was talking to a woman who was dark-haired, attractive, and wore a short dress that was almost the same color as the blush wine she was drinking. Her head was tilted back and she was laughing. Rob was watching her, possibly admiring the curve of her throat. Then he turned and saw me settle on one of the bar stools. His eyes narrowed slightly, then he looked back at the woman, excused himself, and moved toward me, one hand in the pocket of his black jeans, the other dragging along the bar. I lit a cigarette.

"What can I get you?"

I shook my head. "Nothing, thanks. I'm looking for Julia Ellison."

"She's not working today."

"You know where I can reach her? It's real important."

He studied me for a moment, drumming his fingers against the bar's surface. I glanced at his hand and he stopped.

"Why don't you try the college?" He took a towel from below and began wiping the bar's shining surface.

"It's Saturday." While that concept registered, I said, "Could you give me her home number?"

He shook his head as if he thought I had a lot to learn about life. "Hey, lots of guys ask for Julia's phone number. She'd kill me if I gave it out."

"Yeah, well I'm not trying to hit on her. And I'm not exactly giddy at the prospect of talking to her. Thing is, she's the one who wants to talk to me."

His shrug said: What do you want me to do about it?

"Do you think you could call her for me?" I tried, without much success, to keep the sarcasm out of my voice. Still no response. "Tell her Quint McCauley needs to talk to her. If she says Quint Who? you can apologize for disturbing her, and I'll be on my way."

He eyed me carefully but when I returned the look, he turned away. Finally he balled up the rag and tossed it under the bar. "I'll be back in a minute."

The woman at the end of the bar had drained her glass of pink wine and held it up as Rob passed her. He stopped to fill it. She lit one of those long brown slender cigarettes and blew the smoke down the bar in my direction. I turned away and concentrated on the line of bottles in front of the mirrored backdrop to the bar. I touched my upper lip and wondered if maybe it was time to grow the moustache back.

Rob was gone a couple minutes and I was getting hopeful. He returned looking as if he'd just eaten something that disagreed with him. Then he took a napkin and, writing in a left-handed backhand, he scribbled down an address and slid it toward me. "She'll meet you at two o'clock. You know where that is?"

Glancing at the writing, I said, "I can find it. Thanks."

God, didn't this woman have a great sense of timing?

When I returned to the table, Elaine was thoughtfully chewing on a bite of her chef's salad and my hamburger was sitting there waiting for someone to eat it.

"I've arranged to meet the Fox. Thing is, she set it up for two." I slid into the booth, watching Elaine. No clues. "The police station isn't far from the Jaded Fox. Can you go there when the press conference is over and wait for me?"

"This woman has it out for me, doesn't she? She doesn't even know me and she's left me stranded in two places. With no provocation." She shook her head and stabbed an artichoke with her fork. "I'm not crazy about your friends, Quint."

"Neither am I."

As we drove to the police station, Elaine began fidgeting with her purse strap. Finally she said, "I've never been to a press conference."

"All you have to do is take notes. Listen. See who's there. Who's running the show."

"How am I supposed to see who's there, when I don't know anyone in this town?"

"Just write down names." I paused, then added, "Chances are they aren't going to say a lot at this point. They aren't holding this thing for the benefit of the press or the public. It's more a cover-your-ass technique — you know, dispel rumors and prevent leaks. That kind of thing."

She nodded, convincing herself. I continued, "Just keep a low profile. If anyone asks where you're from, just tell them you're a stringer for the *Foxport Chronicle* and you report to Tim Skillman."

"Shit, I don't know why I'm all of a sudden nervous. This is stupid."

"Pretend you're working your way through school using the low profile system. Just sit in the back and don't ask any questions."

"That I can do."

It was easy to spot the police department. Several vans from Chicago area news stations were there and a group of reporters were milling about outside the building, apparently waiting for someone.

Elaine took a deep breath. "Wish me luck."

Before I had a chance to censor myself, I leaned over and kissed her. Not hard, but she knew I meant business. I backed off. "Thanks. Really."

Once the startled look dissipated, she gave me an uncertain smile and said, "It's okay."

"You don't have to ask any questions but . . ."

Her look darkened. "But what?"

"I'd be real disappointed if no one asked if there was a connection between Novotny's and Reaves's deaths. I'm sure they'll mention it or someone will ask."

"Let's hope so." Then she got out of the car, adding, "See you at the shop," adjusted her purse, and strode toward the police station like there was no way she was leaving without her story.

Heavy, dark clouds were moving in from the west as I executed a U-turn. It occurred to me that now would be a good time to replace the car's cardboard window with a real one, but instead I drove off to keep an appointment with my favorite terrorist.

Chapter 14

I TRIED TO SHAKE the mood I'd descended into. It wasn't doing me any good, but like the disturbing remnants of a bad dream, it refused to dissipate. I needed to refocus my efforts to get Jeff out of jail. For all the success I'd had, he might be on his way to setting a new record for doing time while protecting the identity of a source.

The address Rob gave me belonged to one of several small, drab-colored townhouses on the eastern perimeter of Foxport's only shopping mall. Glass bubbles surfaced like huge blisters from the top of each unit — sun roofs for the sedentary. Since there wasn't room in the driveway for much besides the maroon van that was parked in it, and there was no on-street parking, I had to drive to the end of the block and park around the corner on Anderson.

When Julia opened the door the first thing that struck me was that she had aged, and for a few distorted seconds I thought it had been years since I'd seen her rather than a day. Her posture had slipped a couple degrees, there were dark smudges beneath her eyes, and the skin there was thin and translucent like tissue paper. For a second I felt something akin to sympathy.

Then she pulled herself up and said, "You're late," and I wondered why I bothered. I shook my head and stepped into the tiled foyer. Before closing the door, she stuck her head out, apparently noting the heavy gray clouds closing in and the breeze that was ripe with the smell of rain.

"I'm so sorry," I said, "I just haven't quite picked up the knack of time travel."

Scowling, she slammed the door shut with her hip. "I don't mean to sound unreasonable, it's just that there's a lot going on." She slumped against the door and stared at the gray pattern in the tiled floor. Her dark hair hung straight and lifeless and, with her head bowed, all but obscured her face.

In the back of my mind something was trying to register. Then, deep in the house, a timer went off and it hit me. After several moments when Julia still hadn't acknowledged the persistent dinging, I inhaled deeply and said, "I don't know what smells better, fresh baked cookies or a locker room after a win."

With a small shake of her head, Julia detached herself from the door. "C'mon in the kitchen." I followed. As we passed the living room and dining area I was struck by the proliferation of wooden shelves, linen wall hangings, and jigsawed hearts painted blue and beige. Foxport's merchants know how to bottle up country charm and sell it by the gross, but I was willing to bet that Julia Ellison wasn't buying. A spinning wheel that looked authentic took up a big chunk of the living room.

"You spin your own fabric too?"

"Hardly. A friend of mine lives here." We entered a small kitchen, made smaller by a round, dark wood table jammed up against the one wall that wasn't claimed by sinks and appliances. A door opened into a tiny back yard, and as I checked out the view I noted that half of the yard had been paved in concrete for a patio. Julia cut the timer off and said, "Cindy's out of town for a couple weeks. I told her I'd take care of her plants." Donning a blue padded glove, she reached into the oven and pulled out first one, then another tray, each covered with obscenely plump cookies, and placed them on a cooling rack. "It seemed a good place to stay for a couple days." She didn't elaborate. "Care for some coffee?"

I accepted and sat at the table, pushing aside a copy of the *Chronicle*. "You know," I said, as she set a mug of coffee down in front of me on a plastic Pennsylvania Dutch place mat, "I expected you to be pouring sugar into the gas tanks of earth-moving equipment or slashing the tires of dump trucks, not baking cookies." I sipped the coffee, which was rich and hot. "How could I have been so wrong?"

"You heard about that?" It wasn't an admission; merely a question.

"You know that's not going to stop them. Just makes them angry and determined. Kind of like hornets." I waited for her to comment but she didn't. "And the head hornet—Rebecca Novotny—is gunning for you."

"Well, she'll have to get in line." She was mixing thick, heavy batter with a wooden spoon. "And if she thinks fouling up the systems of a few machines is as far as we're going, she's made a serious error in her estimation of the enemy."

I watched as she scraped clumps of dough from a wooden spoon onto yet another cookie sheet. She reminded me of a soldier—slightly shell-shocked but still zealous. "You really enjoy it, don't you? The monkeywrenching, or whatever you call it."

She looked at me for a minute before she said, "Yes, I do. In ways it's better than sex." I frowned, and she continued. "There's this kind of feeling that takes over when you do an action. I get a high out of it. I can be up for a couple days running on that high. Everything's calm, clear. And pure—yes, that's the word—pure. It's an incredible life experience."

"I don't know," I said. "I guess I'll just have to take your word for it."

She shrugged and went back to the dough. After a few moments, she said, "Anyway, I can't stand waiting. I have to be doing something. I can't sit still or my skin starts to crawl." She planted four more dough balls on the sheet. I watched her. I wasn't naive enough to believe that she'd suddenly been struck by an overwhelming desire to cooperate with me in my efforts to get Jeff out of jail, but there was something going on that made me believe the stakes had changed. And though the baser part of my character wanted to be as perverse as she'd been at our two previous meetings, and to point out that she wasn't the only one who had trouble with waiting, I knew that wasn't going to buy me anything. I took another swallow of coffee and set the mug down. While I really wanted to ask her if she remembered a reporter named Barlowe, I suppressed the urge and said, "So what it is you need to talk about?"

She didn't answer right away, but scraped the remaining dough out of the bowl and onto the cookie sheet, slid the sheet onto a shelf in the oven, and set the timer. Using a metal spatula, she transferred about a dozen of the freshly baked cookies onto a plate and set the plate on the table. Then she poured some milk and a lot of sugar into her own cup of coffee and joined me. I waited. She engaged me with her eyes, then reached across the table, and removed a white envelope from a brown leather handbag. "I'd like you to deliver this to the police after I'm gone," she said, and placed the envelope next to my coffee mug. "It's a letter from me identifying myself as the Blue Fox with enough details to prove it."

I leaned back in the chair and crossed my arms over my chest.

She studied me for a moment, her expression bemused, then nudged the envelope toward me. "Go ahead, read it. It's not sealed."

After a minute I did. Curiosity would not allow me to do otherwise. Besides, I wasn't sure I believed her, and I actually was more surprised than pleased to find that she was on the level. The letter contained a detailed account of a number of her excursions, with instructions on where she kept the paint and the other tools of her trade. Not one to pass up a forum, she'd printed in large letters at the bottom of the page: I am one of Earth's soldiers. I am of the Earth, no more and no less than the trees and birds. I am the Earth fighting for its own existence. I will not cease until my body is returned to the Earth.

My sane, rational self told me not to open a discussion on her final statement. It also told me to take the letter and run. End of assignment. But she seemed ready to talk, and the part of me that doesn't close my eyes during horror movies wanted to listen. I returned the letter to its envelope and sealed it. "Why now? Why not before? Why not never?"

"Because now I can hear the baying of the hounds." She lifted her mug, holding it steady with the fingers of her left hand. "They're closing in."

"If they're closing in, why are you sitting here, baking cookies?"

Acknowledging the question with a small smile, she said, "I've got some time. No one knows I'm here except you and Rob."

"Is that your van out front?"

She shook her head. "The neighbors park it in Cindy's driveway when she's out of town. It makes the place look lived in."

"Where's your car?"

"It's not here. Rob dropped me off. If they're looking for me, that'd be a good way to spot me."

"Have you ever thought of turning yourself in? Might be easier that way." Then I added with a shrug, "Can't run forever."

"No," she almost shouted the word. Seconds later the rumble of thunder emphasized her point. She took a deep breath and said in a softer voice, "I can't do any good if I'm locked up."

"How much good can you do now?" I gestured toward the envelope. "After the cops get this, the Blue Fox's identity isn't going to be a secret anymore."

Wrapping her small, square hands around the coffee mug, she said, "I've got plans."

"You want to tell me about them?"

"I don't think that's a good idea." She studied the mocha-colored liquid in the mug as if it contained all the answers. "Let me just say that there's a lot to be done."

"What do you think you can do now? You're not an environmental vigilante anymore, you know. You're wanted for murder."

Her mouth twisted into a smirk. "Oh, so then I'm supposed to act like I've done what they say? Is that what I'm supposed to do?"

I held her gaze and said, "Did you kill Novotny?"

"No," she answered, unflinching.

"You were there. That was your hair they found wrapped around his shirt button, wasn't it?" She didn't answer. "You had to be there. Part of the message you left was a couple dead ducks lying on his desk. If it was someone trying to make it look like you, would they go to the trouble of finding ducks that had died of natural causes? They autopsied those ducks, for God's sake."

She started to protest, but I wasn't finished. "And then I hear about the hair they found on his shirt cuff." I gestured toward the *Chronicle*. "Surely you've read all about it. They say it's a woman's hair. We're looking for a dark-haired woman who couldn't kill a duck."

After a moment, she looked at me and, with an acrid smile, said, "Okay, so I was there. But I didn't kill him."

"You fought with him?"

"Wasn't my doing. He walked in on me and went crazy. Grabbed my arm and my hair. Yanked my head back."

"What did you do?"

"I kicked him in the balls and got the hell out of there. Then I went home and waited for the police to show up. A few hours later I heard on the news that he was dead." She lifted the mug of coffee and breathed in the steam, but didn't drink. "And, you know, when I first heard the news, all I felt was relief. I thought 'now he can't identify me.'" Abruptly she set the mug down, but didn't release it. "And then I felt elated. And that's how I still feel. I'm glad he's dead. One less son of a bitch out there raping Earth." I just stared at her and she continued, "The only thing that bothers me about the death of Leonard Novotny is that I've been framed for it."

"You know," I said after a minute, "if you turn yourself in, all you've got to do is tell them what you told me. Maybe they'll believe you."

For some reason, that took the wind out of her. She sighed. "It's not that simple."

"I didn't say it was simple. You're going to need a good lawyer. Cal Maitlin could help you."

She shook her head. "You don't understand. They're also going to arrest me for David's murder."

After a moment, I said, "Why?"

She rubbed her thumb along the smooth surface of the mug. "Because my fingerprints are in that motel room." I didn't respond, and she didn't look away. Her voice barely registered above a whisper when she said, "I was with him last night."

I decided that wasn't a hard line to swallow.

She leaned forward and for a moment I thought she was going to tell me something so secret that it had to be whispered. Instead, she took one of the cookies, breaking it in half but not eating it. She stared at one of the halves, then as if she were telling me a well-known fact, said, "I've been set up. Twice. Whoever killed David set me up too."

"How do you know that?"

"They knew I'd be there."

"Wait," I held up my hand. "Before you go spilling your guts to me, I'd like to know why."

She took a bite of cookie and chewed on it carefully, then swallowed and said, "Because I need help. I trust Jeff Barlowe and he trusts you, so I guess I've got to trust you. And there are some things I'm going to tell you that have to remain confidential."

"Just now you were still going to deny being with Novotny before he was killed, yet it's okay to tell me you were with David. I don't get it."

"That's simple. I want you to believe me. I was afraid if you knew I'd lied to you before, you might think I'm lying now."

"Have to admit, it's crossing my mind."

"I lied to you before because I didn't think I needed your help, so I decided you didn't need to know."

"Are you trying to hire me?"

"Yes. Once they find my fingerprints in the room where David was killed, I'm going to be a suspect. And I'm willing to bet that the same gun used to kill Novotny also killed David. That's probably all the evidence they need. They'll concentrate on finding me and forget about any other possibilities. That's where I need you. You were already trying to prove that the Fox didn't kill Novotny. I just want you to keep looking into it. Because I didn't kill him. Or David."

"You're pretty confident I'm going to help, aren't you?"

She shrugged and I studied her, coolly trying to hire a private investigator the afternoon after her lover has been shot. Finally she said, "Do you want me to continue?"

"That's up to you."

"Will you take the case?"

"I won't know that until I hear what you've got to tell me."

"If you decide not to, will this remain confidential?"

"Within reason. But don't go telling yourself that I'll go down with the ship like Barlowe did. I've got no protection the way a lawyer does. Like I said, talk to Cal Maitlin."

"No. Not yet."

"Well, maybe you should think about it. I warn you, they call me before a grand jury, I'll sing in any key they want to hear." I didn't know if I would, but I didn't want her to think otherwise.

She finished the cookie and shrugged. "Maybe you would, maybe you wouldn't. I guess I'll take the risk."

The fact that *I* might not want to take the risk never occurred to her. If the contents of the envelope were all Jeff needed to become a free man then, technically, I was finished. But she was still talking, and I was still curious. "Whoever set you up; how would they know you'd be there?"

She bought some time by taking another cookie and breaking it in half just like the other. "I've lived in this area all my life and so has David, so I knew who he was, but that was about it. Then I heard he was running for office and that he was an environmental advocate. I admit I was skeptical until I went to hear him speak. Then I was impressed. I talked to him afterwards, asked him some tough questions, and I was even more impressed. I started doing volunteer work for him then." She told me that after the election she continued to work for him. Eventually the friendship evolved into something more. "We were very discreet, though." She turned her attention back to the cookie. "Whenever he could get away to meet me, he'd call me at school and if he couldn't get hold of me, he'd leave a message at the school for me." She rattled on, describing elaborately coded responses they used in the charade as if it were all very logical and well thought out. I caught a flash of lightning out of the corner of my eye, but didn't recall hearing the thunder. I couldn't look at Julia because I was sure my eyes would give away what was going on in my head. She had impressed me as being a bright woman, now I wasn't so sure.

"Did you always meet at the same place? Cedar Street?"

"Yes."

"So, what happened last night?"

"I was there first. I always got the room. You know," she shrugged, "people might recognize him. It was late. After that fund-raiser and all. Maybe twelve, twelve thirty. He brought a bottle of scotch and made us drinks. Everything like always, but there was something wrong. You know how someone acts when they've got to tell you something bad, but they don't know how to do it. Or don't have the nerve. It seemed like he couldn't look me in the eye for more than a half second at a time." She sighed and reflected for a moment. "I thought he wanted to break it off. I even asked him if that was it. He said that wasn't it at all, and there was nothing wrong." Then, with a shrug, she added, "I said good-bye, you know, figuring he'd open up." She stopped.

"Did he?"

"No, he didn't say anything. It was like he wanted me to leave."

"So did you?"

She added a teaspoon of sugar to her half-filled mug. My jaws ached for a second. After stirring it she took a sip and set it down. "Yes, I left. Told him he could call me when he felt more sociable." She propped her chin on her fist and, after a moment, said, "That's the last thing he heard me say. 'Call me when you feel more sociable.' "

"How long were you together?"

"No more than fifteen minutes. More like ten. I barely started my drink."

The rain had started and the window on the door was taking a pounding.

"Julia, was there a pattern? Did you always leave first?"

After wiping at her eyes, though I saw no traces of moisture, she said, "We never left together. I always left about ten minutes ahead of him."

Elbow propped on the table, I braced my forehead against the palm of my hand. How dumb could a bright person be? I was reminded of the old ditty that ended something like: Love may be blind, but the neighbors ain't.

I folded my hands on the plastic mat in a prayerlike gesture. "You really think no one knew what was going on?"

Her eyes widened. "Of course not. We weren't kids. We were discreet."

Shaking my head, I looked away from her. "You know, when you just said that you and Reaves were having an affair, I wasn't surprised." I turned back to her. "And I'd only seen you two together once. I'm not saying I knew it then, but looking back, you two were communicating on levels that defied any other explanation." Her eyes narrowed. "And if I noticed something, then people who were around you more often would have to be blind to miss it. And those little notes you leave everywhere, they don't fool anyone, at least not for very long." Her look hardened and I raised a palm in a gesture of truce. "Okay, let's not go into that now. But obviously someone knew about you and David. And they knew where you went. Who do you think that was?"

She held onto my gaze for a few seconds, then looked away and shook her head. "I don't know."

"Julia, did David know you were the Blue Fox?"

I interpreted her silence as a yes and pressed on. "Is there more than one Fox?" When she didn't answer, I prompted with: "How do you expect me to investigate this if I don't know the score?"

"Then you're working for me." It was more a statement than a question.

"You stop talking now and I'm not."

After a moment's hesitation, she said, "No, not at any one time."

"What do you mean?"

She hesitated, then said, "The original Fox retired about seven years ago. David knew him. He knew what he was doing." She went on to explain how David had approached her about becoming his successor a couple years ago, after they'd worked together for a while.

"Who was the original Fox?"

She drained the last bit of glucose from the mug and said, "I can't tell you that, Quint. And, really, you don't have to know."

"Your father?"

"No."

"Was the original a man or a woman?"

"A man," she said and quickly added, "That's all you're getting."

It was more than I had before, so I decided to settle. "Did David suggest your activities as the Fox?"

"Sometimes. Sometimes I acted on my own."

"That raid on Novotny's office. Whose idea was that?"

"David's."

"Did it ever occur to you that maybe David was trying to frame you?"

"Of course, I thought about it. But no. He wouldn't."

"How can you be so sure?"

She opened her mouth and the phone rang. Jumping to her feet, she said, "That'll be Rob," then stood next to it and let it ring five times before picking it up.

A second after she said hello, I could tell it wasn't Rob. Her expression clouded over and she turned her back to me. Then I heard her say, "What are you—" She stopped and listened for a few more seconds, then hung up the phone, but held on to the receiver as if using it for support. She stayed that way for maybe a minute and I listened to the rain slashing against the door. When she turned around, her mouth was set in a thin line and her eyes were cold.

She reached in front of me for her purse and I had to lean back in the chair to get out of her way. In one smooth movement, she withdrew a .32 automatic and brought it to bear on me. I swallowed.

"Give me your car keys," she said.

"What?"

"You heard me."

I stood slowly and dug into my jeans pocket. When I started to remove the car keys from the ring, she stopped me. "Don't bother with that. Give me the whole thing."

"How am I supposed to get in my house?"

"You've got an extra set, don't you?"

"Yeah, but they're in the house."

"Break in. You're probably good at it." Still I hesitated and she gestured with the gun. "Put them on the table. Slowly."

I finally did. There was something in her eyes that cautioned me not to take her lightly.

"Back up," she instructed and after I'd retreated several feet, she took the keys and pocketed them. "Now take your pants off and give them to me." I didn't move. She wet her lips and when she spoke her voice was a pitch higher. "Do you have trouble hearing?"

I shook my head, going with the hunch that she didn't have time to argue. "I gave you my keys. You want my pants you'll have to take them off my body." No reaction so I added, "It's a black Honda and it's parked on Anderson."

Finally she reached for her purse and hooked it on her shoulder. Still keeping the gun on me, she backstepped to the door and opened it. A gust of wind swept a sheet of rain in. "Julia," I said and she stopped. "Find yourself another P.I."

She regarded me impassively for a couple seconds, then stepped out into the storm.

I didn't follow. Maybe I still had my pants, but she had the gun and was starting to remind me of a cornered animal. Thunder rumbled and a flash of lightning followed seconds later. Shit. I wasn't sure what Julia had been running from, but I didn't want to stick around to find out. As I was folding her confession into my wallet, the cookie timer went off. I almost ignored it. But even though I didn't know this Cindy who lived here, I was sure she didn't deserve to have her house burn down, plywood hearts and all. Just as I was transferring the tray to the cooling rack, the doorbell rang. Whatever they were selling, I wasn't interested. If the back door was good enough for Julia, it was good enough for me.

I stepped out into the storm. I expected to get soaked. I expected to be cold and miserable and to curse Julia Ellison with every step as I sloshed my way home. What I didn't expect was to find myself eyeball to eyeball with Ed Carver.

Chapter 15

NEITHER OF US MOVED for several seconds. I watched the rain run off his khaki mackintosh in little rivers and their tributaries. He's only got a few inches on my six feet, but he's lean and angular and has always seemed taller than that. When I looked up at him, trying to read his expression, the rain pounded my eyes shut.

"What in the hell . . ." Carver broke off and pushed past me into the kitchen. Standing there dripping on Cindy's black and white tiled floor, he surveyed the small room, dwelling on the racks of fresh cookies. He reminded me of someone who had just woken in a strange place and was trying to get his bearings. He turned to look at me, his features pulled together in puzzlement. Possibly he was wondering why I continued to stand out in the rain, which struck me as an immensely logical question and I stepped back into the house.

After more intense scrutiny, Carver spoke. "Where is she?"

"You just missed her."

The doorbell rang again, buying me a few moments to think. Did I owe anything to a woman who tried to hire me, then held me at gunpoint while she stole my car? And tried to take my pants? I heard Carver give instructions to check the upstairs, then he stepped back into the kitchen.

"What does she drive?"

"She's driving a black Honda Accord, license number QMC1701." He squinted at me from under his cap. "Isn't that your car?"

"I'm afraid so."

"You gave her your car?"

I shifted slightly and glanced at the empty hallway before answering. "Give isn't the word that comes to mind. When someone points a gun at you and asks for the car keys, I think it's called taking."

His expression didn't change. "What kind of gun?"

".32 automatic."

"Damn." He made a fist and slammed it against the counter. The cookies jumped. "We had her. How long ago?"

"Less than ten minutes."

He snatched the phone from its receiver and as he stabbed the buttons, said, "Give me a description of her and what she was wearing."

"Five eight, a hundred and thirty pounds, dark shoulder-length hair. Eyes maybe hazel," I paused and added, "kind of sleepy-looking." Carver gave me an odd look but didn't say anything. "She was wearing jeans and a gray sweatshirt." The rumble of thunder prompted me to add, "She's probably wet right now." I hoped she was miserable as well.

When he finished phoning in the all points bulletin on Julia Ellison, he turned back to me. "You want to tell me what you're doing here?"

I took the envelope out of my wallet and handed it to Carver. "I guess I'm the messenger." Then, as an afterthought, added, "I'd rather you didn't shoot me."

One of Carver's officers joined us in the kitchen. "There's no one upstairs and Collins says it's clean downstairs too." He was a grim-faced little man with large eyes and a nervous twitch.

As Carver studied Julia's confession, I said, "That should be enough to get Jeff Barlowe out of jail."

He regarded me over the top of the paper, then reached underneath his mack, and pulled out a pair of glasses. Holding onto one arm, he snapped them open. Then he put them on and turned away as he read. When he was finished, he removed the glasses and said, "Jeff Barlowe's not my biggest concern right now."

"He's in a bad way. We need to get him out of there."

"Yeah, well I'm in a bad way too. And I'm going to be worse if I don't get this Julia Ellison in for questioning." He looked around the room, as though he'd forgotten something, stopping at the table. "Which mug was she using?"

I told him and he hooked the mug's ear with a pencil and dropped it into a plastic bag. "If she was in such a damned hurry, what's she doing baking cookies and drinking coffee?"

"She didn't know you'd found her." I told him about the phone call and her subsequent actions.

"Why don't you give me that letter? I'll see about getting Jeff out of jail." As I made the request, I knew it was a futile one.

Sure enough, Carver shook his head. "You're coming with me. We're going looking for Julia Ellison. I've never seen her. You've been eating cookies and drinking coffee with her." Then, almost as an afterthought, he added, "And God knows what else."

Once my reason for a hasty retreat was no longer so urgent, I had no desire to step out into the rain. But I didn't think Carver would care much for my suggestion to wait until the rain let up. Not likely. Even though Carver was parked in the street—one of the privileges of his rank—I got enough of a soaking to wish I had one of those natty mackintoshes.

As I sat in the squad car, I ran my hand through my soaking hair, trying to squeeze some of the wet out. Carver glanced at me. "You should've worn a raincoat."

"Thanks for the tip." I dug my cigarettes out of my pocket and was elated to find one with a dry filter.

Carver gave me time to light up before he said, "Don't smoke in here."

I smiled grimly and snuffed it out in his ashtray. Bad enough riding around town with Ed Carver, now I had to do it without the support of a cigarette.

"I don't care if you want to kill yourself with those things, just don't do it in my air."

"I'm deeply touched by your concern."

We drove slowly down Prairie, heading east toward the river. I was looking for my black Honda, but not hopeful. Not only was Julia probably halfway to wherever she was going now, but due to the heavy rain, visibility was poor. I squinted out into it and kept looking.

"Did you enjoy your little charade the other day?" Carver asked.

"That wasn't a charade."

"Don't give me that crap." I didn't argue and after a few moments, he continued, "I suppose you'd never heard of her before today."

I shrugged and wiped the condensation from the passenger window, briefly wondering how much water was soaking into the back seat of my car. "She didn't need a private detective until today."

"Yeah, and I suppose she just came across your name in the yellow pages."

"No, she knows I'm a friend of Jeff Barlowe's. That's why she called me and not the Acme Agency." I paused and added, "Or you."

"What did she hire you for?"

"She tried to hire me to find out who killed Leonard Novotny and David Reaves. Says she didn't do either."

He snorted. "Oh, well, let's call it off. The lady says she didn't do it." He shook his head and added, "Why should she confess to you, anyway?"

"Why would she bother to call me if she did kill either one? Why wouldn't she just cut out of town?" I couldn't believe I was defending the woman.

"Maybe she needed a car."

He had me there. "Who tipped you off?"

"None of your business."

We crossed the river at Grant, heading into town, then turned south on Route 35. We'd be driving past my place and I wondered if that was intentional.

"River's high," Carver remarked. We'd gotten a lot of rain that summer and with each new rainfall the level got a bit higher, and the river more restless. Now it was roiling in its banks, flowing fast and angry.

We had just passed the point where the road dips down near the river when Carver slowed, and at first, I couldn't see a reason. Then I saw a car pulled over on the river side of the road with its flashers going. Another car, a station wagon, was pulled off just ahead of it. I assumed we'd come upon an accident, but as we moved past the two cars I could see no damage to either. Then I saw two people standing on the narrow riverbank, staring off into the river. A man wearing a bright red windbreaker looked over his shoulder, apparently saw the squad car, and began waving frantically, then turned and gestured toward the river. Carver and I exchanged looks and he pulled over just ahead of the station wagon.

As we got out of the squad, the man was yelling something, and the other person, a short, squat woman, was gesturing and yelling, but I couldn't make any of it out.

The wind whipped at me and I was cold and soaked right down to the bone. The grass was slick and I sidestepped my way down the bank. The man in the windbreaker said something about "twenty feet out . . . it's sunk deeper." And then I saw it. At first it looked like a dark tree limb that had gotten snagged on the bottom, but that was wishful thinking because I'd really known what we'd find as Carver pulled the squad car onto the soggy riverbank. Now I stood and stared through the rain at the fender of a black Honda, bobbing up and down in the river's current like a toy submarine.

Tilting my head back, I opened my mouth and let the steaming shower water run down my throat. After a minute, I shook my head and swallowed, blinking the water from my eyes. I tried to adjust the tap but it was already as hot as it would go, and now that it had peaked, the water was dwindling to warm. I stood there, one hand braced against the shower tiles, and wondered if I'd ever be warm again.

It was almost five hours since we'd spotted my Honda; four hours since they'd hauled it from the river, empty, with the driver's window rolled down; an hour and a half since Jeff Barlowe walked out of Abel County Jail. And at least twenty minutes since I'd stepped into the shower.

I heard a distant pounding and chose to ignore it, concentrating instead on the water running off my shoulders and chest, willing the cold out. Then someone called my name, once, then again only closer. I reached down and turned the water off.

"Quint? It's Elaine. Are you all right?" She was on the other side of the shower curtain.

"Yeah," I said, wiping the water from my face.

She seemed to hesitate. "I was downstairs with Louise when I heard you come in. I came up a minute later and you were in the shower." She paused. "You've been in there awhile, you know."

"Yeah, I know. I'll be out in a minute."

"Oh, that's okay. I just wanted to make sure you, you know, hadn't gone down the drain or anything." She laughed tentatively. "Um, well, I'll just be in the living room." She stepped out of the room and closed the door.

I'd anticipated the jolt of cold air as I climbed out of the tub, but that didn't make it any easier to handle. I toweled myself off quickly, thinking I shouldn't have been so short with Elaine, but knowing I didn't have much conversation in me. When I went to dress, I realized I hadn't brought dry clothes in with me. I didn't want to touch the damp ones, not even to push them out of the way. I secured the towel around my waist, and made a quick jog to the bedroom, but when I turned to close the door, Elaine was standing there with a glass partly filled with an amber liquid. No ice.

Her gaze dropped to my towel, then back up to my face. She smiled and offered me the glass. "It's whatever you've got in that decanter I gave you."

I took it from her, thinking I should thank her and turn away, but not wanting to. The first swallow went down like liquid fire and I shuddered involuntarily. "Scotch," I said. "Unblended."

Her hands were thrust in the pockets of her black skirt and her blouse was open at the neck, the ends of the collar bow draped down her chest. She'd removed her jacket and shoes. "We heard what happened. God, how awful. Did they find her?"

"Not yet. The river being the way it is, she could be in the Mississippi by now."

"How's Jeff?"

"He'll pull it together. At least he's out of jail."

She nodded, watching, tentative. "And how are you?"

After a moment, I said, "I'm cold."

Elaine closed the door. Then she stepped up to me and kissed my cheek, hesitated as her gaze faltered, took my face in her hands and kissed me on the mouth. I opened my arms to her and she moved against me, her silk blouse soft against my skin and her hand cool and dry as it came to rest on my chest. I felt her shoulder blade move beneath my left hand as my right clutched the glass of scotch. We were still locked in the kiss as she ran her hand down my chest, slowly. Her touch against my stomach made me gasp. When she got to the towel, she gave it a quick tug and it slipped past my legs to the floor. I moaned and drew her closer.

We were only a couple feet from the bed, but it took us hours to get there. Her clothes seemed to drift to the floor as I slowly recalled the curves and hollows of her body and burned them into my memory. The touch of her hands on my skin was like a warm rain. When I tried to turn her, to ease her onto the bed, she resisted, and murmuring something about who was calling the shots, gently pushed me down on the sheets. I succumbed.

Later, I held Elaine in the dark, feeling the steady rise and fall of her chest against mine. The rhythm hypnotized me, lulling me to sleep, and as I drifted off, I was vaguely aware of the scratching at the door. I decided not to let it bother me.

Chapter 16

DOGS DON'T SLEEP IN. That's their single greatest flaw. Even when they stay up with you to watch the end of some obscure late movie starring William Bendix, at six thirty they're reminding you that you'd have been wise to stick with water and a rawhide bone too.

Elaine murmured something and I brushed the hair back from her face and kissed her forehead. She didn't stir, so I lay there watching her sleep, fist curled under her chin. Then, at Peanuts's insistence, I carefully maneuvered my way out of bed, trying not to jostle it. I put on a pair of jeans and cracked the bedroom door. Peanuts shoved his way in and proceeded to jump at my feet, reading me the riot act with good-natured snarls. Before I could get him out of the room, he'd squirmed past my legs and bounded onto the bed. Elaine responded with a groan and pulled the covers up over her head. I grabbed his collar and dragged him out into the hall.

The grass was soggy from the heavy rain we'd gotten, but otherwise all signs of the dousing were gone. The sky was an early morning shade of blue—pale and hazy with tinges of gold. I tossed the Frisbee for Peanuts—I admit it, I felt guilty. The disk spun through the air and arched back to earth, and he met its descent with a leap Michael Jordan would be proud of.

Peanuts was the only one who really had to concentrate when we did the Frisbee thing, so while he went at it, I thought about last night. What had it been, anyway? Love? Lust? Something in between? Since she'd moved in with me, I'd been walking around just aching for her. Maybe she'd felt the same way. Last night we'd just liberated our hormones. Nothing more. In any case, too much analysis wasn't going to help, so I simply enjoyed the gentle euphoria that had settled over me and threw the Frisbee for my dog.

The river was running high and fast and as I stood at its bank, I wondered if it was possible for Julia to have gotten out of the car and made it to shore. Then I conceded that while it was possible, it wasn't likely. The current in the river is deceptively dangerous, even on a day when the water's calm and easy. But until they found her body, you couldn't count it out.

After about twenty minutes, my arm was getting tired and I'd assuaged my guilt. Besides, Peanuts wasn't putting quite the spin into his leaps anymore. As we walked back to the house, I was thinking that I hadn't been to the office in a few days; maybe it was time to make an appearance. Then I remembered that it was Sunday. Pleased with this revelation, I decided to take Peanuts with me to buy the *Trib*. It was looking like a good day to relax with a fat newspaper. Besides, maybe I was a multimillion-dollar lottery winner and didn't know it yet. The notion cheered me momentarily.

Until I remembered I didn't have a car anymore. The feeling that had kept me slightly off the ground deserted me, and my spirits fell with a thud. There wasn't much you could do with a car that had been soaking in river water for better than an hour. Its body might dry out, but the electrical system would be shot. At the time it seemed small of me to be worrying about the cost of a car when a human being had lost her life. Now I was wondering if it was possible to salvage those new tires.

When we returned, Elaine was up and had a pot of coffee ready.

She was sitting on the couch wrapped up in her blue robe, drinking from a bright red mug. Smiling, she looked up from *The Little Drummer Girl*, but didn't speak.

"You hungry?" I asked.

"I guess so."

"Bagels?"

"Sounds good."

I put a couple in the toaster oven and fed Peanuts. Then I joined Elaine on the couch. She was watching me through the steam rising from the coffee. "So," I said. "How'd you sleep?"

"Real good. How about you?"

"Great." I gestured toward Peanuts, stretched out across the rug. "How'd you like your wake-up lick?"

"It must be hard to oversleep with him around." She rested her head against the back of the couch and drew her knees up to her chest. "I can't believe I stayed up. Seven o'clock on a Sunday morning and I'm wide awake."

I put my feet up on the coffee table, "Well, we did go to bed kind of early last night." I was thinking of some way to express my feeling other than "Damn that was great," when the toaster dinged.

I turned on WFMT, which was broadcasting a concert of baroque music, and brought out the bagels and a tub of cream cheese. Elaine had moved over to the window and was standing there, her arms resting on the sill, taking in the view. She turned to me. "I saw you out there, looking at the river."

"I do that a lot."

She watched me setting things up on the coffee table, then came over and sat on the floor cross-legged. "Why is it," she said with a wry smile, "I feel like I'm in Japan when we sit down to a meal here?"

"The real challenge comes when I force you to eat your bagel with chopsticks." Taking one of the bagels, she said, "Her name was Julia Ellison, wasn't it?" I nodded, and she continued. "Do you think she's dead?"

I smeared my bagel with creamed cheese. "Yeah, I do. It's possible she's not, but I doubt it."

"What if they never find her body?"

"Then I guess we'll never know for sure."

She took little pats of cheese and applied them to her bagel until it was covered. "Do you think it's possible that she could have faked the whole thing? You know, run the car off the road and jumped out at the last minute?"

I thought about it as I chewed. Then I swallowed and said, "If she did, and I find out, she's going to wish she'd gone down with the car." While Elaine's suggestion had been floating around in the back of my mind somewhere, I hadn't allowed it to be seriously entertained. Stubbornly I shoved it back there again. "I don't see how she could have done that by herself, and I don't think there would have been enough time for her to recruit someone else."

Elaine looked disappointed, then shrugged it off, and asked what she was like.

"Committed. Single-minded to the point of obsession."

"She was that woman I picked out at the SOW rally, wasn't she?"

"Yeah, you guessed right."

She smiled her satisfaction. "I knew it. You know, I saw her just that once. But there was something about her, I don't know, unsettling I guess. It was her eyes."

Sleepy, I thought.

"Snakey," Elaine said. "She had snakey eyes. Serpentlike. Shifty. Cold." She took another bite, then said, "What happened at her house?"

"Well, it was actually her friend's house." I went on to describe my meeting with Julia, figuring there was no reason to hold back anymore. I finished with, "She got this phone call that apparently warned her the cops were on their way, and the next thing I know she's pulled a gun on me and is asking for my pants and my car keys." I waited.

Her eyes widened. "Your pants? What in the hell did she have in mind?"

"Either my total humiliation or a way to keep me from following her. Or both."

Satisfied, she went back to her coffee and finding it empty, went to for a refill. While she was in the kitchen, I asked her about the press conference.

"Oh, that went fine." She held up the pot. "You want any?" Without waiting for a response, she filled my cup. "It was real crowded and I figured I'd pretty much blend in with the crowd. Then Chief Carver noticed me."

"Oh, yeah. What'd he do?"

She shrugged. "Just said hello. That's all."

"How decent of him."

She returned to the floor and tucking her robe under her feet said, "Are you in trouble with him?"

"No more than usual," I said. "He can't prove I was concealing her identity. So go ahead, what did they say?"

"Well, the same gun that killed Novotny killed Reaves, and the cops believed they were very close to bringing a suspect in."

"So they had to admit there was a connection."

"That they did. Then they said they were analyzing some things found at the scene and would have some results by Monday. After that, nobody had much to say. Mostly reporters asking questions no one had answers for."

We talked some more about the investigation in general and Julia Ellison in particular. Then we'd exhausted the topic, and I was sitting back in the couch, my feet up on the table, feeling a little drowsy and comfortable, thinking that it would be really nice to take a nap with Elaine. As I was searching for the words, I heard Elaine clear her throat and, from out of nowhere, she said, "Quint, about last night." I opened my eyes. She was gathering bagel crumbs together and pushing them into a pile on the coffee table. She continued without looking up at me. "Well, I really enjoyed it."

"I did too."

As if she'd expected me to say that, she continued, "The thing is, if I don't start earning some money, and soon, I'm going to feel like I'm making love with you because I owe you and not because I want to."

"Elaine—" I started to protest, but she stopped me.

"Wait. Let me finish. I know you'd never expect anything like that, but I can only be a . . . a . . . kept woman, or whatever you want to call it, for so long before I start feeling inadequate." She hesitated, then in a softer voice added, "and I don't need to feel any more inadequate than I do right now." I slid a couple feet closer to her, but she stopped me before I made contact. "I know you don't think I'm inadequate, but right now, I do. And, when it comes to that, my opinion is the one that counts more."

She was sitting up against the couch, her arm resting on its cushion, waiting for my response. Finally I said, "Do you know what it is you want to do?"

She sighed and pulled at a loose thread on the cushion. "I'm not sure. I'd like to talk to a couple of the caterers around here, maybe get a job with one of them for a while, then start my own business. You see, despite the fact that our business out in Santa Fe was ultimately a disaster, I believe we had a good product."

"You really want to work for someone else first?"

"No, not in the least. But I don't know any other way to get started. I need money first."

I wanted to offer her some, but I had little or no cash reserves. Besides, something told me that wouldn't be a good move anyway. I said, "You know you can stay here as long as you want. And sleeping with the landlord isn't required."

"I know. I just want to know that I'm staying here because *we* want me to, not because I don't have a choice."

"So, when do you want to talk to these caterers?"

"Soon as possible. I'd call today, but it's Sunday. They're either closed or they're working a party."

"Well, you're going to try to start your career tomorrow, and I'm going back to mine. What are we going to do with today?"

She shrugged.

"The Bears and Green Bay are playing at noon. I usually watch the games at a place called the Tattersall. Have a couple beers, some popcorn."

"You don't have a car anymore."

"No matter. The Tattersall's close. We can walk there."

"That sounds good."

We were both silent for a minute, then I said, "What do you want to do until then?"

She eyed me, warily. "What did you have in mind?"

I shrugged. "Oh, I don't know. Elaine, I just want you to know that your options are open. And while sleeping with the landlord isn't required, it's not discouraged either."

She didn't say anything and it took almost a full minute for her smile to materialize. I'd begun to worry.

I'd been checking my phone messages faithfully, but there were a couple waiting for me on Monday morning when I got to my office. I got there around nine thirty because I decided I'd imposed on Louise's good nature enough and broke down and rented a car. I rewound the tape on my answering machine, hoping there'd be the promise of some work. I needed a client if I was going to eat this weekend. A paying client. I figured Jeff would kick in something for the time I'd spent, but he'd probably go on my easy payment plan.

One call was from a man who wanted me to check out his brother-in-law. I jotted his number down. The other call was from Mary Mulkey. I returned her call first and was beginning to wonder if Novotny and Associates was closed. Finally after about eight rings, someone answered. She sounded rushed and put out; not at all like the accommodating Mary Mulkey. When I asked for Mary, there was a long pause then a terse, "She's not here," followed by a click. The voice might have belonged to Rebecca Novotny and I began to worry that I might have been a bit indiscreet in confronting Rebecca about the disk. Where else could I have learned it but from Mary? Mary's home number was listed so I tried there. No answer. All I could do was wait for her to call me.

I sent friendly reminders to a couple late-paying clients and played phone tag with the man who was suspicious of his brother-in-law. We finally connected around eleven and he explained that the guy in question was actually his future brother-in-law and was marrying his little sister in a month. The guy lived well, really well, on an accountant's salary.

I was finishing the conversation and telling him that it might take a few days and I'd need a picture, when Jeff Barlowe walked in through the outer office door. When I'd picked him up at the jail, he'd been distraught. Someone had already broken the news to him about Julia. And though he'd thanked me for my help, when I dropped him off at his apartment, it seemed as though he'd simply replaced his anxiety with despair. But now, as he stood in the doorway, wearing his signature tan corduroy jacket over jeans, he looked reasonably composed. Maybe it was the meditation.

He waited until I hung up, then stepped into my office. I asked him how it felt to be a free man. Jeff passed up the one comfortable chair and straddled the wheeled typing chair, draping his arms over its back.

"Great. You have no idea." He chuckled. "You're not going to believe this. I spent all day yesterday on the phone. Seems I've become something of a legend. *Midwestern Journalism Review* is doing a feature on me." Shaking his head, he added, "Incredible. One day you're some poor slob banging out copy and the next day they're writing stories about you."

I leaned back in my chair and loosened my tie. I always wear one to the office, but it never seems to last past noon. "Well, enjoy your fifteen minutes."

"No kidding," he said, then regarded me for a moment and added, "Wanted to thank you."

I shrugged. "It's okay. You'd have done no less for me."

He chewed on his lower lip and rested his chin on his arm. "You were the last one to see her. What did you think?"

"You mean do I think she's a murderer?" Jeff nodded. I sighed and reached across the desk for my pack of cigarettes. "Hell, I don't know. Doesn't matter now, does it?" His expression didn't change. "She had opportunity for both murders. Motive for Novotny. Maybe Reaves too. Maybe he was dumping her, they had a fight. Wouldn't be the first time someone got the bad end in a lovers' quarrel."

He shook his head. "Don't tell me what you think logically. What's your gut feeling?"

It had been so long since I'd examined my gut I wasn't sure I had one anymore, but I gave his question some thought. "I think she was a fanatic, and I think that if someone stood between her and her goals, murder wouldn't be beyond her." I gave Jeff a there-you-have-it shrug and waited.

He digested what I'd said slowly, then glanced around the room as if checking for eavesdroppers and open doors. "Tell me if this changes the picture. All hell is breaking loose down at the police station."

"What happened? Did Carver buy a round at the Tattersall?"

"I'm not supposed to know any of this, but I've got a contact down there . . ."

I held my hands up to stop him. "Whatever you do, don't tell me who he is."

He waved off my paranoia and pushed his glasses up by the bridge. "Wait'll you hear this." He paused for greater effect. "They did an analysis of the drinks found in Reaves's motel room — you know the two glasses of scotch." I nodded. "One of those glasses had enough chloral hydrate in it to put a linebacker's lights out permanently."

"Real nice." There were even more layers to Julia Ellison than I'd imagined. "He didn't feel like a drink, so she shot him."

He smiled and shook his head. "I don't think so. There were two glasses. Both had Reaves's prints on them. Only one had Julia's too. And that was the glass they found the chloral hydrate in."

I stared at him for a minute, playing it over in my head, thinking I must have heard wrong. But Jeff was nodding, so I hadn't. "There must have been a mix up."

He emitted a disgusted snort. "You know who you sound like? Ed Carver. That's who you sound like." Before I could take offense, he continued, "But the guy who bagged the samples swears he didn't screw up. And I believe him. He's careful, methodical to the point of being tedious."

"Who you talking about?"

"Dave Kubus. He's the best there is."

I'd only run into him once or twice, so I'd have to take Barlowe's word for it. Even so. "You saying this guy's perfect? Everyone makes a mistake."

"And maybe he did. All I'm saying is he's careful enough so they ought to give some serious consideration to the possibility that David Reaves was trying to kill Julia Ellison."

"Why?"

"Good question."

Since this was Jeff's call, I wasn't going to make any suggestions. "Are they going to release this information?"

Jeff smiled. "If they don't, I will."

"That sounds like an easy way to get slapped with a libel suit."

"Can't libel the dead. Besides, truth is a defense."

"Maybe, but you'd better be damned sure before you print anything. That man was well liked." I lit a cigarette. Jeff watched me, cool and slightly amused at my conservative reaction. "You want to believe this Kubus, don't you?"

"Maybe I do," Jeff said, shrugging it off as inconsequential. "But, tell me. It doesn't make sense for her to bring a gun, with the intention of killing Reaves, and then slip him a Mickey Finn. Why?"

"Maybe she wanted to poison him, but he wasn't drinking. The gun was a backup."

Jeff shook his head. "You're reaching."

"Why would Reaves want to kill Julia?" I couldn't keep the question down. When Julia described her last meeting with Reaves, she said that something was wrong with him. He'd acted in an odd way. And when she left, he didn't try to get her to stay. "I don't know, Jeff. And seeing as how they're both dead now, I guess we'll never know who was trying to do who in."

"Oh, that's great. There's a murderer out there somewhere, but that's okay because all the victims are dead."

In an odd sort of way, he was making sense. And I felt I was a part of the cover-up. If that's what it was. Still, I couldn't afford to take up every cause that came along. Not when there was a paying customer wanting to do business. "Look, Jeff, I'm sorry it had to end the way it did, but I don't know what I can do for you. I can't afford to work on this case anymore. I hate to sound mercenary, but I've got to make a living."

Jeff bowed his head. "Look, I know I owe you. Just let me know how much and I'll start paying you with my next check."

"I didn't mean that, Jeff. I'm just saying this could take a long time. And I don't think I've got a long time before I go bust."

"Yeah, man. I understand. It's okay." He stood and swung his leg off the chair as if he were dismounting a Shetland pony. "You hear about Catherine Forrester?"

I shook my head. "No. What about her?" But I thought I knew.

"She died yesterday. Early afternoon." He shook his head. "Too bad. She was the best of the family."

I agreed with him and was a little surprised to find that I was saddened more by Catherine Forrester's death than Julia Ellison's. Then I considered how strange it was that while she was dying, I was sitting in a bar watching the Bears as they clobbered Green Bay and hoping, like everyone else, that Harbaugh was the answer to our prayers.

Jeff had moved over to the door and was resting one hand on the knob. He stopped, as if caught by an afterthought. "Yeah, and of all things. You know that wetland Rebecca Novotny was about to obliterate?"

"Yeah."

"The one that SOW group was rallying around?"

"Yeah."

"It belongs to Martin Novotny now."

Since he was making no move to leave, I figured that wasn't his exit line. "So?" I prompted, hoping I wouldn't need instruments of torture to get this out of him.

He chuckled to himself. "You know, I never would have thought him the type."

"Jeff, cut the crap. Spit it out."

"Well, you know what he did with it? All seventy-five of those wet little acres. He donated them to the Nature Conservancy." He opened the door. "Isn't that the strangest thing?"

"Jeff. Get your ass back in here."

Smiling, he closed the door.

I had the feeling it was going to be a long day.

Chapter 17

ONCE JEFF WAS SETTLED again, I asked if Martin had mentioned what had prompted his fit of generosity.

"As a matter of fact, he did. It was his aunt's last request. He was there when she died."

"No kidding." I stared at Jeff for a moment, thinking about Catherine Forrester. "Did anyone witness this last request of hers?"

"Yeah. The nurse, Gretchen, was there." He shrugged. "Not that it mattered. The land is Martin's now. He can turn it into a nudist colony if he feels like it. You know, that's what bothers me. You've met Novotny. Does he strike you as the kind of person who gets hung up on commitments?"

"If I were to go on the basis of our one meeting, I'd have to say the only long-term commitment he seemed interested in was to a bottle of pretty decent cognac. In all fairness though, that commitment was profound."

"Tanked, huh?"

"Yeah. It was early too." I had some trouble fitting Martin Novotny into the philanthropist category, but who knows? Maybe Martin was out there on the West Coast planting trees while his father and sister were chopping them down. Something else occurred to me then. "How's Rebecca Novotny handling all this?"

Jeff smiled. "She's spitting nails."

"I'll bet she is."

I tapped the eraser end of a pencil against the wooden desktop, as I thought about what a messed-up family the Novotnys were. "I tell you, Jeff. I'm not going to let myself be bothered about any of this. You want me to start gnashing my teeth and cracking my knuckles, you'd better give me a good reason."

Jeff frowned. "Well, you saw Catherine last week. Was she talking about donating this land?"

I recalled Catherine's small sitting room and the smell of gardenias. "No, but she was saying that Leonard had evoked a lot of bad feelings and thought maybe he shouldn't have made an issue out of it."

"But she never said she went along with any of this SOW business?"

"Nope."

"Then doesn't it bother you that she suddenly got generous? Just a little?"

Smiling, I shook my head. "Not enough to scratch." Then I added, "Aren't you forgetting something? If Martin's going to lie, wouldn't it be in his best interests to lie the opposite way?" I inched the knot in my tie down. "That land's worth nothing but a tax write-off to him now."

"I thought of that. And you know what it made me think of?"

"I can't wait to hear."

Ignoring my sarcasm, Jeff continued, "It made me think how we were talking the other day about the property adjacent to the wetland being in a blind trust?"

I sat up. "You know who owns it?"

"Well, not exactly. But I checked the deed and I know who sold it."

"So?"

As he pulled his notebook out of his pocket, he said, "So, whoever sold it isn't under an obligation to keep his mouth shut about who he sold it to."

"Don't these developers have some kind of code of ethics they follow?"

"I doubt it." He licked his thumb and paged through about a third of the notebook. Folding it open, he said, "Why shouldn't they be just as bloodthirsty as the rest of us?"

I shrugged. "So, what do you need me for? You think you've got a story. Maybe you do. So, go for it."

He shifted in the chair and raked his hair with the fingers of his left hand. "Well, there's a little problem." He paused, chewing on his lower lip for a moment. "I'm off the story. My editor's been getting a lot of flak and if you add that to the fact that he's a wimp, well, my nosing around could cost me my job. And I can't afford that."

"God, Jeff, you're getting cautious in your old age."

"But if you get something that looks good enough," he continued, "Tim's not going to be able to tell me to forget it anymore. I can go with it. And then if you turn up a zero, I'll back off. Maybe it is nothing." He stopped then and came up with an expression that was somewhere between imploring and hopeful. I had to laugh.

"Knock it off, Jeff. You look like Lassie getting bawled out for peeing on Timmy's bed."

Smiling, he shrugged and resumed a more normal appearance.

"This is really important to you, isn't it?"

Jeff nodded. "I know it's not finished yet."

Against my better judgment, I reached across my desk. "Okay, let's have it."

Maybe I should have told Jeff to forget it, but I was also curious about who owned that piece of land. It was probably no one we'd ever heard of and we could set this whole thing to rest. Let the cops pin both murders on Julia Ellison. Maybe she deserved it. Still, if Jeff were right and Reaves had intended to kill Julia, then I was missing more than a chunk of the whole picture.

Bernard Avery worked in Naperville, a suburb southeast of Foxport, in one of those big glass buildings you can see from the I-88. I got off on Naperville Road and backtracked a half mile to the address Jeff had given me.

Avery and Associates took up several offices on the sixth floor. I had to promise his secretary that I only needed a few minutes of her boss's time. I hoped it wouldn't take much longer, seeing as I actually had a paying customer to take care of.

Bernard Avery was bent over a long table, studying what appeared to be a map, which was spread out across it. He was a heavyset man with dark, almost black hair that was starting to go gray. His splayed arms braced him above the table and the sleeves of his shirt were rolled up to just below his elbow, revealing thick, hairy arms. Barely glancing at me, he returned to the map. "Only got a minute."

"Same here," I said, stepping up to the table. Then I saw that the map was actually a detailed drawing of some kind of corporate complex. "About three years ago you sold about seventy-five acres between Route 41 and Ridgeland in Foxport."

He looked at me, eyes squinted, and I noticed he was chewing on a toothpick. "You a lawyer?"

"Hardly."

"That's good." He stood up straight and began to unroll his shirtsleeves. "Like they say, all sales are final. I sold that property at a good, fair price. Not my fault what goes on around it." He removed the toothpick from his mouth. When he did, he eyed me again. "What did you say you do?"

"I didn't. I'm a private investigator," I told him and before he could question me further, I continued. "Mind telling me who you sold that land to?"

"Why's that your business?"

"I guess you could say that recent events have made me curious."

He squinted at me again, irritated. "What're you talking about?"

"I take it you haven't heard the latest on that wetland area right next to it?"

His toothpick found the corner of his mouth again. Then, stabbing a shirt cuff with a gold cufflink, he chuckled. "Sure I have. They're going to start digging any minute now."

I watched him insert the other cufflink and give each sleeve a yank, adjusting with a shrug. "Then you haven't heard the latest."

"What're you talking about?" He seemed more interested in the stain he'd noticed on the pocket of his silk sports jacket. Cursing, he got his secretary on the line and asked her to see what she could do about it.

She was young with lacquered hair and long, red nails and she took the coat gingerly, studying the small stain as though it were a calculus problem.

"I need that in five minutes," he called after her.

"What were you saying?"

"There are new plans for that prairie," I said. "Since Catherine Forrester died, the property belongs to her nephew, Martin. And he's decided to donate the seventy-five acres to the Nature Conservancy."

For the first time since I'd entered his office, I had Bernard Avery's undivided attention. I knew this because the toothpick went rigid. After a minute he said, "What?"

I repeated what I knew about Martin's benevolent gesture and waited while Avery decided how to handle the news. Another minute passed, during which his face turned an unhealthy shade of red. He made a bitter sound that was somewhere between a laugh and and choke. "Son of a bitch," he said.

"Mr. Avery, who'd you sell that property to?"

He looked at me and I saw that the toothpick was bobbing up and down again. "A guy named Nick Guthrie." He went thoughtful for a moment. "I'd never done that before." He paused and added, "Or since." He shook his head. "That's what I get."

"You'd never done what? Sold property you knew was going to decrease in value?"

"Call it what you want. It's done all the time. Guthrie'd have done the same to me without batting an eye."

"You sold because you knew Novotny was going to develop that area into an industrial park?"

He thought for a moment then shrugged as if it didn't matter any more. "Yeah. Guess it makes no difference now. Len told me. We were pretty good friends and he and Guthrie'd had a falling out. Guthrie wanted to bring some outside investors in or something like that. Anyway, Guthrie was real interested in accumulating some Foxport property. Then when Len hinted to me that it might be a good time to sell, well, Guthrie was there."

"How much more is that land worth without the industrial park next to it?"

"I don't even want to think about it." Then he looked up toward the ceiling. "Oh, let's see, that's seventy-five acres. Prime location. Guaranteed not to be developed around." Dropping his gaze to me, he shook his head sadly, and said, "It's gotta add several million onto the value. You know, when Len and Guthrie split up, I figured Guthrie'd be down the tubes," he snapped his fingers, "like that. Len had the brains, the connections. Guthrie was flash. All flash. Suddenly Guthrie's got this money to invest in some nice property. Before you know it, he's tapped into the upscale market with that Yorkshire Estates. At first Len figured it was some rich widow bankrolling him. Guthrie had a way about him. What's that Len used to say about him?" He consulted the ceiling. "Oh, yeah, he'd say 'Guthrie never met a woman he couldn't use.' "

"That true?"

"What? That he was set up by some woman?" I nodded. "Nah, he got some outside investor interested."

"You remember who?"

"Oh, let's see. Some outfit in Elk Grove Village." He rubbed his forehead. "Securities place. A & R Securities. Yeah, that's it."

"Guthrie didn't have much of a track record by himself. Why would a company invest in someone without a track record?"

He shrugged. "Not unusual. Like I said, the guy had lots of flash. Guess he impressed them." Then he chuckled softly. "Who knows, maybe the outfit's run by a rich widow."

Avery's secretary returned, his jacket draped over her arm. She approached him cautiously. "I'm afraid I might have made it worse, Mr. Avery. I think it needs to go to the cleaners."

He glanced at the area in question which now had a water stain in addition to the original spot. "What difference does it make?" he muttered.

* * *

I called Jeff and told him what I'd learned. He said he'd see what he could find out about Guthrie. I decided to go straight to the source. When Guthrie's secretary told me he was out to lunch, I took a stab in the dark and asked if he was at the club. She said he might be, and there he was, sitting in the mirrored bar with its floor-to-ceiling windows that overlooked the golf course. He seemed glad to see me, which I couldn't understand. I'm not that much fun to have around.

It was mid afternoon on a weekday, but several tables of the lounge were filled with casually dressed men and women. Guthrie introduced me to the man sitting at his table. He looked to be in his early fifties and had thinning gray hair and an extremely dark tan. Unlike the other occupants of the bar, he was wearing a gray light wool suit and a shirt he probably had laundered professionally. "Quint McCauley, this is Mel Vincent. He's helping me celebrate, but he's got an appointment in a half hour so I've got to recruit someone to take his place." Vincent stood and we shook hands. His grip was firm and dry. Most of the ice had melted in the glass tumbler which sat on the table in front of him. Most of a bottle of Heineken's was in a beer stein Guthrie was holding.

I took a seat at the table, feeling I was dressed just right. I still had my sports jacket on, even though I'd shed the tie a while ago. "Let me see if I can guess what the celebration's for."

"Be my guest, but Mel here's the only one I've told so far." He drank from the stein, winked at Vincent who regarded him impassively, and added, "Not that it's a big secret anymore."

"It wouldn't have anything to do with the increased value of that piece of land you own next door to the wetland."

Guthrie's smile remained frozen on his face for a moment. It slowly disintegrated and he looked at Mel, who was watching me. Guthrie's smile returned, only now it conveyed curiosity rather than mirth. "Okay," he said, "I'll bite. Who'd you hear that from?"

"Bernard Avery," I said and apparently made Guthrie's day.

His laughter whooped throughout the country club bar, and a number of people glanced our way to see who was making the noise, then with studied nonchalance, each turned away again. Vincent looked like he either wanted to crawl under the table or gag Guthrie.

"I'd forgotten about that added bonus. He's probably having fits."

"He almost swallowed his toothpick."

Guthrie liked that. He had to set his beer down, he was so overcome with amusement. When he'd settled down, he said, "So Avery coughed my name up. Just like that."

"Only after I told him about the wetland's change of status."

Guthrie smiled and shook his head, still enjoying the warmth of the moment. Then he turned to Vincent who was watching him. "I'd heard that he was having some money problems, so I figured that was why he was parting with a choice piece of land like that. Then I find out that Novotny's got plans to develop his area." He shrugged. "So much for my upscale subdivision."

Vincent, still watching Guthrie, nodded.

"Novotny tipped Avery off then?" I asked.

Guthrie took a quick drink of beer. "Yeah, well it worked out in the end."

After a moment, Vincent pushed himself away from the table, "I hate to leave the party just as it gets going, but some of us have to work this afternoon." Vincent excused himself and left the room, stopping briefly at another table.

Guthrie watched his retreat and sighed, then noticed his glass was getting dangerously close to empty, and waved at one of the waitresses. "What are you drinking?" he asked me.

"Scotch on the rocks." He ordered one for me and another beer for himself.

Resting his arms on the table, Guthrie tilted the beer stein, perhaps studying the stand of foam on an inch of beer. Then he shifted his eyes to me. "What made you check out Avery?"

"Well, I figured whoever owned that property next to the wetland was getting the best end of the deal. I guess I was curious. Did some checking and found out who sold the property." I shrugged. "Guess I didn't have to go to all the trouble. You're making no secret about it now."

"Don't have to anymore. I mean, that's why I had it in a blind trust. I figured once Novotny knew I owned land next to him, he'd do something like this. Then he does anyway, and I figure he must have known. I even confronted Avery about it. He denied knowing what Novotny was going to do, but he's not much of a liar." He smiled and shook his head in utter amazement at his good fortune. "Justice prevails. Let's hear it for justice."

The waitress brought our drinks and Guthrie told her to add them to his tab.

I nodded my thanks. "You must hate this guy, Avery. And Novotny too, for that matter."

"Sure I do. Well, of course I wanted to nail those two sons of bitches when I found out what Novotny planned to do with his land." He frowned. "But there wasn't much I could do. I was good and screwed. Avery knew it, Novotny knew it, and I knew it." He paused and added, "Everyone knew it. Then I heard that there's this groundswell of public sentiment against doing anything to that wetland. I figured I'd just go with the flow. Why do you think I joined a group like SOW? My civic responsibility? Give me a break."

"Yeah, I gotta admit I had a little trouble making that picture work." He toasted me and stopped chuckling long enough to take a drink.

"You know what this means to me? God, I think I'm going to name this development after Catherine Forrester." He paused, reconsidering. "Or maybe a couple streets. Well, whatever. But the beauty of it is that I was going to go ahead and build there anyway, just on a smaller, not so grand scale. You know, I could've handled the wrath of a bunch of suburbanites whose basements were flooding. It would've been a little unpleasant, but I'd manage. But not only is that not a problem anymore, I own one of the hottest pieces of property in Abel County. In the western suburbs. Hell, in the whole U. S. of A. This place is going to be bigger than Yorkshire Estates. More exclusive. You won't be able to touch a home for less than seven fifty. And I can do it. Do you know what people will pay to live next to a place that is guaranteed never to be more than a wet prairie? In this area? I can sell a lot for better than a hundred grand."

"You financing this new development through A & R Securities?"

He stopped, peered at me over the rim of his glass, took a long draught, then set it down, and licked the foam from his lip. "Avery tell you that?"

I nodded. "Is it true?"

"Must be. Seems Mr. Avery knows all there is to know about Nick Guthrie."

"That wasn't exactly an answer."

Frowning slightly, he said, "No, I'm not going through A & R this time. Though they're good folks. This is a bigger investment than they're used to handling. Besides, now that I'm established here in Foxport, I like to go through the local banks. You know, keep it in the community. Buyers seem to like that."

"You financing this through Foxport Federal?"

"That's the plan."

"So, tell me about this new place. What's it going to cost me to build a second home there?"

I listened to Guthrie ramble on for a while and decided that, like Mel Vincent, I also had a meeting in a half hour. As I drove back to my office, I reasoned that unless he could make something of the poison in Julia's drink angle, Jeff didn't have much of a story. Guthrie's actions were logical, if a bit self-serving.

There was another message from Mary Mulkey and this time she left her home number. When I reached her, she was beside herself. She was also royally ticked off. At me.

"Why did you tell Rebecca about that disk I found?"

"Why? Well, the only way to get it out in the open was to confront her. What's wrong?"

"She fired me. That's what's wrong."

"Rebecca fired you?"

"Yes. After more than thirty years. I just can't believe it." Then she began to go on about what a faithful employee she'd been to Leonard and how she just didn't understand this daughter of his. I was feeling slightly guilty, but also defensive. What had she expected me to do with that information? While Mary was rambling, Elaine walked in. I motioned for her to sit.

When I finally had a chance to interject a word, I jumped in with, "Mary, I'm sorry Rebecca fired you, but you didn't tell me to keep the information about the disk to myself. And she'd have found out sooner or later, if not from me, then from the police." Then she started in again on what she was going to do and how she needed the job to get by. I interrupted her. "Mary . . . Mary, listen to me. Maybe she's just reacting emotionally to all this. Rebecca's been through a lot lately. And maybe she'd just learned that Martin was going to donate that area she was planning to develop. And she took it out on you."

Mary sighed and was silent for a few moments. Elaine was giving me a sympathetic smile. Finally, Mary said, "Maybe you're right. Perhaps she's just upset. But I can't go talk to her now. I don't think I have the nerve. She was quite, um, vehement."

I rolled my eyes heavenward and said, "I'll go talk to her, Mary."

"Oh, would you?"

"Yes. I will."

"Do you think you can convince her to give me my job back?"

"I don't know, but I'll try."

"When? When do you think you could see her?"

I glanced at my watch. "Well, it's four thirty now, so I'll probably wait until tomorrow."

She heaved a deep sigh, but didn't say anything.

"Mary?"

Another sigh and then she said, "It's just that I'm sure I won't be able to sleep tonight, what with all this on my mind, but that's all right."

"Okay," I said, "I'll go see her now."

She began to pour her thanks out to me and I had to cut her off with promises to call her after I talked to Rebecca.

"What was that all about?" Elaine asked as I hung up.

"Rebecca fired Mary because she told me about the disk that proves someone was in Novotny's office diddling with a computer the day he was killed."

"Hmm," Elaine said, "that's a pretty strong reaction, don't you think?"

"That's what I'm hoping." I shrugged into my jacket. "How'd your day go?"

"Interesting. Can I come along and tell you about it?"

"I don't know. This might be kind of unpleasant. Why don't we talk over dinner?" I held the door open for her as she collected her purse from the floor.

"I can't. I've got plans." As she walked past me, she added, "I'm having dinner with Ed Carver."

She had reached the sidewalk before her announcement registered. And she'd turned around, waiting, before I found my voice. "Ah, listen, Elaine, how unpleasant can this be? Why don't you come with me?"

She shrugged. "Sure. Don't forget to turn the lights off."

Chapter 18

I DIDN'T KNOW WHETHER to be angry or just confused, so I kept my mouth shut and sulked. Elaine was fidgeting with the strap of her purse. After a minute, she said, "It's not what it looks like, Quint."

"It's not, huh?" I suddenly realized I needed to be in the left lane and cut off a white van to get there. I was admonished with a sharp honk and saluted with an extended finger. "You know he's still married?"

"Separated." I glanced at her and she shrugged. "I ran into him in town this afternoon. It was a pretty bad day. For both of us. We had coffee."

The light changed to red just as the car in front of me began to turn left. I followed it through the intersection. "Gee, you'd think things would be looking pretty rosy, what with this murder being all wrapped up. You'd think he'd be drinking champagne instead of coffee."

The ensuing moments of silence were deadly. The ice was pretty thin so I tried to backslide a few steps. "Sorry. I take it your job hunt didn't go well." No response. "What happened?"

She seemed to hesitate, and I thought she had decided to ignore me, but finally she said, "Well, after you dropped me off in town this morning, I went to the three catering businesses, you know, to see if I could get some work. I did a lot of walking and had absolutely no luck. Two of them told me to come by as it got closer to the holidays and the third was almost rude. I can't afford to wait until the holidays, Quint." She sighed and continued, "Well, after meeting with total rejection, I was doing some window shopping, looking at all the things I may never be able to afford. You know, panty hose, stuff like that." She paused.

"And?"

"Well, I passed that little cluster of offices on south Second and who steps out of one of them but Ed Carver. He acted kind of strange at first, almost embarrassed, but then he started walking with me and we got to talking. I told him I was looking for a job. I also wound up telling him some of what happened in Santa Fe. Not the drug part. Just the part about the business failing. He was real nice."

"So you had coffee with him."

"Well, he asked and I didn't want to be rude. Besides, there wasn't anything else to do."

"I see. So, you were just killing time with good old Eddie."

Elaine didn't respond and when I glanced at her I knew that I'd pushed it too far this time. "That's out of line," she said as I turned back to the road. "I can kill time with whomever I want."

We were only a couple blocks away from Rebecca Novotny's office and I didn't want to confront her with these bad feelings hanging over my head. I looked again and saw that Elaine was staring out the passenger window, her arms folded across her chest. I turned back to the road. "So, he asked you to dinner."

"Yes. He did." Her attention was still focused outside the window. Or, more likely, away from me.

"Didn't he ask you if we were, you know, seeing each other?"

"No," she responded without hesitation, adding, "Your name never came up."

I noticed Novotny's office slip by and had to brake hard in order to make the corner. I was rewarded with another honk. From the sound of it, it might have been the van again, which meant he probably waved at me too. But I didn't look. I drove around the back of the building and saw Rebecca's little Honda parked next to the office's back exit. It was almost five, but for some reason I figured it didn't make much difference to Rebecca. She probably spent most of her life there.

When I pulled into one of the parking spaces in front of the building, Elaine was still looking out the window. There was more to be said, but this wasn't the place for it. "You want to come in?"

She slowly turned, regarded me for a moment, then nodded. Her eyes left me cold. I'd considered leaving her there to brood, but I remembered how Rebecca had responded to Elaine when they met briefly in the parking lot at the SOW fund-raiser. It wasn't exactly friendly, but maybe not quite so defensive. "Just let me do the talking, okay?" As soon as that was out of my mouth, I knew I sounded like a jerk. But I guess that was the voice I was looking for because I didn't regret it. Elaine hesitated, but followed me in, and I could feel her anger hanging over my head like a clenched fist.

What hit me when I walked into Novotny's office this time, wasn't the smell of paint. It was the smell of cigarette smoke mingled with the warm, cheese and tomato smell of pizza. A large cardboard box with two slices remaining was open on a low table near the reception desk, which had been moved out from the office where Mary Mulkey and I had talked. There was a light on in Rebecca's office and the door was open. I glanced at Elaine, but she wouldn't make eye contact.

As I stepped into her office, Rebecca looked up startled, then collected herself, and dropped a pizza slice onto a paper plate. Wiping her hands with a paper towel, she watched us as she chewed. Her eyes had the hollow look of someone who'd been up for a long time. She wore a gray sweatshirt and, though she was sitting behind the desk, I would have bet that she wasn't wearing a skirt and heels. Swallowing, she wadded the paper towel and tossed it in the waste basket. "What do you want?"

Her desk was covered with books and some of the clutter from Mary's office seemed to have moved here — file cabinets, bookcases. As I approached Rebecca, I noticed that her eyes were not only tired-looking, they were also red-rimmed, as though she'd been staring at a computer screen for too long. Or crying.

I had a lot to ask her, but decided to start with my excuse for being there. "I talked to Mary Mulkey this afternoon. She said you fired her because she told me about that disk. I guess I feel responsible."

Before I could continue to grovel, Rebecca cut me off. "That's not why I fired her. I fired her because I'm running the business now, and I don't have to have people around who don't like me. It's that simple." She took a swig from a can of Diet Coke.

"Her telling me about the disk had nothing to do with it?"

Shrugging, she said, "It gave me an opening. If that hadn't happened I'd have found another."

I stepped deeper into the room and helped myself to a seat. Rebecca's flat stare didn't welcome me, but I try not to be sensitive about those things. I saw that Elaine had found a chair against the wall.

"Mary was with your father for thirty years."

Rebecca snorted. "So?"

"Doesn't that count for something?"

"I'd been with him all my life. It didn't count for much."

I wanted to bring up the disk again, but decided to go with the indirect approach. Maybe she wouldn't see me coming.

I wasn't sure how to word my next comment, but I knew I didn't have much time so I blundered ahead with: "I guess your brother's donation sort of messed things up for you." I didn't think that came out well, a notion that was seconded when I heard Elaine shift in her chair and caught her arching a hand across her brow.

A muscle in Rebecca's jaw moved and she took a deep breath.

"Believe me, we're not finished yet. I've already consulted a lawyer. The Nature Conservancy shouldn't start counting their lily pads yet."

I smiled. "Lily pads. I like that."

"Why are you here?" she asked, looking from me to Elaine and back again.

I crossed an ankle over my knee and tried to appear comfortable and oblivious to her disposition. "Did Martin talk to you about this before he made the announcement?"

"Hardly. Martin and I haven't said much to each other in the last twelve years. But he'll hear from me. Through my lawyer." She lit a cigarette and leaned back in her chair, puffing away.

"Why haven't you and Martin spoken in the last twelve years?"

Rebecca brushed a crumb from her desk.

"I mean, I know that he and Leonard had a falling out—"

Suddenly I had her attention. "Where did you hear that?"

"Nick Guthrie."

Her eyes narrowed and I kept going. "But why were *you* alienated as well? God knows, your mother wasn't. What did he do to you? To your father?"

"Nothing. It's none of your business."

"Did it involve the business?"

"No it didn't." She lurched forward, almost upsetting the can of soda. "This is my family. You don't understand. You never will. So don't even try." As she spoke she jabbed the air with her cigarette, emphasizing each word. She glared at me then and knocked an ash off over the paper plate. It landed on a pepperoni. "Now why don't you leave?"

"One more question. Why did you lie about being here the day your father was killed?"

"Who said I lied? You did. And who cares what you think?"

"Then who else would have been in here working on one of your accounts?"

"Mary Mulkey, for one."

I shook my head. "No. Why would she lie?"

"Why would I lie? Now get the hell out of here before I call the cops."

I dug my cigarettes out of my jacket pocket and lit one, pulled her marble ashtray toward the edge of her desk, and dropped the match in it. "Go ahead. I'll just wait."

She gaped at me and I could feel Elaine watching me too. I glanced

171

at her and thought for a second that she was angry. I inhaled deeply and ran the smoke through my lungs. Then I shrugged and said, "I wonder what they'll have to say about that disk. They're probably going to be more curious than me." I stood and began to move around the room, glancing at the book titles on her desk, taking in the view of the parking lot and the single young birch growing in the parkway.

Rebecca jammed her cigarette into the pizza slice, yanked another from a pack, and lit it. "What if I was here? Doesn't mean I killed him."

"You're right. But it does mean you lied." I had walked behind Rebecca and she turned in her chair to face me. "I want to know why. That's all." She glared at me. I shrugged and leaned across Rebecca to drop an ash on her pizza plate. "Convince me or convince the cops. It's your call."

Rebecca turned to Elaine who seemed to be reserving her coldest looks for me. She gave Rebecca a wan smile. "He's known for his wonderful rapport with the police."

I thanked Elaine for the endorsement and waited, wandering around the room, not sure what I was looking for, maybe just wanting Rebecca to get uncomfortable. I didn't need the cigarette as a prop anymore, and I couldn't bring myself to use her pizza slice, so I moved around the desk and extinguished it in the ashtray. Rebecca never took her eyes from me. After a minute, she sighed and, staring down at her desk, began to talk. "I came in that Saturday to finish up a contract and to make a few calls to some other developers I know. I was thinking of leaving. You know, going to work for another developer. There had been a lot of friction between us lately." She paused, then went on, stammering out the first couple words. "I found out by accident that he was talking to some outside investors. I overheard him on the phone. I couldn't believe he'd make a financial decision like that without talking to me first. But he did."

"Rebecca," I asked, "who were these outside investors?"

"I don't know," she snapped and I shut up.

After she glared at me for several seconds, she continued, "Anyway, I didn't want my father to know I was here, so I parked in back behind one of the other offices. In case he decided to come in. I'd finished the contract and put the disk on Mary's desk. Then I went back in the office and made a couple phone calls. While I was doing that, I heard someone — at the time I assumed it was Father — go in his office. Then about five minutes later, I heard someone else come in. I knew this person was my father because when he stepped in his office he exploded. I heard a woman's voice hollering back, and there was a fight. Things being knocked over. Then a door slammed and someone ran through the office and out the back. My father was slamming things around, swearing God's vengeance. I left before he knew I was there."

"You left right away?"

"A minute or so later." She paused and added, almost to herself, "I forgot about that damned disk."

"Did you see who was in his office?"

She shook her head. "No. She was gone before I got out to the parking lot. I only heard her voice."

"You didn't hear a gun shot?"

She hesitated. "No."

I was pacing beside her desk, trying to read a lie in her eyes, but she wouldn't look at me. "So you know that the Blue Fox, aka Julia Ellison, didn't kill your father."

Now she wrenched herself around in the chair to look up at me. "I don't know that. She could have come back and killed him because he could identify her. It could have happened that way."

"Oh, c'mon, Rebecca." I bent down so we were almost at eye level. "You can't believe that. If Julia Ellison killed your father, she did it out of panic, not premeditation." She opened her mouth to protest, but I kept going. "What I want to know is why you were so damned positive the Blue Fox killed your father. When you knew she didn't. Why, Rebecca?"

"She could have come back," she faltered.

"But she didn't. Why were you so damned insistent? Taking out an ad in the newspaper for God's sake. You were trying to cover your own ass, weren't you? Because if anyone sat down and looked at it, they'd see you had a damned good reason to want your old man dead. Not only was he cutting someone else in on the business, but he blamed you for everything that was wrong with it."

Something like a shadow passed over her eyes and their expression changed from furious to confused. There was still some anger, but now she was fidgety as well—taking deep, short puffs on the cigarette, forgetting about the inch and a half ash. She didn't notice when it fell to her gray jogging pants. I moved closer, resting my hand on the edge of her desk, and smelled the faint, sweet odor of sweat and saw the drops of moisture on her upper lip. There was something there, just below the surface, but I was afraid if I pushed too hard I'd lose it. I ventured a quick glance at Elaine. She was watching, waiting. "Not only

173

did he blame you for everything that was wrong with the business, but for everything that was wrong with your family as well. That's one hell of a burden especially when you consider the family. There's a mother who's mentally estranged from all but her son and a son who managed to get himself blackballed from the family."

Rebecca shrank back and looked away. I leaned closer. "That's what hurt your father the most, wasn't it? He could live with a distracted wife, but losing the son who was supposed to step into his shoes, well that was the last straw. The family took a nose dive." I stopped, and waited for Rebecca to look at me. When she did, I said, "And Martin's leaving. That was all your fault, wasn't it? What did you do to the guy?"

She glared at me, her eyes narrow and her mouth a thin, red, angry line. "*I* didn't do anything to *him*." Then her hand moved suddenly and I felt a stab of pain in mine. I let out a yelp and grabbed it, cursing. She'd extinguished another cigarette, only this time she hadn't used the pizza slice. When the white hot flash in my head fizzled I saw that Elaine was no longer content to observe. As she pulled her chair up to Rebecca's desk, she ordered me to run some water on my hand. Nothing doing, I thought as Elaine leaned on the desk.

"Rebecca, what did he do to you?" she was asking her.

Rebecca wouldn't look at Elaine. "Just go away."

Undaunted, Elaine kept talking. "Your father blaming you, that wasn't fair. You know, people are sometimes so bent in one direction, pigheaded I guess, that they can't see another side." She continued talking in a calm, soothing tone, as if she were trying to ease a wild-eyed colt out of a barbed wire fence. I let her see what she could do while I wrapped a handkerchief around my hand. As I paced the back of Rebecca's office, nosing around the boxes and files, trying to concentrate on something besides pain, I saw the edge of a picture frame in a corner next to a cabinet. I eased it out, expecting to see Leonard Novotny's haughty countenance. What I saw wasn't what I'd expected, but I wasn't as surprised as I might have been a few minutes ago. It was the oil of Leonard all right, but now he had one neat, black cigarette burn right between his eyes.

I brought the picture out and stood with it behind Rebecca's chair. Elaine was talking to Rebecca who seemed to be listening. I cleared my throat. Elaine looked up, at first annoyed, then when she saw the portrait, her mouth dropped open.

"You bastard!" Rebecca jumped up, grabbed the picture and awkwardly wrapped her arms around it, as far as they would go. "I didn't invite you in here. Get out!" I didn't move. She turned to Elaine, who had stopped gaping. "I didn't kill him." Elaine just watched her. "I didn't kill him," she repeated, this time in a soft, insistent, almost childlike tone. She lowered herself into the chair, slowly, still gripping the picture, resting her chin on its frame. "He couldn't love me, but I didn't kill him."

Elaine leaned on the desk, hands folded. "Why? Why couldn't he love you?"

Rebecca, staring off into some personal black hole, didn't respond.

I tried to blend into the file cabinets. It was Elaine's show now, and I wasn't too much of a jerk to admit it.

Leaning farther over the desk so she didn't need to speak above a whisper, Elaine said, "Rebecca, your father was really upset with you one day because you wore makeup. Wasn't he?" Elaine waited a few seconds, then said, "He was afraid if you wore makeup, men would find you attractive. Men like Martin."

Slowly, Rebecca turned to Elaine, her small, thick hands flat against the back of the portrait.

"Martin found you attractive, didn't he?"

Rebecca blinked but otherwise didn't move.

Elaine put a hand to her mouth. I could tell she was fighting the urge to lean back into the chair. Instead, she moved her hand to the desk, palm down, extended toward Rebecca. She wet her lips and looked away for a second. "Rebecca . . ." she broke off, but Rebecca had opened her eyes and was watching her now.

"Rebecca," she tried again, "did Martin, ah . . ." Before she could finish, Rebecca looked away, fixing her gaze on the wall, but Elaine took a deep breath and kept going. "Did Martin molest you?"

When Rebecca finally spoke, her words were dull, plodding. "Not really."

"What do you mean, Rebecca? He either did or he didn't. Right?"

"Yes, well I didn't tell anybody. Not for a while."

"That doesn't mean it didn't happen."

Unconvinced, Rebecca lifted her shoulders in a small shrug.

"Why didn't you tell anyone?"

"It was my fault."

"Don't say that."

"Well, it was. I could have screamed or hit him or something. I didn't."

"It's not that easy. How old were you?"

"Eight."

"And Martin?"

"Fourteen."

"There's no way. I've got a brother seven years older than me, and there's no way I could have protected myself." She faltered for a second. "If I'd had to." Rebecca squeezed her eyes shut. "Who did you finally tell?"

"Father." She opened her eyes. "After a while he sent Martin away," she whispered and began to cry without making a sound, "but he never forgave me." She was still shaking her head. "He should have sent me away too. He should have."

"Why?"

"He couldn't look at me. He would only talk to me when there were other people around. He was so ashamed."

"But it wasn't your fault."

Rebecca nodded. "Yes. Yes it was." Elaine moved around the desk so she could be closer to Rebecca. On the way, she motioned me to get out of the room. I didn't argue.

I stood outside Rebecca's office, trying to understand the kind of man who would send the son packing and figure the daughter would just mend herself. And then I reflected that times had changed a lot since then. Things might have been different if it had all happened twelve years later.

I hoped Elaine would talk to Rebecca for a while. Not only did she probably need someone like Elaine right now, but I wanted some time to check out Leonard's office.

This was my first opportunity, and I wasn't about to waste it. The room was cool and dry and, fortunately, the dead ducks had been removed, although no one had painted over the fox's head yet. I took a moment to judge it critically and decided that Julia didn't do any better drawing foxes than I did. I began to go through Novotny's desk, working quickly, but thoroughly, knowing what I was looking for and not at all sure I'd find it. After forty-five minutes, I'd worked my way through every file the guy had and I was frustrated at my lack of success and ticked off at my reaching for straws. I leaned back in the contoured chair that didn't fit quite right, and looked across the surface of the big oak desk which was empty except for a telephone and a Rolodex. I hesitated, then reached for the Rolodex, flipped it open to the As, and was immediately rewarded. I smiled at how good it felt, then I helped myself to Novotny's phone.

Sgt. Patrick O'Henry and I didn't have a long history together, but it had been an eventful one. We'd met on a professional basis and, after a rough start, had managed to work together pretty well. Last summer we'd gone to two ball games. One Cubs and one Sox.

O'Henry always liked Elaine and, before he could ask about her, I said, "She's back."

"No kidding. What's up?"

"Wish I knew, but if she's here long enough, why don't we meet you and Kay down at the White Hart one of these days."

"Sounds good. That why you called?"

I smiled. "You know better than that. You ever hear of a firm called A & R Securities?"

"Nope. And since when did you have some money to invest?"

"I don't. I just wondered if you could, you know, make a couple calls. Do your magic. See if you can dig up something on them."

A pause. "What d'you smell?"

"I don't know. Maybe nothing."

"Okay, give me your number."

I told O'Henry I'd call him back in an hour.

"Thanks for the generous deadline."

I'd just gotten out to the parking lot when Elaine came out. She just looked at me, shook her head, and got into the car. "If you ever hear me complain about what a creep my dad was to ground me for a month for staying out past curfew, you have my permission to smack me upside the head." She turned to me. "It's bad enough you've got a brother who's raping you, but you top that off with a mother who's so cold you don't know how to tell her about it, and a father who thinks you've irrevocably offended God! Shit, I wouldn't blame her if she massacred the whole lot."

"What else did she tell you?"

"God, I can't believe what I heard. I just can't. This went on for years. She said she was eight when he started. Jesus. She could never tell her mother. I guess the woman dotes on Martin. And then . . . when she finally does tell her father, he doesn't believe her at first. Can you believe that? Can you?"

I didn't answer.

"Shit. You know when he finally believed her? He caught Martin in the act. And then instead of killing him, he just sends him away. And then he treats Rebecca like a pariah. What a creep. Shit."

I waited a moment to make sure she was finished. "You know, I'm not trying to defend the guy. Let's face it, he didn't act like Robert

Young on 'Father Knows Best,' but it wasn't exactly that kind of family, either."

"Whose side are you on?"

"There aren't any sides here. All I'm saying is it's real easy to write this guy off as a creep. He ignores the situation as long as he possibly can, then when he finally acts, he does the worst thing possible for everyone involved."

"So why isn't he a creep?"

"I suppose Martin denied it was his fault."

"Of course he did, but . . ."

I held my hand up. "Just hear me out. I'm trying to figure this out for myself here. Maybe there was always a doubt, maybe just a shred; maybe he was never convinced he'd done the right thing. And he couldn't ever look at Rebecca without thinking that maybe he shafted his son." Elaine was watching me, her eyes narrowed, and I couldn't tell whether she was angry or just thinking. "I mean, think what it took to send Martin away. He's his only son, he's pinning his business future on him — his shot at immortality. And Martin was apparently the only thing he and Amelia shared. Okay, maybe it was a bad decision, but it definitely wasn't the easy way out."

"Why are you defending this man?"

"I don't know. Seems like I don't question things as much as I used to. That bothers me."

"Leonard lost a son, but what about what Rebecca lost?"

The silence stretched out for a minute, then two. Finally I said, "Yeah, you're right." I shifted in the seat and wanted a cigarette, but my wounded hand reminded me of the health hazards. "So what did you say to Rebecca?"

"I told her to go see a rape counselor. I said she had to start believing in herself and that what other people do to you isn't necessarily your fault. She should stand up for herself. I said she had to, you know, have conviction. Not let people walk all over her. Take charge."

I recalled Rebecca's behavior at the SOW fund-raiser and said, "I think she'll have no trouble doing that."

Preoccupied, Elaine didn't respond to my comment. She made a little snorting sound. "All this advice sounds kind of funny coming out of me, huh? How to turn your life around by Elaine Kluszewski." She paused for a moment, then said, "I had the feeling she might be having some other trouble on top of all this. Like with a boyfriend."

"A boyfriend?" I hadn't meant for that to come out sounding as incredulous as it did.

Elaine was watching me. "You know, Quint, just because she's not up to your standards doesn't mean she can't have a relationship."

"You're right. I'm a pig," I conceded.

After a moment, she said, "I guess I know what you mean, though. I was a little surprised too. After what she's been through and all."

"Do you think she might have killed Leonard?"

After a moment she said, "I don't know. Maybe, but I doubt it."

"Why?"

"I think deep down—and I mean really deep down—she loved him and hoped that someday he'd come around. Forgive her. Maybe that's why she was thinking about leaving the business. You know, force him to beg her to stay." She began to rummage around in her purse and pulled out a hairbrush. "God, all I am is broke. That poor woman's going to spend the rest of her life trying to forgive herself for being a victim. Someone should castrate the son of a bitch." As she spoke, she ran the brush through her hair. It snapped with electricity. "I told her we'd buy her dinner, but she said she had work to do." She began to brush the underside of her hair, stopping to work out a snag with her fingers. "We're going to have lunch tomorrow."

"You know, you've taken a lot on, don't you?"

"Yeah, I know. It's okay. Someone needs to." Then she said, "She's terrified you're going to tell someone about this."

I pulled the car out onto Charlemagne. "I'm not going to mention it to anyone who doesn't already know."

"Martin?"

"Yeah. I can't wait to hear how he tries to justify this."

"His side of it is that he's a sick bastard. You think it's got anything to do with what's happened?"

"Maybe," I said.

Elaine had finished brushing her hair and had opened a small compact and was applying lipstick.

"Where you want me to drop you?"

She hesitated. "Beijing Gardens." She blotted her lips with a clean tissue and dropped it and the compact into her purse.

We rode in silence for a couple blocks. And then, because I needed an answer before I let her go, I said, "What happened between us the last couple days. Was that just because the moon is in some weird phase?"

"Quint, you know that's not true."

"Do I? Then explain to me what's happening here. This thing with Carver."

"I tried to explain before, but you were too busy being bullheaded to let me finish."

"Go ahead. I'll be quiet."

"Okay, here it is. I have a lot of male friends. You may not realize or understand that, but it's a fact. I grew up with three men. Ed Carver is going through a bad time right now, and he just needs someone to be a friend. Someone who doesn't know his past history, who's not going to judge him. I'm just having dinner with him as a friend. That's all."

"Does he know that?"

"If you mean, did I say 'Ed, I just want to be friends,' well no. But I never indicated that I wanted anything else."

"If he's just separated, then he's not picking up subtle messages. Trust me, I've been there."

"Quint, he knows I'm living with you. He understands the situation. No one had to bring it up."

I was proud of myself for not mentioning the fact that Elaine living with me probably made this all the sweeter for Carver. Somehow I sensed that would reduce the level of civility we'd attained. But I wanted one thing said before I dropped her off. "Elaine, maybe I am being a jerk about this, but I'm the one who lives here. In Foxport. This is where, as you say, I've put my roots down. I have a business. I'm staying for a while. I may not have the best relationship going with Carver, but if you're going to come in here, make it worse, then leave, well I guess I don't exactly appreciate that. And I know you wouldn't do that intentionally, but it could happen. Just know that." I pulled up in front of Beijing Gardens. At least this was a moderately priced restaurant and he wouldn't be spending a bundle on her.

"Quint, believe me, I know what you're saying. And I know what I'm doing." She hesitated before she got out of the car, leaned over and gave me a kiss, which I accepted with a moderate amount of enthusiasm.

It would have been easy to spend the rest of the night brooding as I sat up and waited for Ed Carver to drop his date off, but I shoved all that to the back of my mind and concentrated on Martin Novotny. He wasn't expecting me, which was good, and seeing as it was almost seven, maybe I'd arrive just as he and Amelia were sitting down to dinner. Maybe they'd set an extra plate for me.

Chapter 19

I'D DONE ALL THAT was expected of me. More really. I stopped at a convenience store and bought some salve and bandages. As I ministered to my hand I was thinking I should just tell Carver that Rebecca Novotny heard Julia leave her father's office while he was still alive. Let him worry about it. Not only would I be aiding law enforcement, I'd also be giving law enforcement something to do besides hit on Elaine. The motives behind gestures such as these can be as simple as that. When Elaine first told me that Carver had asked her to dinner, I'd immediately concluded that this was Carver's way of paying me back. That's the kind of self-centered schmuck I can be. But then I thought about how attracted I was to her and how so many things about her surprised and excited me, and I had to concede it was probably more than a grudge move on Carver's part. And if I wasn't careful, I'd be the one trolling the mean streets of Foxport in search of a sympathetic ear.

As I drove to the Novotnys, I forced myself to concentrate on something I could control, or at least consider rationally. Rebecca's story. While it was possible that Julia had gone back to kill Novotny, it didn't work for me. I could see her panic and then shoot him, but I couldn't see her leave the building, think it through, go back, and do it. And if Julia didn't kill Novotny, then she probably didn't kill Reaves either, since the same gun was used in both murders. So who did? And then there was her story about Martin. I thought about the photo I'd seen in Catherine's sitting room. No wonder Rebecca seemed to be trying to squirm out of her brother's embrace. I found myself trying to make Martin fit as his father's killer, then realized I wasn't looking at this rationally either.

There were about ten cars parked along the curve of the Novotnys' driveway. Not only was I about to interrupt them in the middle of dinner, I figured this was a big dinner. As I rang the bell, it occurred to me that this might be some sort of memorial service for Catherine.

The maid who answered the door was the same one I'd encountered on my last visit, and she didn't look any too thrilled to see me. But she didn't slam the door in my face, and I waited in the foyer again. The sounds of people laughing and talking drifted out from one of the two main hallways. Maybe it was an Irish wake. I turned toward the window. It was almost dark, and you couldn't see much of the gardens, but I recalled the red-faced little man and idly wondered what he did in the winter.

"What are you doing here, Mr. McCauley?" It was Amelia. Damn. She was wearing pearls and a tight-fitting dress that stopped several inches above her knees. It was black, but I doubted that she was doing any mourning in it. In her left hand she carried a flute of champagne. "This is not a good time."

"Yeah, I can see that. Well, I guess it can be tough losing your husband and sister in the same month."

The corners of her mouth turned down, adding about a dozen tiny lines to her face. "Please leave."

For a moment I had a flash of what it might have been like growing up with this woman for a mother: competitive with her daughter — pushing Rebecca to make more of herself, yet at the same time slamming her down every time she threatened to overtake her. Martin had been her favorite, but with a distant husband and a daughter she wouldn't let herself get close to, her love must have been suffocating. I blinked the picture from my mind. "Actually, you must have gotten the message wrong. I came to see Martin."

"I know who you came to see. Martin's busy now, so I'm afraid you'll have to leave."

I shook my head and dug my hands in my pockets. "Can't do that."

"Then I'll have to call the police." She paused, then added, "Chief Carver."

In spite of myself, I smiled. "Go ahead. I'll have to talk to him sooner or later anyway."

She stared at me, not moving except for the little finger of her left hand which was tapping the stem of the glass she held. I returned her stare. This standoff had all the makings of a long one, but, mercifully we were interrupted.

"Amelia, what's keeping you?" A tall gentleman, balding but with a perfectly shaped dome, emerged from the hallway. He gave me an odd look, then favored Amelia with an affectionate one. "You're missed."

"I'll be right there. This gentleman was just leaving."

He regarded me, apparently curious about this guy Amelia was so anxious to be rid of.

"Actually," I said to the stranger, "I needed to talk to Martin. Is he back there with you?"

Without consulting Amelia, he said, "Sure," then turned and called for Martin. That done, he glanced at Amelia and was stopped cold by her glare. He looked at me—I smiled and nodded my thanks—then back to Amelia. "What's wrong, dear?"

She shook her head and turned away from me. "Nothing."

"Yeah, Arnie, what's up?" It was Martin, looking casual in a pair of khaki chinos and a gray shirt open at the neck. When he saw me, his expression went from eager to distressed. I have that effect on people.

"I just wanted to talk to you for a couple minutes."

"Yeah, well I'm," he waved his hand toward the noise, "kind of busy."

"Like I said, just a couple minutes."

He hesitated, then said, "Okay, we'll go in my study."

I thanked Amelia and Arnie, neither of whom said 'you're welcome.'

As I suspected, Martin's study turned out to be the one his father used to call his own. No standing on ceremony in the Novotny household. When offered, I accepted a snifter of cognac. Traditions can't be ignored. Besides, I didn't want to offend him. Yet.

"I see you've still got a bottle or two left."

"There's plenty more where this came from," he replied and winked at me. I shuddered and took a sip. It burned its way down to my empty stomach, and I decided to spend most of my time swirling it in the bowl and breathing it in. Besides, I didn't plan to be there long enough to finish.

Martin studied me over the rim of the snifter as he took a drink. "I guess you should get an apology. To tell the truth I don't remember much of what I said the last time we met. So, whatever you do, don't hold me accountable for any of it." He wiped his upper lip with the back of his hand and took another drink. Short and quick.

"That sounds like an old excuse," I said, then continued before he had time for questions. "Well, that's not why I'm here. But I'd like to say that you did a pretty good job on 'Waltzing Matilda.' Many a sober individual has done much worse."

After a moment, he accepted the compliment and raised his glass for a toast. I did the same and we drank to the wonders of a drunk whose lips could get his mouth around the phrase "billy boiled."

I was standing next to a globe done up with gold oceans and earth-tone continents so it wouldn't clash with the oakwood stand. I spun it slowly on its axis. "Pretty generous of you, giving up that piece of land."

He shrugged. "Didn't have much of a choice. It's what Aunt Catherine wanted. How could I refuse a dying request?"

"You had a witness, didn't you? The nurse. What's her name?"

"Gretchen," he said.

"That's it? Just Gretchen?"

"Warren. Gretchen Warren." He sat on the corner of the big dark wood desk, bracing himself with one foot on the floor. "Believe me, I'd rather be the owner of a prosperous industrial complex than a generous citizen with a tax write off. What could I do though?"

"Your sister's not too happy about it."

"What can she do?"

"She's talking to a lawyer."

"Let her." He shook his head. "It's my land now. What I say goes." He cradled the snifter in the palm of his hand, his long, slender fingers rising up the sides of the bowl like a spider engulfing an orb.

"Yeah, well that figures. You're pretty good at getting your way, aren't you?"

Martin set his brandy snifter on the desk and laced his fingers together, folding his hands in his lap. "What's that supposed to mean?"

I gave the globe a hard spin and walked away from it. "Rebecca had a few things to say about you."

"You can't believe much of what she says, you know. She's always had a pretty active imagination."

"Aren't you even curious about what it was she said?"

Frowning, he shrugged it off, then crossed his arms over his chest. "Why should I be?"

"Seems like a natural reaction to me."

He managed a lopsided grin. "Okay, go ahead. What did my dear sister accuse me of now?"

"Rape."

After a moment, he sighed and shook his head. Then he said, "Quint, between you and me, I think we can chalk that off to wishful thinking."

"I didn't say she told me you raped *her*."

Taking the snifter up again, Martin swirled the dark liquid and took a drink. "Maybe not, but that is what you're talking about, isn't it?" I didn't respond. "Rebecca had an unfortunate childhood. Mom didn't care for her much, and no matter what she did, she couldn't get Dad's attention. In her loneliness, she turned to me. I suppose it's only natural that in her imagination, she made that relationship more intimate that it actually was." He chuckled as if this were the only natural conclusion and an amusing one at that. Then he shrugged. "What do you think?" The light from the desk's lamp cast shadows against the features of his face, carving hollows that juxtaposed the toe-in-the-rug grin.

"I think that Rebecca may be inclined to go a little easier on herself these days. She may even get to the point where she can talk about it. And there's probably a few people who'd be real interested in what she's got to say."

He held my gaze for several seconds, then turned to his drink. "It's her word against mine."

"Could get messy. Real unpleasant. What would your mother think?"

"You think I care?"

"Yes. I do. I think you care a lot." His fascination with the contents of the glass encouraged me. "Not only is she your mother, she's a major source of income. Sure, you've got the property your aunt gave you, but that's not much compared with your mother's holdings. Someday that'll be yours. If you don't piss her off."

Bracing one hand against the edge of the desk, he studied me for a minute. Finally he said, "You got a sister?"

I nodded.

"C'mon then. Don't tell me you've never, you know, thought about it."

"Martin, don't even try to put me in your category."

"But you know what I mean, McCauley. You're trying to work your way through puberty, having wet dreams, and there's this sweet young thing running around half dressed."

"She was eight years old."

"What're you supposed to do?" he asked, as though he hadn't heard me.

"Not what you did." He looked away again, shaking his head as though I were either incredibly dense or self-righteous. I set my glass down and stepped up to him. "You'd better tell me why you donated that property to the Nature Conservancy, 'cause I don't believe for a minute that it was your aunt's dying request. She was way too practical. And if you don't tell me, I'm going to tell anyone who'll listen what you did to your sister." I was bluffing, but I pushed on so he wouldn't have time to consider that possibility. "Starting with your mother. Then I've got a friend who's a reporter. The papers would love to get their hands on something like this. And I also have a friend who's tight with the chief of police. And that's only the beginning. I'm going to talk to your employer, make it hard to go back to Malibu. Then I'll check out your record in California. Maybe you didn't stop with Rebecca." Never underestimate the potency of stream-of-consciousness rambling. I could tell from the brief look I got of Martin's eyes before he turned away — surprised and panicked — that I'd hit paydirt. "Yeah, I think that's where I'll start. Unless, of course, you want to answer my question."

It was a full minute before he responded. Then he smiled the smile of one who's been dealt one blow too many. "Isn't it amazing how a half-truth can destroy you?" I didn't answer and he continued, "And it is a half-truth. It wasn't rape. Well, maybe the first time she was a little reluctant. After that she wasn't what I'd call enthusiastic. I doubt she'll ever be. But I can tell you she wasn't fighting me off."

"So, how's it destroying you?"

"Nick Guthrie," he stated simply and with disdain. "Somehow he got wind of what had supposedly happened. I don't know how. Possibly my father said something." He gazed into his glass, maybe hoping he'd find a better response there than the one he had in his head. "He approached me, and blackmailed me, the same as you're doing now."

When he stopped to glare at me, I said, "My heart's bleeding for the victim. Keep going."

Shrugging, he continued, "He called me out in California. Said if they started to build on that property, he'd be sure that my mother, and anyone else who'd listen, got a detailed account of what happened, you know, between Rebecca and me. I told him the land wasn't mine. Apparently he'd done his homework, because he knew who was getting the property after Catherine died. At the time we talked, she was in the hospital, and it didn't look like she'd make it. I came back, and she recovered. As much as a person that ill can recover."

"What would Guthrie have done if they'd started developing the property before Catherine died?"

"I don't know."

I couldn't tell from his bland expression whether he was lying. "The timing of her death was pretty convenient then, wasn't it?"

Shrugging, Martin said, "I guess you could call it that."

"Some might say too convenient."

He stood and stepped toward me. "I didn't kill my aunt, if that's what you're getting at. I loved that woman."

I made a noncommittal noise. "The nurse. Gretchen Warren." I was half talking to myself because somewhere in the back of my head something clicked and I was trying to coax it out. "She must have been in on it too." Martin didn't confirm or deny it and then I knew why that blond woman who'd drifted into the SOW fund-raiser with Guthrie, and quickly detached herself from him, had seemed familiar. "Guthrie's girlfriend and the nurse are the same person."

"I didn't tell you that."

"Did Guthrie tell you why he wanted you to donate the property?"

"No, but I figured it out."

"If your father had been alive, could you still have gotten away with it?"

"Sure. Like I said, it's mine now."

If that was true, Guthrie had just tumbled from his brief, but promising position at the top of my suspect list. Easy come, easy go. Just as quickly, another person wormed his way up there. "You were pretty much exiled from Foxport as long as your father was alive, weren't you?"

"So? What's so great about Foxport?

I shrugged. "What kind of car do you drive in California?"

Crossing his arms over his chest, he said, "Who cares?"

"You've got a whole stable of cars here." I lifted the glass of cognac. "Good liquor. You'd pay ten bucks for this in a restaurant." Sweeping the room with my hand, I added, "All this can be yours. Didn't take you long to settle in, did it? Amazing how little time it takes to acclimate yourself to the good life."

Martin chewed on his lower lip and studied me for a moment before he said, "You've got some wild theories, McCauley, but you're a long way from proving any of them."

"I don't know about that, Martin." I glanced at my watch. "Well, I've kept you from your company long enough. Thanks for your time and the brandy." He finished off the brandy in one gulp and turned away as I walked out.

I managed to find my way to the door without anyone's assistance. For a moment, I stood there and listened to the sounds of the party as a piano accompanied a group of not-so-gifted singers belting out "Oklahoma." I was just about convinced this wasn't a memorial service for Catherine.

My rental car was parked at one end of the long-curved drive and as I approached it, I noticed a faint glow beneath the car. At first I thought the moonlight was reflecting off something in an odd way, but as I drew closer, I saw a pair of feet sticking out from under the car and realized the moon wasn't involved at all. One of the feet was moving back and forth as though keeping time to some silent melody.

I cleared my throat. The foot stopped. "Unless you want two useless kneecaps, move out from there real slow." The only means I had of doing damage to his knees or any other part of his anatomy was by kicking them. But he didn't know that, and when he hesitated I didn't want to give him any time to think so I started to count. "One . . . two . . ." fortunately he began to slide out. That threat loses a lot of its punch when you have to go past ten.

As he squirmed his torso out, I relieved him of his flashlight and a small knife, both of which he relinquished without a struggle. Then I grabbed his jacket and yanked him the rest of the way. He squinted as I shone the light in his face.

"I don't mean to sound ungrateful, but I really don't need an oil change just yet," I couldn't figure out where I'd seen him before. He had a small build, a broad nose and a pale, pencil-thin moustache.

"I, uh, I lost something. I was just looking under your car." His voice was soft and from the way he stammered and averted my gaze, it seemed he wasn't used to lying. I found that kind of refreshing. There was something about the way he looked up at me with his head slightly bowed that was familiar. "You're the gardener, aren't you?" He didn't deny it. "C'mon." I pulled him up by his jacket. "Let's go back to the house and see who's the least happy to see you."

I figured he had to be working under orders from either Amelia or Martin and, as luck would have it, they were both coming out the door as we climbed the steps. Amelia appeared strident and Martin confused. When Amelia saw me gripping the gardener's arm, her mouth dropped slightly but she quickly snapped it back into place and pulled herself up. Martin continued to look perplexed as he pulled the door shut behind him. The four of us stood beneath the porch light for a minute without speaking. Finally I said, "You'll never guess who I found weeding under my car." I held up the knife. "It's bad enough you make him do it in the middle of the night, but all you give him to work with is a lousy pen knife." I shook my head.

Amelia's mouth was one thin, tight line. Without taking her eyes from me, she said to the gardener, "It's all right, Thomas, you can go back to your room."

I released him and he nodded at Amelia, turned and fled.

"What was he doing? Cutting the brake line?" Martin turned to his mother who continued to regard me with her icy gaze. The porch light shaded her face in harsh angles.

"Well, that's pretty stupid, isn't it?" I said. "This isn't San Francisco or the Grand Tetons. This is Foxport, Illinois. The land is flat and the speed limit's thirty-five. The odds of my killing myself when the brakes go is pretty slim, isn't it?"

She folded her arms over her chest. "Who said anyone was trying to kill you?"

"No? Then what were you trying to do? Scare me? Okay, I'm scared. Now why do you want me scared?"

"Mother, what's going on here?"

We ignored him and Amelia's mouth twisted into a smile. "Mr. McCauley, you're an unmitigated pain in the ass, but you're not stupid."

"Why, thank you," I said, adding, "You know who killed your husband, don't you?"

"This is a Novotny affair. It's not your concern. We take care of our own."

"That's exactly the conclusion I was coming to."

Amelia's glare intensified. "I'm just about ready to file a complaint against you and your tactics. You've no business meddling in our family."

"Go ahead. I'll wait. And then I'll tell them how your hired help flattened my tires, busted my windows, snaked my car and was in the process of carrying out this last feeble gesture when I practically tripped over his feet."

"Why should they believe you?"

I pointed in the direction the gardener had gone. "You think *he's* going to lie for you?"

Martin put his hand on his mother's shoulder, "Mother, what is he talking about?"

"Be quiet, Martin," she snapped and I thought she was going to bite him.

"Maybe you didn't kill him, but you're protecting whoever did." I shifted my stare to Martin who continued to view the exchange as though he'd walked into a movie an hour late and was trying to figure out the players.

"What the hell is he talking about?"

"Martin . . ." Amelia was rapidly losing her patience.

Martin moved between his mother and me. "How come you two are the only ones who know what the hell's going on here?"

"I said be quiet." The command was all the more threatening for the slow, deliberate way she delivered it.

She wet her lips and turned to me as though Martin weren't there. "Mr. McCauley, how much do you earn in a year? A good one?"

"You mean what's it going to cost to keep me from telling the police that your son killed his father?" I was watching Martin when I spoke, expecting to see the shock of disclosure written all over is face. I didn't.

Instead, he turned to his mother, his face screwed up in confusion. "WHAT?" I almost believed him when he said, "What are you talking about?" He looked at me. "I swear to God, I don't know what she's talking about."

"She thinks you killed your father."

"I know what she thinks." Then, in a softer tone, he said to his mother, "I just want to know why."

Amelia shifted uncomfortably. "It's all right, Martin. I understand and I realize that it was the only way. And," she shot me a nasty look, "he can't prove a thing."

"I know he can't, because I didn't do it."

"Mr. McCauley, why don't you leave?"

Martin moved close to her, and there was an edge of menace in his voice as he said, "Mother, answer my question. Why do you think I killed him?"

She looked up at him, disconcerted. "You think I don't know why your father sent you away? Those stories your sister told about you. This is all her fault." I could barely hear her next words. "She is a liar, isn't she?"

Martin gazed at her and shook his head in disbelief. "God, yes, Mother. You can't doubt that."

His eyes were wide and his tone so sincere that I decided that incredulity he'd displayed earlier could just as easily have been an act. But I figured I'd gotten all I could for the moment and I'd had just about all I could take of the Novotny family. As I turned to leave, I said to Amelia, "One of your kids is a liar, but you've got the wrong one."

I decided it was time to dump all this on Jeff Barlowe. I was beginning to think he knew more than he was letting on. Sometimes I'm a little slow on the uptake.

Jeff doesn't live in Foxport. Most reporters for the *Chronicle* can't afford the rent. Most moderately priced P.I.s can't either, and if it hadn't been for Louise and her low-rent package, I'd probably be ten miles west of town in the little farming community of Chandler, possibly living in the same apartment complex as Jeff. As I drove out there, I kept testing my brakes and by the time I reached his place was convinced that the gardener hadn't achieved his objective before I came along.

Jeff's building has got a security door, but someone insists on propping it open with a brick. I went right up to his third-floor apartment without ringing the bell. The sounds of Monday night football filtered through the door. I knocked. After a minute and some movement, Jeff asked who it was.

"It's me. Quint."

"Just a sec." It seemed to take longer than necessary for him to remove the chain and unlock the deadbolt, but I was patient.

When Jeff finally got the door open, he looked a bit frazzled, but that wasn't unusual for Jeff. "What's with the Fort Knox—" I started, then was stopped cold. I breathed deeply the rich, warm smell, recalling the last time I'd experienced it and thinking this entire episode was forever going to pollute my opinion of chocolate chip cookies.

Chapter 20

I ALMOST LOST IT. And when Jeff stood there, one hand on the door knob and the other nervously pushing his hair back from his forehead, and said, "What are you doing here?" I was the closest I've ever been to breaking a person's glasses when they were still on his face.

I summoned up a casual smile. "I smelled the cookies."

After gaping at me for a minute, Jeff backed up, opening the door wide enough for me to enter. "Sure. They're almost done. I think."

I stepped past him into the living room. "Since when did you become so domestic?" I scanned the cluttered room for signs of another person. It was hard to tell.

"What?" He was partially behind the door, holding it open as though preparing for me to leave in a hurry. Or maybe hoping.

"The cookies. I thought your culinary skills stopped just short of Hamburger Helper."

His laugh was forced and he looked past me as he said, "Yeah, well, you gotta try everything once. I just figured . . ."

"Forget it, Jeff." The bedroom door had opened and Julia Ellison stood there, wearing a pair of baggy jeans and a plaid flannel shirt. "He knows about me and cookies."

Jeff hung his head. Then he sighed and with a toss of his head, looked at me. "I'm sorry. I didn't want to do this."

"I made him promise not to tell anyone. Even you." Then she turned to Jeff. "For God's sake, shut the door."

Startled, Jeff obeyed.

"No, Jeff," I said, "Leave it open. I was just on my way out. I've had it with you two." Jeff didn't move. "Open it, Jeff. I'm about two breaths away from going through anyway, using one of you as a battering ram."

Still, he hesitated. "You've got to listen . . ."

"I don't *got* to do anything except get out of here before I lose it. What the hell do you think you're doing? Is this some kind of game? Is she," I jerked my thumb toward Julia, "calling the shots here? Since when?"

Julia stepped forward. "None of this is Jeff's fault, so get off his case, okay?"

I whirled on her, and she stepped back, eyes wide. "I'm not getting off anyone's case. I've been used, goddammit, and I'm pissed off. I've been running my ass off all day and the two of you have been shacked up here—"

"Hold it," Jeff said and at the same time Julia uttered something about my guttertuned mind.

"I'm not going to hold it," I said to Jeff. "You used me and I don't like it. And you," I turned to Julia, "you owe me a car. What the hell are you two doing to me?"

"Nothing, Quint. I swear I didn't know she was alive until I got back from your office this morning. She'd walked here from Foxport."

As if lending validity to that statement, Julia sneezed. "That's true. I didn't know where else to go."

Jeff began to pick papers up off the battered sofa, tucking in the blue ribbed spread he used as its cover. "C'mon, Quint, sit down." He tried to take my arm. "Let's talk. Okay?"

"No, it's not okay. I don't like being used."

Julia sighed and crossed her arms over her chest. "Forget it, Jeff, he isn't interested in the truth. Only in his fragile ego."

I was stunned and I gaped at Julia for a moment. She didn't blink. I finally found my voice. "You've got a helluva lot of nerve talking about egos here, Miss 'I'm too important to go to jail' Ellison. And don't give me this higher cause crap."

Jeff had disappeared into the hallway that was his kitchen and now emerged with a can of beer. "Here, Quint, drink this. You'll feel better."

"The hell I will."

"Look," Jeff said, one hand on his hip and the other extended to me with the can. "Go ahead and rave for a while. I guess you've got the right. But when you're finished, you've got to listen to us. You know something's wrong with this whole investigation. You know she didn't kill either Novotny or Reaves. And whether you'll admit it, it's bugging you just as much as us."

I looked at Julia. She was waiting for my reaction and I was unable to read her expression. Maybe it was somewhere between hopeful and hostile. Finally, I snatched the can from Jeff and threw myself down on the couch. As always, the cushion felt lumpy and the springs tenuous. Jeff appeared visibly relieved and Julia sat in a fan-back rattan chair. How fitting.

I lit a cigarette and blew the smoke in her direction. She wrinkled her nose, but didn't say anything. Jeff sat on the opposite end of the couch, holding his own can of beer.

I took a long swallow of the beer, which, at this point, was more to my taste than cognac. Then I took a deep breath and asked Julia, "What about your buddy, Rob?"

Frowning, she said, "Well, when I thought about it, I realized he must have been the person who gave me away to the cops."

"What made you decide it wasn't me?"

She studied the back of her hand for a moment, twisting the silver filigree ring on her middle finger. "I guess I figured whoever sold me out, did it for the money. Rebecca's ten thousand dollars. Rob's got lots of money problems right now. It made sense."

I ignored the fact that she'd come to this conclusion based on someone's bad qualities rather than my good ones. "Don't suppose this hit you before you put my car in the drink?" When she didn't respond, I added, "That was intentional, wasn't it?"

This time she looked me straight on and said, "Yes, it was."

I glanced at Jeff then back to Julia. "Well, I guess if a human being's expendable, then a car must be too."

Julia just stared at me, cool and composed. I interpreted her silence as agreement. "When we were at your friend's house, you got a call warning you. If that wasn't Rob, then who was it?"

She shifted. "That was someone else who knows about me."

"Who?"

She blinked and cleared her throat. "The original Fox."

"Who's that?"

She shook her head. "I can't tell you. It could get a good person in trouble."

"I thought you trusted me."

"That's not the point. I gave my word."

I remembered how I trusted Elaine, but still wouldn't tell her. But, damn I wanted to know. "Can you give me his initials?"

A smile pulled at her mouth. "Sorry."

I regarded Julia for a moment. She appeared a little more vulnerable, but still too sure of herself for someone in her situation. Sneezing again, she pulled a tissue from her jeans pocket to wipe her nose.

"Quint," Jeff said. "Did you talk to Guthrie?"

"Yeah, he's so elated over his good fortune that he can hardly see straight. Thing is, I'm not sure whether he's happier because his land has just increased in value ten times or because he pulled one over on his old nemesis Leonard Novotny. He must figure poor Leonard's spinning so fast in his grave that he's drilled himself halfway to China by now." When I looked, both Jeff and Julia seemed to be waiting for more, so I continued. "I had much more interesting conversations with Rebecca and Martin Novotny and a brief but meaningful encounter with their mother." As I related Rebecca's story, I told Jeff it was off the record, but added that it might be worth his while to see if Martin had any kind of record on the West Coast. When I mentioned Nick Guthrie's coercive measures and his relationship to Catherine's nurse, Julia and Jeff exchanged looks. I finished up with Amelia and her threats.

Neither Jeff nor Julia spoke for several minutes. I went to the refrigerator for another beer, saw that there was one Guinness left and took it. When I returned to the living room, Julia was shaking her head as though she was having trouble working it out. She said, "So Amelia doesn't believe that her son raped his sister, but she does believe that he killed her husband? And she understands?"

"That's what it sounds like."

"What do you think?" Jeff asked.

I leaned back into the couch and drank from the bottle before I said, "I think Martin's a sleaze, but I don't think he's a killer. When Amelia said she understood why he'd kill his dad, he looked shocked. Really." I paused and added, "Besides, I don't see any motive for him to have killed Reaves. And they're saying the same gun was used."

"Right," Jeff said, nodding to himself, apparently caught up in his own thoughts. "That's right."

"So," Julia said, "you're convinced I didn't kill either man?"

"Sure," I said. "And I'll bet the cops will believe it too. So why don't you try talking to them? It's not like your identity is a secret anymore."

"I can't do that."

"Why not?"

"Because I want to stay dead."

I stared at her for a minute until I was convinced she wasn't going to crack a smile. Then it all seemed to make sense. "That's easy, isn't it?"

"No. As a matter of fact, it's not."

I thought about that. Somewhere she probably had grieving friends. One or two anyway. "So, what's stopping you from leaving now?"

Sitting there in the fan-back chair, with her elbows resting on its wicker arms, she looked, as I supposed she felt, like some island native queen addressing one of her more querulous subjects. "I've made contact with a group out on the West Coast. We've got similar ideas and methods. They want me, but they don't want someone with a price on her head." With a little shrug, she explained, "In case I'm identified."

"I see. Credibility among the radical fringe."

"Something like that."

"So, we're clearing your name so you can go out and spike trees."

She regarded me for several moments, before she said, "I know you don't like me, and I really don't care, so I don't know why I want you to know that there are certain tactics that even I find objectionable."

I raised my eyebrows. "I had no idea." Julia scowled at me. Before she got her retort off, I turned to Jeff. "Did you find out anything about Guthrie?"

"Some. Apparently he financed the purchase of the property in question with the backing of this A & R Securities. He borrowed heavily from Foxport Federal to finance Yorkshire Estates and is in the process of arranging another large loan, which shouldn't be a problem seeing as his credit rating is A-1."

"You learn anything about A & R?"

He frowned. "Just the usual kind of investment firm. Into a little bit of this and a little bit of that."

"You know," Julia spoke slowly at first, "I'm not sure, but I think David handled some legal matters for them."

"Let me use your phone." Before Jeff could answer, I was in the kitchen dialing. "What'd you find out?" I asked when I got through to O'Henry.

"Well, nice talking to you again too, McCauley."

"Sorry," I said. "What'd you find out?" As O'Henry proceeded to fill me in, Jeff watched, trying to read something into my monosyllabic responses. Julia pulled at a loose thread on the cuff of her shirt. "You get any names?"

He rattled off a list of the principals, none of which interested me much until he got to Mel Vincent. I love it when things like that happen.

Jeff looked hopeful when he heard me tell O'Henry I owed him one.

"I've lost count," O'Henry said before hanging up.

I returned to the living room, taking my time finding a comfortable spot on the couch.

"Well?" Jeff prompted. In the quick glance that Julia shot me, I noticed that her face was taut, strained.

"Well," I finally said, "Apparently A & R Securities is one of the mob's more respectable enterprises. O'Henry didn't have many details, but he had a few names, one of which belonged to a guy having a couple victory drinks with Guthrie at the country club. He got the information from some guy who's heading up an organized crime task force who, incidentally, was real interested in why O'Henry was asking."

"Did he say?" Julia was looking a bit alarmed.

I shook my head.

She slumped down in the chair and drew her right leg up under her. Her gray wool socks looked too big for her and I surmised that most of her outfit had been provided by Jeff. "David," she said, speaking so softly it was barely audible.

Jeff's eyes went wide. "Reaves was involved too, wasn't he?"

She shook her head, slowly, like she was trying to deny it herself. "He never said anything to me, but, like I said, they did some legal work for A & R. I'm sure of it." She seemed to hesitate then and wouldn't make eye contact with us. "It's no big deal, it wasn't anything really."

"What wasn't?" Jeff and I crowed in unison.

She said to Jeff, "You remember just before the last election when they broke that story about Barry Haller's affair with one of his campaign workers?"

He nodded, then turned to me. "The *Chronicle* wouldn't touch the story. Didn't think we had enough evidence. Apparently the *Westender* had photos. Still, it was pretty sleazy journalism. What about it?"

"Well, the night before that story ran, I came back to the office late because I wanted to pick up some flyers to distribute the next day. David was sitting in his office, the door was open, but the light was off. He was just sitting there, in a dark office, looking out the window. I asked him what was wrong, and he said, 'I'm going to win this election.' I told him that I knew he was going to win, so what was the matter? He said, 'No, I'm positive I'm going to win. I just hope I'm not giving up more than I'm getting.' I asked what he meant and he wouldn't say.... The next day, that story ran and David almost immediately overtook him in the polls and, as you know, went on to win the election two weeks later." She sighed and shook her head. "Now I'm wondering . . ."

"You and me both," Jeff finished.

"Do Reaves and Guthrie have any connection besides A & R?"

"Guthrie was a campaign contributor the first time David ran and they seemed to know each other pretty well. They both were active in SOW."

The three of us sat for a minute. No one spoke. Finally, I said, "Okay, here's what I think we've got here. Let's say Reaves knows about A & R's mob ties. They help each other out. Maybe more. Guthrie and Reaves establish some kind of friendly, mutually beneficial relationship. Guthrie's an up-and-coming developer and community planner. Reaves needs one of those on his side. Guthrie's looking to buy some land, but none of the banks are willing to risk him. Reaves introduces Mr. Guthrie and A & R Securities. Is this making sense so far?" Jeff nodded and Julia just watched me. Encouraged, I went on, "Maybe A & R is still financing some of his investments. One of their first mutual ventures is investing in that area next to the wetland. Guthrie finds out what plans Novotny's got for the area and he can see his property's value dropping like a brick. So he digs this stuff up on Martin. I don't know how, but he does. We know that already. Maybe instead of approaching Martin, who's not even in town, he takes this bit of information to the senior Novotny. He's a self-righteous guy who sure as hell doesn't want this to get out about a member of his family. But instead of capitulating, he sees what he can get on Guthrie. Let's say he finds out that A & R is run by organized crime and these homes Guthrie's building for Foxport's elite are being financed by drug money. What's that do to Guthrie?"

"He's dead in the water," Jeff picked up. "He'll never get that bank loan he needs so bad, and I'll bet there aren't too many citizens who would be caught buying one of those homes if they knew they were built with mob money."

Julia finally spoke. "You're saying that Guthrie killed Novotny."

"If Guthrie knew when you'd be paying a visit to Novotny's office, he had the perfect dupe."

"David," she whispered, almost to herself.

"What about Reaves?" Jeff asked. "Why would he kill Reaves?"

We both looked to Julia. "I don't know," she said at first, then slowly shook her head. "What you're saying, about my being set up, that makes sense, but I can't believe David would agree to that." She paused and added with more certainty, "No, he wouldn't do that to me."

"Maybe that's it then." Julia waited for me to elaborate. "He just sent you to Novotny's office on his buddy's suggestion. Maybe he didn't know what was going down until after it happened. Then he figured it out and got a bad case of the guilts. Guthrie didn't think he could trust him to keep his mouth shut, so he decided to test him."

Jeff nodded, eyes widening. "That's it! Julia was the test. Poison her, and he's as guilty as Guthrie. Back down, and Guthrie figures he can't afford a loose cannon, so he takes care of him."

"Poison her?" It was Julia, and her coloring had paled a shade. "What are you talking about?"

"Uh, oh, yeah." I watched Jeff stammer around for a minute and decided I didn't feel like helping him. I took a drink, sat back into the couch, and waited. "Well," Jeff cleared his throat and took a couple swallows of his beer. Then he explained to Julia about the chloral hydrate in her glass. When he finished, she just sat there, mouth open, then looked to me, perhaps hoping I'd tell her it was all a bad joke on Jeff's part. I nodded.

Shaking her head in slow, deliberate denial, Julia said, "I don't see . . ."

I decided to help. "He was trying to kill you."

"No," she spoke without much conviction. "You're wrong. There's a mistake." She looked at Jeff who wouldn't meet her gaze.

"Did you put chloral hydrate in his drink?"

Jerking her head around to me, she snapped, "Of course I didn't."

"Then there's no mistake." Jeff continued to stare at the floor, but I kept going. "I guess that's the way it happened. To tell the truth, my money was on your trying to poison Reaves. I figured the cops just got the glasses mixed up."

Slowly, her disbelief was diminishing. "He must have been acting on Guthrie's orders." She pushed herself out of the chair and began to pace the room, arms crossed over her chest, making sharp, angry turns every couple yards. Jeff and I watched her expression change with her emotions — from the pinched, puzzled look of anguish to kicked-in-the-gut fuming. "I can't believe that son of a bitch tried to kill me."

"Well, if it's any consolation, he didn't try too hard." She stopped dead and stared at me. I shrugged. "There's lots more efficient ways to kill someone than sleeping potions. Besides, he didn't make an issue when you left after barely touching your drink."

Julia took up her pacing again and Jeff turned to me. "So, maybe Reaves had a change of heart, Guthrie couldn't trust him, so he offs him." He nodded, liking the sound of it. "Have we got enough for the police?"

I was doubtful. "What have we got really? A bunch of suppositions." Jeff and I glanced at Julia as she passed by us on her room laps, muttering something about Reaves's lack of sexual prowess. "Besides," I turned back to Jeff, "there's more. We're missing something. I can feel it."

Jeff drained his can of beer and crushed it. "Me too. So, what do we do?" He watched Julia, pacing and muttering. "Hey, I know what. We get Julia all wired up, you know, then she appears at the foot of Guthrie's bed with seaweed in her hair and a flashlight under her chin. Scare a confession out of him."

Julia stopped pacing long enough to say, "Forget it, Barlowe."

After a minute, I said, "You know, I think I like that."

"No way, McCauley. Just because—"

"Not you," I waved her silent. "But I like the wired part."

"Yeah, well, if we don't have enough for the cops now, they sure as hell aren't going to be happy to wire us."

"I know, but what if we gave them enough proof?"

Both Julia and Jeff spoke at the same time. "How?"

"If we do just what Novotny tried to do. Blackmail the sucker."

"Who?" This time only Jeff spoke.

"Well, we can't send her in." I poked my thumb at the Julia. "Despite the fact that it's her butt we're saving, and she's so anxious to help, she's not the best person. There's no way Guthrie's going to believe that she's not setting him up. And you," I turned to Jeff, "you went to jail to keep her out, so you're not too likely." I trailed off.

"That leaves you," Jeff offered.

"I'm as good as we've got right now."

"I don't know," Julia, having worked through her gamut of emotions, had returned to the fan-back chair. "You a blackmailer. It's pretty obvious that money's not a big priority of yours." She paused, then added, "I'm not sure what is, but it's not money."

As she watched me with her snake charmer eyes, I noticed they were cool and not so much amused as skeptical. And she was waiting for an answer. "Fame," I said. "My agent encourages me to solve high profile cases like this." Snapping my fingers, I added, "Solve this puppy and I can write myself a one-way ticket to the talk show circuit—Oprah, Phil, Geraldo—next thing you know all three networks are begging me to star in my own series." She continued to regard me, unblinking, so I kept going. "And then . . . maybe then I can afford to buy a new car."

Chapter 21

I<small>T WAS ALMOST TEN</small> o'clock by the time I got to Nick Guthrie's house. On the way there, I'd stopped at the apartment to pick up my gun. Not that I anticipated needing it, but I felt more secure with it clipped to my belt. Besides, I wanted to see if Elaine was home yet. She was stretched out on one end of the couch, reading. As I walked in the door, Peanuts jumped down from the other end. He looked a bit sheepish and probably would have brushed telltale hairs from the cushions if his paws could have managed it. Elaine didn't look at all sheepish. In fact she immediately started quizzing me about my evening, her questioning becoming more urgent as I dug my .38 Smith and Wesson out of the kitchen drawer.

"What are you doing?" She bent over me, still clutching her book.

"I'm going to see how convincing I am as an extortionist." As I loaded the gun, I quickly filled her in on the evening's events, whereupon she insisted on going with me to Guthrie's place.

"No," I told her, "I don't want him to get any idea that this is a setup. He might figure that anyway. If he sees you sitting out in the car, he's going to know." She started to protest. "Please, Elaine," I said and she stopped long enough for me to add, "Besides, if you don't hear from me by," I glanced at my watch, "midnight, call the police." She looked disappointed, but agreed. "By the way, how *is* the police?"

"We had a nice dinner. He's a nice man." She shrugged. "What do you want me to say?"

"You had a lousy time," I suggested.

"I had an okay time," she allowed. "That's all."

Guthrie lived on the east end of town in a Georgian brick that was nice, but nowhere near as impressive as the homes he was building out west. I guess I'd expected to find him in some kind of avant-garde place, or at least one that looked less like a normal family's home. I rang the bell and, as I waited, tried to fit myself into the appropriate mind-set for extortion.

He answered the door wearing a lightweight beige sweater and jeans. "What is this? I walk in the door, the phone's ringing. Two minutes later, it's the doorbell." Stepping aside he waved me in. "Well, at least I got to the door in time. Don't you hate it when they hang up just before you get there?"

"Sometimes that's best," I told him and before he could ask me to clarify, I continued, "I was afraid I wouldn't catch you here. Figured you'd still be out celebrating your recent fortune."

"No," he said closing the door, "I allow myself one brief celebration, then don't dwell on it. Just keep going." We were standing in the foyer and now he regarded me with some curiosity. "What brings you out here? And don't tell me you were just driving by."

"You're right. I wasn't. Just had sort of a business proposition to discuss with you. If you've got the time, that is." I mentally kicked myself. Extortionists weren't supposed to be that considerate.

Guthrie's eyebrows shot up and he studied me for a moment. "This should be interesting. A P.I. and a developer talking business." Then he shrugged and added, "Why not?"

I followed him past a flight of stairs and down a hallway into a large room that was half kitchen and half family room. At one end of the family part of the room was a red brick fireplace surrounded by bookshelves containing almost as many beer mugs and clay pots as books. The dark green of the other two walls was broken by large oil paintings of the Old West, one of cowboys, another of Indians, and yet another with both. The artist had painted the humans with rather passive expressions and there was a certain sameness to them all; it was the horses — white-rimmed eyes and nostrils flared — that drew my attention.

"What are you drinking?" he asked and before I could answer, the phone rang. Guthrie motioned me into one of two gray leather armchairs. "This must be the mystery caller." He picked up the phone in the kitchen, said hello a couple times, then with a disgusted look, slammed the receiver down. "Man, I hate that. Why can't a wrong number just say so and hang up," he commented to no one in particular. Then he turned to me, repeating his question.

"Nothing, thanks." I figured there were certain conventions to be observed here, and having a drink with him first didn't seem appropriate.

"Well, I think I'll have one. Make yourself at home." I spent the time he was gone staring at the charred logs in the fireplace and wondering how in the hell I was going to pull this off.

"More to look at if there's a fire going, you know."

"I suppose," I said, glancing at his ice-filled glass brimming with bourbon.

"So, what's the business venture you're talking about?" He took a drink, sunk one hand into his pocket, and waited.

I turned back to the fireplace. "These developments you've got going, they're going to be pretty lucrative I imagine."

"Yeah, they are. So?"

"I was pretty impressed with what you were saying about the price of lots in the area next to the wetland."

He chuckled softly, but I could feel his gaze still on me, intent. "You want to buy one?" he asked, feeling for the bottom.

"Not exactly."

I paused and Guthrie waited several seconds before he said, "So what is it?"

"Well, I was thinking you might want to cut me in on the business. You know, make me a silent partner or whatever you want to call it."

The silence expanded and I became aware of the ticking of a large clock. Still I waited. Finally, Guthrie said, "What are you talking about?" I didn't answer, continuing to stare at the fireplace. "Why would I want to do that?"

After a moment, I looked at him. "Because I've got a real big mouth."

His expression was a mixture of confusion and amusement. "So? Why should I care?"

"I know too much." Bracing myself against the fireplace mantel with one hand, I ran the other through my hair. Then I shook my head and said, "You were counting on nobody looking past some whacked-out environmentalist."

Smiling a thin smile, Guthrie shook his head. "I'm afraid you're going to have to spell it out for me. And you'd better do it fast because you're starting to irritate me." He drained half the glass and waited.

"I know that you killed Novotny and I know why. I also know that you killed Reaves and I know why you did that too. How's that for spelling?"

I thought I saw something scared in his eyes, but just for a second. I clung to it. "I'm surprised you got out of grade school," was all he said.

"Yeah, well I admit it didn't come to me right away. I'm not the quickest study in the world, but I got around to it."

"Now I understand why you didn't want a drink. You weren't planning to stay long. Well, you were right there. You know where the door is."

"You're not even curious about what I know?"

"Mildly. But only in the academic sense."

"It seems like you haven't exactly got a lot of leeway when it comes to being indignant about extortion. Hell, this is a real opportunity for me. I could learn at the feet of the master."

His eyes narrowed and he took a quick drink. Then he turned and began to walk out of the room. I kept talking. "You tried to blackmail Leonard Novotny. Somehow you found out that his son raped his daughter, and then you learned that Martin didn't exactly have a spotless record on the West Coast either. But Novotny wouldn't take it lying down. Not Leonard. He came up the hard way and wasn't going down easy. He did some of his own digging and found out that A & R Securities isn't your average investment firm." Guthrie had stopped walking, but kept his back to me. "If Foxport Federal learns about those mob ties, you can kiss that bank loan good-bye." Then I told him how I figured he knew that Julia was the Fox so it was easy for him to frame her for murder. "And when Reaves didn't play the game, when his conscience started to get to him, then you decided to test him. You had to get rid of Julia anyway, so why not have Reaves do it? You've convinced him he's as guilty as you are, or that it would look that way to anyone who knew what happened. But he doesn't play ball. He's maybe basically a decent guy, aside from his mob connections. I'll bet he wasn't happy about that either. I think David Reaves was living on borrowed time the minute he sold his soul to A & R Securities. And he did. He wouldn't have gotten elected the first time if he hadn't. But I'll bet he was sick of the whole business."

Guthrie turned and stared at me with a bland expression. I waited.

"Is that it?"

I didn't answer.

"Surely you can come up with a more colorful story than that." Stepping toward me, he continued, "Something that would put me in the schoolyards, selling cocaine to eight-year-olds. Or, I know, I'm burying the poor slobs who cross the mob under the foundations of my houses. There's something worth exploring." When I didn't answer, he shook his head. "What the hell do you expect me to do here? It would be nice if I could sue you for slander, but there's no one to hear this. I can promise you one thing though, you talk about this, you get that reporter friend of yours to print this, I will sue. You don't give a shit about a man's reputation, do you? The dead or the living." He was right in front of me now, drink in hand, pacing, doing a pretty good indignant. "You threaten to go to the cops with this asinine story, and I'm supposed to hand over a million dollars or whatever you're asking?" He stopped pacing and got right in my face. "Get the hell out of my house. That's what I think of your threats."

I held my ground, but it wasn't what came natural. He was so convincing, I began to doubt my convictions. But it was too late to excuse myself. I held his gaze for several long seconds, then said, "I've got no plans to take this to the cops. I've got better places to go." I paused then and waited for something akin to doubt to creep into his eyes, then decided I didn't have that long, so I kept going. "No, I'm going straight to A & R Securities. See if they're interested in my theory on who killed their fair-haired politician. They probably don't know that you killed Novotny either. Novotny *and* Reaves. Kind of trigger happy. It also makes you a loose cannon, doesn't it. Sloppy, too. Well I'm betting those guys don't like loose cannons."

Other than the muscle in his jaw, Guthrie wasn't moving. Finally he said, "If they do have organized crime connections . . ."

"Oh, they do. I've been assured of that. Reliable source."

His eyes narrowed and I felt like a student who'd spoken out of turn. He continued, "*If* they do have these connections, what makes you think they'd be remotely interested in what you—a third-rate private investigator—have got to say?" He didn't give me a chance to tell him. "When I let you into the country club with that half-baked story about the bow, I guess I did it because I was amused by your cheek. I'm not amused anymore. I'm annoyed." He stepped back, swirling the ice in his glass. "Now get out of here."

I tried to look very tired with the game he was playing, which was a challenge. What would it take to force his hand? I decided to try one of the oldest poker plays in the book. "Julia Ellison saw you entering Reaves's motel room that night after she left."

"That's bullshit . . . Ellison's dead."

I shook my head. "Afraid not. That's just what she wants everyone to think. She's as alive as I am. More than you, because she doesn't have to answer to guys like Mel Vincent. And I think he'll be real interested. 'Cause when I combine that with the fact that Rebecca Novotny heard Julia leave her father's office before the gunshot was fired, well, I think that's a story worth listening to. Something I'm sure they'll pay to hear." Guthrie didn't move or speak. I was encouraged enough to play my final card. "Well, Nick, it's been nice talking to you. I guess I'll be on my way now." I walked past him and, just before entering the hall, shot back at him, "Next stop Elk Grove Village."

I was halfway to the door when he called my name. I stopped and waited for him to come to me. "You're wired, aren't you?"

I raised my arms, "See for yourself." And he proceeded to frisk me. When he got to the lump at my waist, he drew my jacket back and looked at the gun. I smiled and shrugged. He reached for it, but I stopped him and he didn't argue. Then he turned and went back into the family room. After a moment, I followed and sat across from him in one of the gray leather chairs.

Guthrie smiled. It was a cold smile, a shark's grin. "I had you figured for a straight arrow. An overgrown boy scout."

"I know. I'm good, aren't I?"

"I'm not sure."

"You'd better be, because I'm starting to feel real chatty right about now. Before you know it, I'll need an audience."

He nodded, regarding me for a moment before he said, "What do you want?"

"Money. Lots of it."

"How much?"

"Hundred thousand." I paused and added, "For starters."

He considered, chin resting in the palm of his hand. Then he said, "That's a problem. You see, those bank loans you mentioned. I need them. Bad. I have no cash."

"I'll bet A & R would be pleased to hear that." It was just a hunch, but I could tell from the slight grimace that I was on target. "I don't even think they'd be interested in your explanation of where their money went. I know I'm not."

"It's still a problem. You're attempting to blackmail a man with very little cash. Novotny thought it would work because he didn't want money. He wanted my silence."

"Instead he got a slug in the chest."

He responded with a modest shrug. I'd have to do better tomorrow if I was to carry a wire. But it was enough for now. I was convinced.

"Until the loan comes through, I've nothing to offer you."

"I think we can work something out."

The doorbell rang. I was at once relieved and concerned. Relieved because I'd have time to come up with an alternative to hard cash, and concerned because for all I knew there was a delivery of AK 47s at the door. "Get rid of whoever it is," I told Guthrie as he left the room, and added, "I've planned ahead for lots of eventualities and if certain people don't hear from me at a certain time, well, you'd just better hope I stay healthy." He nodded, looking more amused than concerned.

I was really at a loss now, not having the vaguest idea of how to negotiate extortion when you don't get cash up front. This was supposed to be simple. Neat like a razor slice. And how was I supposed to know he wasn't putting me on? I'd seen that look in his eyes and I believed that A & R might not be too happy if they knew what he'd done with their money, but maybe he was jerking me around as well. As indecisive as I felt, I knew if I let it show, I'd be sunk.

I didn't hear voices right away, which struck me as odd, because I wasn't that far from the door. After a couple minutes, I ventured a look down the hallway. No one there. Maybe he'd split. Or maybe he had other plans. By telling him I'd shared this information with someone else, I figured I'd covered my ass. But I was dealing with a man who'd killed twice and probably wouldn't have any trouble writing me off his conscience. As I walked down the hallway, the carpet silenced my steps. Halfway to the door, I heard two voices, hushed but angry, coming from one of the rooms off the hall. A woman's voice was saying, "Don't give me that, Nick. I think I always knew you were using me, now I know why."

I knew the voice, and I cursed myself for not letting Elaine come.
Guthrie said, "Becky, honey, what am I hearing?"

"Don't you 'Becky, honey' me. I trusted you, I told you things I've never told anyone else and it was all you wanted. You needed a way to get to my family and I gave it to you. You're worse than Martin, you know that? He's sick. You're a greedy, self-serving bastard."

I stepped into the room. Rebecca looked shocked; Guthrie relieved. She wore a black trench coat over her gray sweats and gripped a .38 automatic in both hands. Using my unexpected entrance, Guthrie moved toward her. A second before he reached her, she saw him coming and jerked the gun up, firing it. The bullet shattered the wall-length mirror above a wet bar and brought Guthrie to a dead stop.

He allowed himself a quick glance in my direction. "Hey, man, why don't you do something. You know?"

"He's beyond your help, McCauley. He's beyond anyone's help." There was something about the way she said that — so matter of fact — that I believed her. "The only reason he's not dead already is because I want him to know why he's dying."

"Becky, hon—" he broke off and started again, "Becky, listen to me.

You do this and you've got a witness. Don't ruin your life over me. I'm not worth it."

"He may be right, you know."

"Who asked you?" she snapped at me.

I looked at Guthrie and shrugged.

"Sit down," she ordered Guthrie. "There," she motioned him with the gun toward an oak chair which went with a game table. Guthrie sat. She approached him. "Put your hands where I can see them. On the arm of that chair." He gave me a disgusted look but obeyed, and I half-expected Rebecca to light up a cigarette. But she didn't. She just stood next to him, her gun pointed at his temple. Her hair was pulled back against the nape of her neck in a ponytail.

Rebecca studied Guthrie for a moment, the way you'd look at some kind of toxic mutation. Then she threw her head back and spat on him. He didn't move as the spittle ran down the side of his face, just swallowed, and wet his lips. "I told you. I trusted you. You used me to get to Martin. Didn't you? DIDN'T YOU?" She screamed the last two words in his ear. Guthrie winced, but otherwise didn't move. "You think you're going to get it all now. That can't happen. I won't let it."

"Martin's not the only one he blackmailed, Rebecca."

"Keep out of this, McCauley," Guthrie warned, but didn't move his head.

"He tried blackmailing your father first." She allowed herself a glance at me, but only a glance. I kept going. "When your father turned around and dug up the fact that Guthrie's using the mob to finance his developments, Guthrie decided he might as well shut him up for good and pave the way for himself at the same time."

"He's full of shit, Becky. You know that."

"You shut up, you bastard." Rebecca clenched her jaw and closed her eyes, then sprang them open wide as though she felt Guthrie watching her. "Catherine," she said and Guthrie flinched. "Wasn't it convenient that Catherine died before we started construction. Or did she? Did you help her along? I think you did." Rebecca may have been a crazed woman, but she was talking sense. "But you know what? No one cares what I think anyway. Just like always, they're going to say, 'Poor Rebecca, she's trying to make it look like it's everyone's fault but her own.' Well, they might say that, but I'll know better. I will, and I will have done what needed to be done."

"McCauley." Guthrie pleaded under this breath.

"You used me. You told me you loved me. You must have choked on it. I told you my most horrible secrets and you used them against me." She took a deep breath and gripped the gun so tight her knuckles went white. "I don't care what happens to me anymore." Straightening her arms, as if bracing to fire, she added, "I just don't care."

I moved closer. "Rebecca, don't do this." She didn't move her eyes from her target — Guthrie's head.

"For shit's sake, McCauley, use your gun."

Rebecca shot me a quick glance, alarmed. I shook my head. "I'm not going to use my gun. I know why you want to kill him and I don't blame you. But I tell you, we've got him. You don't have to kill him."

She shook her head in a staccato movement, but didn't speak.

"Between what you know, what I know, and what Julia Ellison knows, he's going away for a long time. And where he's going, he'll find out first hand what it's like to be used. Nice-looking, well-built guy like him. He won't last the day."

"You don't get it, McCauley, do you? I've got to kill him. I need to do this for myself. I need to do something for myself and this is it. I know. I have to."

"You're better than that, Rebecca."

"I know what I have to do." Her words were slow and measured as she pressed the gun to Guthrie's temple. Guthrie closed his eyes and I could see beads of sweat on his upper lip.

"You do that and you lose your choices for good." She didn't move. "You do that and he wins. Your family wins. They've done all these things to you. You can't let them win."

Eternities passed. Mountains shifted and lakes evaporated. Rebecca eased the gun away. Guthrie, feeling the cold metal lifted, sighed. Rebecca took a deep breath, clenched her jaw, and fired. A fifth of Jack Daniels exploded. Guthrie jerked and moaned. Lowering the gun to her side, she watched Guthrie bury his face in his trembling hands, then she looked at me, not speaking.

"Let's go," I said and she nodded and walked past me into the hall without a backward glance. I followed her.

Just as we reached the door, Guthrie called after us, "Nice try, McCauley. An extortionist, my ass. Go back to school. Now take that pathetic little loser and get out of here before I laugh myself to death."

Rebecca hesitated and I gently pushed her out the door and followed.

Once the cool night air hit me, I realized I'd been sweating. I wiped my forehead with the arm of my jacket as I walked Rebecca to her car, then watched as she removed the clip from her gun and dropped it in her pocket along with the gun.

She looked up at me. "You should have let me kill him. No one would have to know. He doesn't deserve to live."

"All that's probably true." I opened the car door for her.

"So, why didn't you let me?"

"It's you who didn't pull the trigger." Resting my arms on the door, I gestured toward the house. "Like I said in there. You're better than that."

Sighing, she lowered herself into the car. "Where's my sense of failure when I need it?"

I closed the door and knocked on the window. "Rebecca." She rolled it a third of the way down. "You know you almost made a joke."

Her mouth twitched into what might have been a smile. "You tell anyone I'll say you're a liar."

Chapter 22

I ENJOY RAKING LEAVES. There's something satisfying about looking back on your labor and seeing a visible difference. Of course, every now and then a big gust of wind comes along and blows a bunch of them back over the grass. I was working on how that applied to more than leaf raking, when a car pulled into the drive. When I first heard the crunch of gravel, I figured it was Elaine returning from the Jaded Fox where she'd been helping Louise. But then I looked up and recognized Cal Maitlin's Mercedes.

Several weeks had passed since Rebecca and I had walked out of Nick Guthrie's house. The next day, she'd gone with me to see Ed Carver. Elaine had come along too, sort of smoothing the way into his office. He listened, and by the time he retraced my steps, talking to Martin and Amelia Novotny, he was convinced that Nick Guthrie and not Julia Ellison had murdered two of Foxport's more prominent citizens. Carver had also managed to get an autopsy performed on Catherine Novotny and, sure enough, she'd had help with her dying. And by the time Gretchen Warren broke down and confessed to giving Catherine a lethal dose of morphine, she realized that, just like Rebecca, she'd been used by Guthrie. So she was more than willing to take him down with her. Knowing that Catherine had died ahead of her time, whether by days or weeks, saddened me and made me angry when I thought about Gretchen's lecture to me about smoking. "She's dying anyway so what difference can it make?" she'd chided me, and probably used those same words to convince herself it was all right to administer the injection.

She admitted she was alone when she did the deed, so Martin wasn't implicated in his aunt's death.

But *his* troubles weren't over. He couldn't take back the wetland donation without losing more face than he had left. And once the news leaked out that he'd accumulated three statutory rape charges in California, he'd have his hands full convincing his mother that each one had been an "unfortunate misunderstanding."

Nick Guthrie was the only question mark. When Carver and two of his men had gone to Guthrie's office to arrest him, his secretary told them he'd gone deer hunting for a few days. No one had heard from him since.

Elaine was still looking for a "real" job, although she admitted that she enjoyed helping Louise out at the Jaded Fox. She was still determined to start her own catering business, preferably in Foxport, but conceded that it could sit on the back burner for a while. But as I watched her forming friendships, I was encouraged. Already she and Louise were tight, and she'd gone out of her way for Rebecca, helping her arrange for some counseling. And then, of course, there was Carver. Although she was determined to get her own apartment, she wanted to stay in Foxport. I told her that was essential because Peanuts had grown quite attached to her, and if she were to leave Foxport, it would be a traumatic experience that he might never recover from. I later admitted that it would be traumatic for me as well. What I didn't tell her was that I hoped she wouldn't achieve financial independence before Christmas.

Now I watched Cal Maitlin emerge from his car. A pile of leaves moved and Peanuts rose up, shook himself off, and trotted over to meet him. Cal was wearing a leather flight jacket and his signature cowboy hat, a combination which would have seemed a contradiction on anyone else. He always looked immaculate and next to him, in my faded jeans and Super Bowl XX sweatshirt, I felt like a slob. But then I was raking leaves and he wasn't.

"There's something reassuring about this chore, isn't there?" he surveyed the expanse of yard and the piles of leaves. Peanuts, having finished greeting Cal, was bounding around in one of these piles, apparently convinced that the leaves were trying to attack him.

"What a life," I said, adding, "when I come back, I want to come back as a dog."

Maitlin smiled and nodded as he watched Peanuts. Then he turned to me with an arched eyebrow. "Heard something through one of my sources I thought you might find interesting. Suppose it'll be common knowledge in a day or so, but you've earned the right to be one of the first to know."

A gust of wind brushed some leaves up against my jeans. I waited.

"Seems that Nick Guthrie's turned up."

"Oh?"

"What's left of him, that is. A couple hunters found his remains impaled to the trunk of an oak by one of his own arrows. Seems he'd been there a while and the elements and the forest creatures, well . . ."

"Revenge of Bambi?"

"Something like that. They found him in a state forest just north of the border in Wisconsin. Right now speculation is centering on his circle of business associates at A & R."

I stood with the rake propped on the ground, both hands gripping its pole. There was something about the beauty of the day that made me not want to dwell on Nick Guthrie's fate. "Don't suppose you've heard anything from Julia?" She'd disappeared from Jeff's place without ever talking to the cops. In fact, as far as most people were concerned, she was still dead. Jeff was so bewildered by the suddenness of her leaving that I believed him when he said he didn't have any idea where she'd gone. I believed him and I felt a little sorry for him because I think Julia had allowed him to believe there was more between them than a story. Maybe there was. If so, it was expendable too.

"As a matter of fact, she called me this morning." He turned slowly from the pile of leaves Peanuts was enjoying. "Didn't say where she was, though I suspect she's made it to California." He paused and added, "I imagine we'll hear from her someday."

"Yeah," I nodded, "she'll probably turn up at the head of some group of environmental outlaws. Either that or she'll run for state senate somewhere."

Chuckling, Maitlin nodded. "Yeah, neither of those scenarios would surprise me. I imagine Julia Ellison can do just about anything she sets her mind to."

I silently added that she wouldn't have to worry about people getting in her way, she'd just mow them over.

"You know," Maitlin said as though reading my thoughts, "she's really not as mean spirited as she seems."

I didn't respond. In the late afternoon sun, I had to squint a little to study Maitlin's face, shaded by the brim of his hat. "She's committed," he continued, "and sometimes people like that tend to be a little, well, single-minded."

"I'll say."

"But we need people like her to balance out the middle. Know what I mean?"

I shrugged. "Yeah, maybe."

With a half grin, he eyed me. "You know one of the reasons she called?"

"I'm not going to touch that one."

"Well, she wanted to say good-bye, but she also wanted a favor."

He paused and I waited. Finally he said, "She wanted me to thank you."

I regarded him for a moment, then nodded. My ambivalence toward Julia Ellison was none of his doing.

He continued, "She also said you kept bugging her about the identity of the original Blue Fox."

"That's right. I guess I figured she owed me at least that much."

"Well, she couldn't tell you because it wasn't her place to reveal that. One thing you could expect out of Julia Ellison was her confidence. People trusted her."

"I understand that. So, she called to rub it in?"

He slipped his hands into the pockets of his jeans. "No, she called the only person who's got a right to tell you who the first Blue Fox was."

I felt my eyes go wide and spent a minute studying the wiry little man in the oversized hat. Then it all clicked and I smiled and nodded.

"Don't look so surprised. I'm in good shape now and I was in even better shape twenty years ago." He shook his head and looked down the stretch of lawn to the river. "I used to take walks by the river all the time. And every day it seemed like it was getting worse. The white-bellied fish, the ducks. The water. Seemed more like the consistency of ink. I'm ashamed to think how easy it was walking along the bank wondering why someone didn't do something." He shook his head, chuckling at his own expense. "Then I finally listened to myself and I asked myself what I was waiting for. I started with one of the chemical plants up the river a ways. DependChem." He smiled at the recollection. "I stopped up their waste disposal system. Hmph. Some system. Just dumped all that crap right into the river. I kept at it. I picked out every single plant that was polluting the river and I went after them. People noticed and started passing laws against the pollution." He laughed a little. "FBI noticed too. So when it seemed like things were going in the right direction, I cooled it for a while. The only person other than my wife, God rest her soul, to know about it was David Reaves's father, John. He's gone now too. Probably a blessing. Anyway, David eventually came to know. Actually, he came right out and asked me. Either he was a smart kid or his old man and me weren't as discreet as we thought. Anyway, after I'd been retired for a while David wanted to start it up again. Thought there was more to be done. And Julia was there, ready to take up the gauntlet like she'd been born to it." He removed his hat and scratched the top of his bald head, then rubbed the inside band of the hat. "A shame about David. I guess you can do

214

something about the pollution of the environment, but people pollution . . . I don't know."

I watched Cal Maitlin looking out on the river and thought somehow I should thank him, but knew he'd be embarrassed. So I asked him if he'd have a beer with me.

"Sounds like an excellent idea," he replied. "Wouldn't have any of that Irish stuff you're so fond of?"

"I think I can dig some up." I found a couple Guinness in the refrigerator and as I opened them and pulled two mugs down, I thought about Elaine and wished she'd get home soon. Perfect fall days are rare.

Maitlin was sitting at the picnic table when I brought the bottles and glasses out. I poured the stout slowly into each glass and we toasted the sun, the season, and the river. Then we drank the thick, silky liquid and watched Peanuts down at the river's edge, as he assembled a group of disorganized, protesting ducks into an orderly, protesting herd.